Praise for *Phytosphere*

"Mackay manages to breathe life into the tired alien invasion genre, deftly juggling hard sci-fi and a bleak tale of postapocalyptic survival. . . . [He] churns up enough high-tech intrigue and old-fashioned suspense to make a fresh read." —*Publishers Weekly*

"This hard-hitting apocalyptic thriller has a strong emotional core. The characters are believable and sympathetic, and while the humans are easy to root for, the Tarsalans aren't so easy to hate. The science is lucid and delivered with finesse, yet Mackay never forgets that his story is ultimately about what makes us human." —*Booklist*

"Refreshing . . . an innovative, well-written apocalyptic science fiction thriller." —Alternative Worlds

"There's a lot in this novel that's intriguing and engaging, and the science is great." —Science Fiction Weekly

"A scary look at a seemingly possible future. . . . Slightly reminiscent of *The War of the Worlds*, this is a book that both hard-core science fiction readers and others will enjoy equally." —*Romantic Times*

"Perfect beach reading; plenty of entertainment and . . . fast-paced." —SFRevu

continued . . .

OMEGA SOL

Scott Mackay

A ROC BOOK

ROC
Published by New American Library, a division of
Penguin Group (USA) Inc., 375 Hudson Street,
New York, New York 10014, USA
Penguin Group (Canada), 90 Eglinton Avenue East, Suite 700, Toronto,
Ontario M4P 2Y3, Canada (a division of Pearson Penguin Canada Inc.)
Penguin Books Ltd., 80 Strand, London WC2R 0RL, England
Penguin Ireland, 25 St. Stephen's Green, Dublin 2,
Ireland (a division of Penguin Books Ltd.)
Penguin Group (Australia), 250 Camberwell Road, Camberwell, Victoria 3124,
Australia (a division of Pearson Australia Group Pty. Ltd.)
Penguin Books India Pvt. Ltd., 11 Community Centre, Panchsheel Park,
New Delhi - 110 017, India
Penguin Group (NZ), 67 Apollo Drive, Rosedale, North Shore 0632,
New Zealand (a division of Pearson New Zealand Ltd.)
Penguin Books (South Africa) (Pty.) Ltd., 24 Sturdee Avenue,
Rosebank, Johannesburg 2196, South Africa

Penguin Books Ltd., Registered Offices:
80 Strand, London WC2R 0RL, England

First published by Roc, an imprint of New American Library,
a division of Penguin Group (USA) Inc.

First Printing, May 2008
10 9 8 7 6 5 4 3 2 1

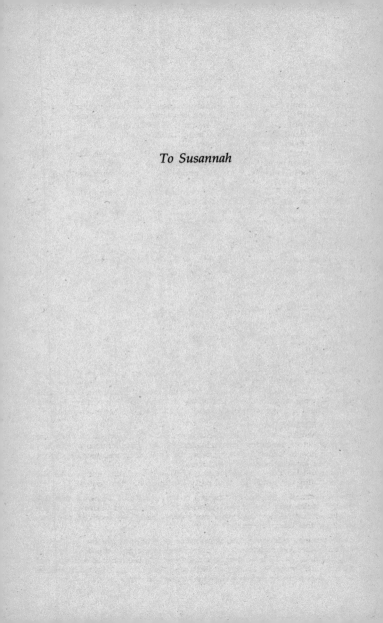

To Susannah

ACKNOWLEDGMENTS

The author would like to thank the following people for the contributions they have made to this novel: Joshua Bilmes, Anne Sowards, Claire Mackay, Joanie Mackay, Colin Mackay, Nicky Scrimger, Ginny Ouellet, and Dan Larsen.

*"When beauty is abstracted
Then ugliness has been implied;
When good is abstracted
Then evil has been implied.*

*So alive and dead are abstracted from nature,
Difficult and easy abstracted from progress,
Long and short abstracted from contrast,
High and low abstracted from depth,
Song and speech abstracted from melody,
After and before abstracted from sequence."*

—LAO TZE, 500 BC

Yin-Yang: "Two primal opposing but complementary principles or cosmic forces said to be found in all nonstatic objects and processes in the universe."

—WIKIPEDIA

PART ONE

The Builders

1

In the lunar valley below, Dr. Cameron Conrad saw Stradivari—ten generators focused on a dime-sized containment field, his life's work, his grand creation, the reason he was here—slowly slip away.

The installation was now obscured by a cloud of dust, ejecta hurtling past, propelled by whatever cataclysmic event unfolded behind Bunker Hill. A meteorite strike? His heart contracted. He saw Lesha, Mark, and Jesus—his workers—staring eastward toward the source of the disturbance. The dust thickened. The first generator, A-Node, fell over, slid along the ground, tumbled a few times, and was gone, disappearing behind a rise on the Moon's western horizon. Lesha clung to B-Node. The node moved, then settled. She got to her knees.

Cam strained to see. "Lesha!" he cried through his suit radio.

The gray cloud thickened. Cam caught one last glimpse of Jesus, aloft, before the gray cloud swallowed him.

Something appeared overhead. Cam looked up in

time to see what looked like a large silver eye peering down at him from the other side of Bunker Hill. He caught only a glimpse; then the eye, the sphere, whatever it was, dipped behind the summit. A new wave of ejecta shot over the hill and rained on top of him. He got to his knees, scared. Sweat came to his brow. Adrenaline rushed through his blood.

"Lesha?"

All he got was the sea-sound of broken static.

He turned east, saw the Gettysburg Scientific Installation, the Moon's only research and military outpost, brightly lit, like spokes on a wheel, tight to the ground, as yet undamaged. He saw the Sumter Module and Command Port. Rocketing dust enfolded the SMCP. Modules and command vehicles bounced away like oversized metal balloons. An oxygen feed broke loose and hissed blue gas.

The ejecta lessened. The weak lunar gravity pulled the dust and flying regolith groundward. The static in his radio faded.

He pushed himself up and keyed a command into his wristpad. He looked at the small screen on his inside visor, where his biomonitors showed the sawtooth dramatics of his heart, then got to his feet.

With the static gone, his radio came back—but didn't come back in the usual way. Instead, he heard commercial radio from Earth, signals that weren't supposed to reach this far or on this frequency, an unnerving anomaly that told him things were truly awry. He heard music, news, weather. English, Mandarin, Arabic. Snippets of various stations as his radio skidded through the band like someone turning the dial with a palsied wrist.

Visuals popped to his visor screen. Network television from Earth, technically impossible because his screen wasn't equipped to receive such signals. A wild flipping of stations. Like someone with a bad case of channel surfing. Television from all over the world—America, Europe, New Sumeria, the People's Republic of North China. His fear deepened. He thought of the silver sphere. Perfect. Too perfect. Too unearthly. He tried to transmit—a standard hail to Gettysburg—but his voice wouldn't penetrate the broadcast pollution.

He took a few steps. In the valley below, more dust settled. Stradivari was wrecked, nodes A through J tumbled like toys. Ejecta patterns streaked Bunker Hill, showing up on the brown surface of the Moon like frost patterns on a window.

"Lesha?"

"Cam?" Her voice emerged through the electromagnetic tide.

"What was that thing? Did you see it? That huge silver sphere?"

Radio sludge overwhelmed her reply.

He took a few steps into Shenandoah Valley and, peering over Bunker Hill, saw the sun. His visor screen channeled appropriate shading. The sun lost its glare and became a small silver sphere.

Then he saw that other silver sphere, much larger than the sun, glimmering along the edge of the valley's south slope, its argent-tinted luminescence reminding him of a dew drop on a leaf.

"Cam?" Lesha's voice came again.

"Do you see it?"

More moondust cleared, the larger pieces sifting

out of the finer particulate, hitting the ground first, leaving a brown veil behind. Shenandoah Valley had fresh white scars everywhere.

A voice struggled to break through the radio interference: "Status . . . status . . . Stradivari Team . . . report." Lamar Bruxner, chief of support at the Gettysburg Scientific Installation, sounded not only frantic but also confused, his voice tight, nasal, just short of panic.

Cam ignored Bruxner, too spellbound by the thing in the valley.

The sphere rose thirty stories, its mirrorlike surface reflecting with uncanny resolution the new gashes in Shenandoah. It spun, seemingly in all directions at once. He was scared. Stunned. Couldn't move for several seconds. But he came out of it a moment later, pawed his wristpad with a shaky hand, engaged his vidcam, and, like a man hiking through the wet forests of the Northwest and catching an unexpected glimpse of Bigfoot, filmed.

"Stradivari Team . . . report . . . report . . ."

Once again he ignored Bruxner's voice. More dust cleared. In the dark sky above, a green shadow moved, bending the vacuum. He blinked several times. In shape it was like a vortex, but being of scientific mind, he was disinclined to give it a label of any kind just yet. Still, the notion persisted. A vortex? A gate? A wormhole? Beneath his fear and bewilderment, he felt some excitement, that rarefied giddiness only a subatomic physicist like himself could feel in such situations, when a new phenomenon— perhaps even a glimpse of the hyperdimensionality

he had always postulated about in his own papers—
was making itself manifest. He bounced a few steps
closer, his vidcam steady in its stabilizer. The dust
continued to settle around the lucid sphere.

Looking up once more, he saw the green vortex
close, as if the thing's arrival—and its presence—was
now frighteningly established.

Inside Gettysburg, Cam waited in the main common room with the other scientific staff. Through the
observation window he saw what was left of the
Sumter Module and Command Port. It reminded him
of a multicar pileup on the freeway, only these
weren't cars but space vehicles, tangled with each
other, heat shields shattered, thrust conduits twisted,
cabin windows cracked.

Lesha sat next to him, hunched over, hand to her
mouth, and stared beyond the window with apprehensive blue eyes. Jesus was still out there. Mark
Fuller paced to one side. Cam raised his hand and
placed it on Lesha's shoulder.

Scientists from the Princeton Team—the only other
scientific team currently conducting research at
Gettysburg—sat in the back next to the kitchen serving area.

A Gettysburg support man named Laborde emerged
from corridor 7 and walked to the Princeton Team.
Team members stopped their low, earnest conversa-
tions. Laborde spoke to Dr. Renate Tennant, Princeton
Team leader. Renate sat forward, a tall woman, back
straight, elbows on the table, hands clasped, a scientist Cam had gotten to know over the past two

months. Laborde motioned toward corridor 7, asking
her to come. Renate got to her feet and the two
retreated.

"I wonder where they're going," said Cam.

Lesha remained preoccupied with Jesus. "Do you
think he's all right?" She pulled a tissue from the
dispenser and dabbed her nose. Cam leaned forward,
put his hand on her knee, and stared out the window,
feeling odd, displaced, and unusually compelled to
go out and look at the strange new sphere, nearly as
if he had a voice in his head telling him to go out
and look at the recent arrival.

Then out the window he saw the Emergency Rescue Vehicle's lights flash out in Shenandoah. Lesha
got up and moved quickly to the window. He rose
as well, hopeful that the ERV might be bringing Jesus
back. Mark and two other team members, Blaine
Berkheimer and Lewis Hirleman, joined them at the
observation glass.

Twice the size of a regular rover, the ERV rounded
the far side of the SMCP at full speed. This made
Cam nervous.

This could only mean that Jesus had been seriously injured.

Cam left the window and headed toward the air
lock. As he entered corridor 6, he clutched the railing
to steady himself in the disorienting Moon gravity.
Lesha was right behind him.

They came to corridor 9, turned right, and arrived
at the air lock. Cam looked through the small pressure window into the garage. He saw several surface
vehicles parked along the side.

A moment later, a red light flashed above the vehicle-entry port and a hissing came from the airlock valve. After a minute, the red finally went to green, and the big door lifted. The ERV rolled into the air lock and the bright overhead lights came on. The door closed. He heard hissing again as the garage filled with air. The ERV eased into a parking spot.

With the ERV now stopped, Lamar Bruxner, head of Gettysburg support, maneuvered out of its cab and bounced to the back of the vehicle. Johnsie Dunlap, Gettysburg's nurse practitioner, emerged from the rear doors. She turned around, gripped a gurney, and pulled. Jesus, strapped to the gurney, appeared feetfirst from the vehicle's rear. Moondust covered his orange pressure suit, and StopGap, a compound for sealing leaks, clung to his left leg like lime sherbet.

"His suit's been breached," said Cam.

Pushing from the other end was Harland Law, a third Gettysburg support staff member. Harland and Johnsie maneuvered Jesus around the side of the vehicle and Bruxner shut the doors. The three hurried to the air lock. Bruxner, a heavyset man in his fifties, typed the necessary commands. The seal hissed, the outside door opened, and the group entered the linking chamber. The chief of support then keyed in another command, and the inside door slid back. Frigid air billowed into corridor 9.

Cam asked, "Is he okay?"

"His condition is critical," said Johnsie.

The three Gettysburg support staff hurried down the corridor toward the infirmary with their casualty.

Cam and Lesha followed. But Bruxner allowed them only so far before he raised his hand. Cam saw Bruxner's broad, meaty face through his pressure suit's yellow-tinted visor. "If you could wait in the common room . . ."

"His leg," said Lesha. "Was there a depressurization?"

"Dr. Conrad, if you could take Dr. Weeks back to the common room . . ."

Harland and Johnsie disappeared through the infirmary doors with Jesus. Bruxner turned around and followed.

As Cam watched them retreat, the three moving through the weak gravity with the skill of long-term Moon personnel, he thought the infirmary looked too small to handle such a big emergency. It was no more than a first-aid station, staffed by only a nurse practitioner, no doctor—with the Emergency Evacuation Vehicle able to transit from the Moon to Earth in less than a day, a doctor wasn't needed.

But now the EEV was wrecked. The whole module and command port was destroyed. This meant they had no way of getting off the Moon until NASA or the Pentagon could launch a rescue mission. Which meant for the time being they were stuck here.

Stuck on the Moon with that strange lucent sphere just over the hill.

And with the peculiar sensation that he now had a voice inside his head.

2

Retired Air Force Colonel Timothy Pittman lifted his phone after three rings.

It was, of all people, General Morris Blunt, his old Orbital Operations commander.

At first he couldn't concentrate on the man's words because he was so surprised to hear the general's voice after four years—they hadn't kept in touch. He thought the general might be calling him simply to say hello, and it took him nearly ten seconds to realize the call was about the Moon, how they might need a military presence there, and how something extraordinarily odd had happened. The general explained that he usually didn't like calling people out of retirement, but this was something special, with its own circumscribed set of problems.

"And because of your spectacular success in the orbital exchanges against the People's Republic of North China four years ago, Tim, we think you might be the man for the job. Orbital, hard-vac, and micro-g warfare are your specialty. No one does them better."

Pittman glanced out the window at his desert

homestead where a coyote nosed around a scorpion. A jet from Peterson Air Force Base five miles away hit the sound barrier, music he usually gloried in—the reason he lived so close to an air base, so he could watch the jets go by and remember his days as a pilot—but which under the circumstances he now found a distraction. "The Chinese have something on the Moon?" For the Chinese would never leave his blood.

It turned out the PRNC had nothing on the Moon. The situation was far stranger than that.

An *entity* had come to the Moon.

Blunt said, "We have no idea what it is. But we know that someone with your particular skills should be the one to handle it. Fye and Goldvogel both agree, and we have Oval Office approval."

It took Pittman a moment to answer, and when he did, it was still with China in his mind. "Has satellite reconnaissance shown any launch activity in the People's Republic of North China?"

"No."

"Have interlunar tracking stations shown any approaches?"

"The thing just appeared."

"And you're sure the PRNC doesn't have any assets on the Moon?"

"You forget how badly we degraded their capability. Believe me, the PRNC was the first thing we thought of. And we've ruled it out. Po Pin-Yen is concentrating on his navy, not his space program."

"Have there been any casualties?" He was already thinking about how he could neutralize this entity—

this *thing*, this potential new enemy—if in fact it had caused any casualties. He was like that scorpion out there. Scorpions stung when attacked, and stinging was what he did best. What he loved. What he lived for.

Blunt, in a voice that was now subdued, said, "We have one man in critical condition. He's not expected to live."

Pittman felt his stinger flexing.

In Arlington, two low-ranking officers took Pittman to one of the smaller situation rooms, no windows, the lights down low, a big screen, the shield of the Department of Defense in blues and greens, and Blunt there with Oren Fye and Brian Goldvogel, Fye looking after intelligence matters, Goldvogel their security head.

In those first few seconds he saw in their eyes the usual judgments, Fye turning his jowly face a fraction of a centimeter, Goldvogel's expression hardening like quick-drying cement, General Blunt—his crisp blue uniform, round red face, and white goatee—appraising him, all of them thinking, *Why did he retire? Why did he desert us?* and none of them understanding how it had been his last desperate effort to put his marriage with Sheila back together. He needed to leave the military, the thing he worshipped most, so he could show Sheila and the kids that he loved them.

The reproach was still in their eyes.

Blunt said, "Soft drink?"

The offer was like the first move in a chess game.

"A Coke."

Blunt nodded to the accompanying officer. The officer went to get Pittman the refreshment.

Move two: Fye and Goldvogel, on their feet now, offering casual salutes—here they were in the Pentagon again, and the rogue colonel, Timothy Pittman, was graciously returning to duty, divorced and single still, at last seeming to understand that the role of soldier and husband simply couldn't be reconciled.

The pleasantries, if such they could be called, ended quickly.

Blunt began. And Pittman was glad he did. For as much as he loved his ex-wife and kids, he was never happier than when he had a military problem to solve.

"At oh nine hundred hours today, an entity appeared on the Moon. We have no idea where it came from, what it is, or what it's going to do." A hint of speculation crept into Blunt's voice. "The Greenhow System detected no approaches until the thing was forty kilometers above the lunar surface." Mention of the Greenhow System, something that was visible from space as Earth's "ring," so sensitive it could detect the movement of an insect under a leaf, an apparatus that had been instrumental in his orbital spearhead against the Chinese four years ago, made Pittman feel as if he had at last come home. "It came to rest less than a kilometer from the Gettysburg Scientific Installation. Brian, if you could give Tim the scoop on Gettysburg."

Goldvogel, every strand of his blond hair perfectly in place as if with laminate, glanced at his waferscreen. "The entity produced significant ejecta on its final approach, and while the eastern slope of Bunker Hill took the brunt of this wave, the fallout circumference was significant enough to destroy much of the Sumter Module and Command Port." Years in Washington hadn't entirely eliminated Goldvogel's Bronx brogue. "This has effectively stranded all scientific and support personnel at Gettysburg, at least for the time being."

"But Gettysburg itself is okay?" asked Pittman.

Goldvogel nodded. "It's built snug to the western slope of Bunker Hill. Damage to the facility was minor."

"Who's up there now?"

"Two teams, both scientific, one under the leadership of Dr. Cameron Conrad, the other headed by Dr. Renate Tennant. Dr. Tennant's under contract with us. Dr. Conrad's with the Brookhaven National Laboratory. He and three of his team were on the surface when the entity touched down. As General Blunt might have mentioned in his telephone call, one of his doctoral students, Jesus Cavalet, was badly injured, and remains in critical condition."

"But no one is dead."

Blunt shook his head. "Not yet."

The officer came back with Pittman's Coke. Pittman took the soft drink, snapped it open, and took a meditative sip.

"Have we had a report from Dr. Tennant? If she's on Pentagon contract—"

"She's sent us a status report and some preliminary safety proposals," said Goldvogel.

"Have we spoken to the North Chinese?" asked Pittman. He still had a hard time accepting that they didn't have anything to do with this.

Oren Fye sighed. "Their space program is in mothballs, Tim. As I think General Blunt explained to you, and I'm sure it's something you already know, Po Pin-Yen is concentrating on his navy."

He didn't like Fye's tone. Fye was speaking to him as if he'd been out of the loop too long. "Do we have any intelligence on this thing? Any live feeds? Anything at all?"

"Dr. Conrad captured some footage," said Fye.

He took another sip of Coke and pondered Dr. Conrad. "No one else?"

"No," said Blunt.

"Do we have it?"

"We do," said Goldvogel.

Goldvogel lifted a remote and thumbed some buttons.

The fuzzy footage of a helmet-cam appeared on the screen. The camera shifted dizzily from Conrad's wrist, then rose into the sun. For a second, the screen went white as sunlight overpowered the digital medium. But then the camera made adjustments, and the moonscape dimmed. Everything was gray, rounded, and bleak.

"This is the eastern arm of Shenandoah Valley seen from the top of Bunker Hill," said Goldvogel. "If you look behind the dust, you'll see the entity."

Pittman was impressed. It was huge. As a possible fighting vehicle it was bigger than anything the U.S. or the PRNC had. Its lower edge appeared first, reflecting the light of the sun. Conrad shifted and the sphere became centered in his helmet-cam lens. The top curve gained definition. Though the image was grainy—the same quality one might expect from a convenience-store security camera—Pittman now discerned texture, color, and . . . movement? The entity appeared to spin in a hundred different directions at once. Was that possible, or was it some kind of optical trick? Perhaps camouflage? Its texture was as smooth as polished marble. The thing reminded him of a giant blob of mercury.

Still impressed with its size, he asked, "How big is it?"

"Gettysburg reports a diameter of at least three hundred meters," said Fye.

"Have we spoken to Dr. Conrad?"

"No."

"And did Dr. Tennant provide anything useful over and above her status report and safety protocols?"

"Nothing of military value, if that's what you mean?"

"And satellite reconnaissance indicates that this is the only one?"

The notion that there might be more seemed to surprise them all.

Cowed, Blunt answered, "So far." As if he was now willing to admit to the possibility of an invasion.

"And we've definitely spoken to the North Chinese?"

"Yes."

"And they deny . . ."

Fye shook his head. "They're just as baffled as we are, Tim."

"Has it done anything since it landed?"

"The Greenhow System indicates it's remained stationary," said Goldvogel.

"Is it emitting energy?"

"A minimal electromagnetic field," said Fye.

"You say Conrad has one scientific team member in critical condition. What is the nature of his injuries?"

"Blunt-force trauma due to flying ejecta," said Goldvogel. "As well as vascular distress from sudden decompression. His suit was breached."

"Is he going to live?"

"The nurse practitioner says it's doubtful. Especially because they can't medevac him to Earth."

Pittman stared at the image on the screen. The camera shifted away to the west arm of Shenandoah. He saw what was left of the SMCP, a mass of twisted metal, destroyed modules, and crumpled space vehicles. That in itself was reason enough for war. But first they had to determine the nature of their enemy, and he was beginning to think that Cameron Conrad might be an asset in this regard. The camera veered northwest, and he saw Gettysburg itself, delineated by its own outside lights, a hub with several spokes built close to the ground, rugged, secure, but now covered in dirt from the thing's moonfall.

"And we're planning a rescue mission?"

"NASA is," said Goldvogel. "It might take a while."

"How soon can we get a *military* presence to the Moon?"

"Ten days for the expeditionary force," said Blunt. "Three weeks for a larger force."

Pittman said, "Put me on the first shuttle. What about these scientists? Can we use them?"

Goldvogel said, "We think we should put Dr. Tennant in charge because she's already under contract with us."

Pittman's brow settled. "I think we should go with Dr. Conrad. He filmed the damn thing. That took guts. And we're going to need guts for something like this. He might be a scientist but he seems to have a firm grasp of military reconnaissance. More so than Dr. Tennant."

3

Two hours after they took Jesus to the infirmary, Cam sat in the common room for a briefing. Dr. Renate Tennant, having come back from her mysterious disappearance with Laborde, conducted the briefing.

"Because I'm the senior scientist here at Gettysburg, and am operating under the auspices of the Department of Defense, I've taken it upon myself to coordinate our emergency response to the development out on the surface."

Her lips were thin mauve lines, her eyes wide and glittery, and her makeup precise, redone since her disappearance, a gesture that seemed superfluous to Cam under the circumstances, but in keeping with the woman's personality, for she was nothing if not precise.

"I've been working to devise, along with Lamar, appropriate measures to ensure our safety, maintain our discipline, and secure our rescue."

Lamar Bruxner, chief of support, stood to one side, his face frozen, looking bewildered by this sudden lapse in routine, as if emergency briefings at a time of day when everybody should have been starting their afternoon round of research constituted a serious breach of Gettysburg etiquette.

Renate continued. "I know many of you are wondering how we're going to get off the Moon, now that the SMCP has been wrecked, so I'll address that question first. I've made initial contact with the Pentagon, and they tell me NASA's planning a civilian rescue mission, but that it might take some time. The Pentagon's chief concern is landing an expeditionary military force on the Moon, which I'm pleased to say speaks to our first concern, that of ensuring our safety."

Cam peered more closely at Renate. "And the Pentagon feels an expeditionary force is necessary? This may not be a military situation." He paused, not exactly sure why he had interjected, feeling only that some outside force had prompted him.

Renate glanced at the chief of support, then turned back to Cam. "They have to consider the . . . the possible danger that the sphere outside presents, not only to us but to the rest of the world, and that's why they're sending an expeditionary force." She raised her chin, and the corners of her lips settled. "We have no idea what that thing is or where it came from. We don't know if it's a threat. We don't know if it plans to do anything, or remain inactive, as it has so far." She motioned toward the observation window. "The Pentagon is looking at the bigger picture. As for us, we have to design protocols that address worst-case scenarios until NASA can arrange a civilian rescue. Lamar and I have discussed a number of approaches. We've generally agreed that it's best to stay inside Gettysburg. It's safest if we remain invisible to it. In other words, no surface activity, and minimal radio communications.''

Cam frowned. Remain invisible to it? Did she have no concept of the historical importance of the thing? He examined her as she continued to outline in exacting detail further security protocols, a tangle of rules that touched on everything from carbon dioxide venting to human waste recycling. Didn't she understand that they had an opportunity here? It seemed perfectly obvious to him what they had to do.

"So we're just going to sit here and do nothing?"

Renate turned to him. "In the interest of safety, Lamar and I feel that would be best."

He felt his face settle. "That's the last thing we should do. We should go out, take a look at it, and try to figure out what it is, where it comes from, and what it wants."

Her face tightened. "Yes, but Dr. Conrad, we can't rule out hostile intentions."

"If we don't go out and look at it, how can we decide if it's hostile? Also, if it's extraterrestrial—and this is certainly starting to look like our best hypothesis—shouldn't we find out what we can about it before it takes off? When are we going to get a chance like this again? How can you even suggest we *hide* from an opportunity like this?" He looked around at everybody, taking control of the room, and in a more hushed voice said, "This is first contact." He motioned out the window. "Do we want it to slip through our hands?" He turned to Renate. "I'll volunteer. I don't mind. I'll go take a look. We could learn so much from it."

Her eyes narrowed with worry. "What if you antagonize it? It may retaliate, and staff could be injured or even killed. Look at Jesus." She shook her head. "I'm sorry, but I believe our security should be our first concern, and as ranking scientist I really must insist on our three-pronged plan of safety, discipline, and rescue. That means no excursions to the surface."

He glanced around the room. The Princeton Team members nodded encouragement. His own team members looked at Renate with growing skepticism.

He pushed his arguments. "To give you an example of just how much we can learn from it, while you were talking to Lamar, I was reviewing the Greenhow tapes, specifically, the thing's approach. It's a most puzzling and intriguing approach. The entity just appears. It comes out of nowhere. It materializes forty kilometers above the lunar surface. How can something do that? What are the physics behind it? Don't you see that this hints at something beyond our realm of understanding? I've particularly examined what I'm calling its point of entry, that spot forty kilometers above the lunar surface, where the sphere is first observed by the Greenhow ring. I've run this point-of-entry sequence through some of our Stradivari software models, ones that weren't destroyed, and I've determined that at the moment of materialization, a viscous impact occurs. This impact has much in common with the five-dimensional black holes we've been creating at Brookhaven. Low-viscosity fields like this curve space and time. In this particular case, the curved space-time field was seventeen kilometers across. We're at the microscopic stage in these kinds of things. But this point of impact seems to indicate a practical stage. If what we have here is a sentient species, then we're looking at an extremely advanced one. Which means an immense opportunity to learn. So let's not blow it by being cowards."

Her brow settled. "In other words, your own field of professional work is motivating you."

"Characterize it any way you like. But don't blame me when the scientific community holds you personally responsible for not exploiting, understanding, and studying this historical opportunity. What we need here, Renate, is a full-blown investigation."

Renate grew still. "Dr. Conrad, we're in an extremely dangerous situation, and in no position to conduct any such investigation. We should concentrate on devising the necessary protocols to see us through safely until the civilian evac team gets here. Then maybe we can consider further study. Until that time, I believe the last thing we should do is antagonize our unexpected visitor with premature research attempts that are unlikely to produce any useful results."

His face settled. He turned to the observation window. The thing called to him. He didn't know how, he didn't know why, but he could definitely sense it in his head now; and while this worried and perplexed him, he also understood he had a responsibility. For whatever reason, he felt the thing had singled him out, and he knew he had to rise to the occasion. "Do what you want, Renate. But I'm going out to take a look at it. With or without your permission."

* * *

An hour later, Lamar Bruxner called Cam and Renate into his office. The big bald man had a tight grin on his face. Renate sat stiffly, the corners of her lips turned downward, her eyes superalert, as if jolted by a megadose of caffeine. Cam, on the other hand, felt unusually calm.

"We've just received a priority message from General Morris Blunt's office at the Pentagon," said Bruxner. In an aside to Cam, he added, "He's the man who's sending the expeditionary force, by the way, and he's also the Pentagon's liaison to the NASA civilian evac team." He then addressed the two of them. "He's now assigned a commanding officer, Colonel Timothy Pittman, of the Orbital Operations branch of the United States Air Force, to oversee any and all responses to the entity." Bruxner peered at Renate, his lips bunching as if he were about to blow air between his teeth. "Contrary to the safety protocols we've been designing, Dr. Tennant, Colonel Pittman has now asked us to conduct a surface investigation, such as Dr. Conrad has suggested."

Cam felt elated, unduly so, and knew the thing was calling him again.

Bruxner turned back to Cam. "But not primarily because he thinks we can learn from it, Dr. Conrad." His elation ebbed. "While Colonel Pittman is prepared to accept the possibly benign nature of the visitation, he won't rule out that the entity poses a potential threat either, such as Dr. Tennant has theorized, especially because we've received nothing in the way of a communication from it, and have no idea what it's going to do. Since such is the case, he thinks we should take a look, but with the focus on military reconnaissance, not scientific study. That's not to say that the two don't go hand in hand, and he understands there'll be a strong scientific element to any such investigation." In a more anxious tone, Bruxner said, "And I'm sorry, Dr. Tennant, but Colonel Pittman believes Dr. Conrad is the scientist best qualified for the job, as he's already uncovered some information for Orbops that has possible military value, particularly his review of the Greenhow tapes."

Cam's elation ebbed some more, as he didn't immediately agree with the apparent martial interpretation Pittman had put on his Greenhow tape review.

"Ma'am, I'm afraid they've asked me to put Gettysburg at Dr. Conrad's disposal, not yours."

Cam turned to Renate. "I'm sorry."

She took it better than he expected, nodding gracefully. But that didn't hide the great misgiving in her face. "I just hope we don't prompt retaliation. I'm perfectly willing to be blamed by the scientific community for not taking a historical opportunity. But I should hate to have on my conscience the deaths of all our team members. And I wouldn't want to provoke a war with it."

Cam said, "The odds that it means to wage war are so infinitesimal that they're not even worth considering."

"What makes you say that?"

He couldn't help thinking that the thing was once again prompting him. "Because it's already sacrificed the element of surprise. If it had any military intent, why would it forfeit that supreme advantage? Believe me, war with humans is the last thing on its mind." He lifted his chin and looked at the pair, even as he sensed the thing talking to him once more, revealing to him in mental snippets and impressions some of its true nature. "My guess is that it's so advanced, and so far removed from us technologically, it probably hasn't taken much notice of us at all. If it has, it's as an inconsequential species of our planet's overall biosphere, nothing more. So I wouldn't worry about war. It would be like us going to Antarctica and declaring war on penguins."

4

Cam, Lesha, Mark Fuller, and Blaine Berkheimer left the exit bay in a Class II rover early the next day, following the road along the shadowed western base of Bunker Hill. They had to use the rover headlights to see where they were going. The road was a rutted track, the lunar particulate compressed from constant use.

Cam inspected the wreckage of the SMCP as they drove by. One of the larger landers looked like a squashed bug, a huge boulder sitting on top, its landing legs in rough formation but now bent, unable to support the weight of the boulder. A small orbital ferry had been toppled on its side so that Cam saw its various undercarriage fixtures. A two-man sled had lost its main engine and now looked like a hollowed-out cigar.

They continued on. Radio channels were open. The airwaves hissed with white noise. They rounded the southern end of Bunker Hill. As he came out from behind the slope, he got a clear view of the entity,

which, for the purpose of a convenient referent, they
had now dubbed Alpha Vehicle.

Alpha Vehicle represented the fundamental ideal
of positively curved space: the sphere. In its elegant
simplicity, it reinforced Cam's growing notion that
he was dealing with an advanced species. It shimmered like a mirror, yes, but seemed to possess a
refractive quality as well, so that its silver tone was
tinged with a variety of other visible light spectra,
including violet, pink, and blue. It defied gravity,
hovering two meters above the ground. It possessed
an immense solidity and, as with his initial impression, seemed to be spinning in all directions at once.
Yet for all its solidity, it didn't cast a shadow, and
that got him thinking of hyperdimensionality again,
his own field of endeavor, how theoretically, in certain higher dimensions, light could travel easily
through solid-body objects uninterrupted, the way
neutrinos from the sun traveled through the Earth.

They drove to within five hundred meters,
stopped, and got out.

They scanned Alpha Vehicle with a variety of
instruments.

It was Mark Fuller who summarized its essential
naked-eye characteristic: "It just sits there."

Yet Cam had the sense that it was more than just
sitting there; that it was in fact trying to talk to him
again, and he found this so odd and unnerving that
for several seconds he couldn't move.

A short while later, the crew moved in for some
closer observations. As the distance shrank, the object
loomed larger and larger. Getting a better look at it

now, Cam saw that its silver surface had a liquid quality, was perfectly smooth, and reflected the Moon's surface, the dark vacuum of space, and the approaching rover with the concave mirrorlike quality of a giant ball bearing.

As they got within fifty meters, Cam heard a strange hiss in his radio, like an audiotape sped up a hundred times, the hiss demarcating itself into delineated sound parcels, a pattern: two, then one, over and over again.

"Stop the rover."

Blaine braked, and the rover came to a stop.

Cam listened to the noise.

Alpha Vehicle rose above them so that looking straight up, he saw he was underneath its equatorial regions. Being so close to it, he fully appreciated its size, thirty stories high, and also thirty stories wide. He got off the rover and approached. He looked up at the silver surface and saw his own small reflection, foreshortened and twisted as if through the lens of a peephole.

The noise faded.

"All right, crew, let's set up."

The crew got off the rovers and busied themselves with their instruments.

Cam, meanwhile, stared at the entity.

He felt hypnotized by the thing. He moved closer. The closer he got, the more spellbound he felt.

He heard Lesha's voice through the radio, asking him not to get too near. Even when Lamar Bruxner came on from Gettysburg Tower, distressed by his boldness, the support chief's worries dwindled to insignificance. Cam was *too* fascinated by Alpha Vehicle. *Too* enthralled to care about the support chief's worries. The thing was indeed calling to him—there could be no doubt of that now—and he meant to answer it.

The object remained stable, unmoving, its surface unblemished.

But as Cam neared its south pole he noticed an imperfection. A node appeared, reminding him of a volcano, warping its silver skin so that it deepened to a cerulean blue. His reflection shattered into a dozen tinier ones, and he saw iterations of himself arranged like the petals of a flower along the slopes of this volcano. He stopped. He backed up and stared at the thing, made dizzy by the way it reflected everything, and by the way he had to hold his head straight up. The node followed him; it was rounded, calm, yet ominous. He backed up some more. The node trailed. Its base now narrowed, its peak rose, and the thing reached for him.

"Guys, I think . . ."

He stepped back, startled, and tripped over impact debris. He fell to the ground while the node reached. He heard Lesha's voice, frightened, telling him to get out of there. He caught a glimpse of Mark Fuller rising from his console, the bend of his knee straightening with a sudden jerk as he caught sight of the struggle happening twenty meters away. Cam pushed back, but before he could get up, the node lunged, and the silver appendage went right through his suit, then his chest.

It penetrated but did not impale. It pierced but did not draw blood. He was skewered but not injured. It was physics twisted on its side, two solid body

objects occupying the same space at the same time,
and he was surprised, shocked, alarmed, frightened,
but also intrigued.

The appendage flexed within him and lifted. He
left the ground. He glanced back and saw Mark and
Blaine loping toward him in the weak lunar gravity.

"It's all right," he said. "I'm okay."

They felt far away.

The node lifted. He traveled up Alpha Vehicle, his
arms dangling, and checked his biomonitor screen.
His respirations were nil, brain activity was dead,
and his heart had flatlined. According to the small
screen he was clinically dead. But he knew he wasn't.
He didn't feel alarmed. He felt at peace.

He gripped the silver appendage, and his hands
went right through it. His radio died. He was lifted
higher and higher. As the node came to Alpha Vehicle's equatorial regions, it drew him inward. He sank
toward its surface, but did so willingly, again trust-
ing that the thing had in some way selected him, a
notion that wouldn't let him alone. He looked at
Alpha Vehicle and saw that a deep pit had developed. The node drew him into the pit. He should
have been afraid, but he wasn't. He heard several
tones fluctuating back and forth in sequences of twos
and ones again. The node pulled him into the pit and
Alpha Vehicle closed over him.

He thought it would be dark. But it was light. And
he had a perplexing view of the solar system—time
and space warped and shifted so that he could see
all nine planets, the multitude of moons, the asteroid
belt, and the sun, all at once. Beyond the solar system
he saw stars, all delineated one from the next, and

they had planets as well, and these planets had moons. The weave and warp of space inside Alpha Vehicle was unlike anything he had ever experienced, and it again reminded him of his own work on hyperdimensionality, trying to create hyperdimensional fields known as anti-Ostrander space, a field with the possibility that the space within might be bigger than the space without.

It wasn't only the planets of his own solar system, or the planets of other systems, or every star in the Milky Way, but also the galaxies of the universe—a backdrop of spirals, ellipses, and irregular conglomerations. Also protogalaxies, Alpha Vehicle probing light generated thirteen and a half billion years ago, just after the Big Bang, so that he knew it wasn't only the warp and weave of space inside Alpha Vehicle, but also a change in the way time was fluxing.

He felt an affinity for it all because this was what he had theorized about, the fluid nature of time and space, viscous layers, hyperdimensionality, phenomena comprehended through the arcane language of higher mathematics and potentially viewed through the lens of a practical anti-Ostrander space field, just as he had hoped to develop with Stradivari. He was just wondering if the thing had in fact generated an anti-Ostrander field when a purple point of light raced toward him out of the cluster of protogalaxies, came right for his head, struck him in the bridge of his nose, and seemed to make a curious numbing sensation right above his brow. Then there came a little head pain, but this was quickly soothed by more numbness, and a few seconds later, he had the bizarre sensation that his body was expanding, that it was reaching out in all directions to encompass the things he was seeing.

It was at this point that Alpha Vehicle revealed something of itself to Cam. It intimated to him, perhaps by manipulating the synaptic nerves in his brain, that it was a vehicle of quantum potentiality. He found himself grinning as he thought of this ability, to be all things, in all places, at all times. It could change. Shift. Perhaps even mutate to suit any occasion or environment. It was a plugged nickel before it had been stamped. A blank waiting for an impression. A mission waiting for its purpose.

After that, his view of the universe disappeared and was strangely replaced with a nearly filmic map of his own personal life.

He saw his mother, his father. He saw the car accident, his father having a stroke at the most inopportune moment so that the car ended up in the Buffalo Bayou outside Houston. Couldn't save his mother, but managed to save his father, even though his father's stroke had been a massive one. Saved him for only one more miserable year before another stroke took him for good. Then the caskets. First his mother's. Then his father's. He felt the old heartache again.

Then plunging forward. All his years at Brookhaven National Laboratory. The teaching posts. The publishing. The indifference of the scientific community. The development of a small and imperfect anti-Ostrander space field generator based on the highly experimental Relativistic Heavy Ion Collider. And more indifference from the scientific community. And always the—the *gut feeling,* yes, that's what it was—that he was onto something, a fundamentally different way of looking at the universe. Alpha Vehicle seemed to dwell on this—his gut feeling about the universe—and it was as if the entity was methodically sifting his mind for clues about it.

Then—suddenly, unexpectedly—Lesha Weeks.

Lesha, materializing from some secret place in his subconscious, never before acknowledged; Lesha with her blond hair and blue eyes. The beach girl who had come to work for him. He saw her at Brookhaven National Laboratory studying the latest microscopic black-hole findings on her laptop, then opening a Tupperware container of vegetable curry, stuff she made at home, too yellow, for she liked turmeric a lot; then giving him a sideways glance as her fork was poised halfway to her mouth; and seeing an acknowledgment in her wide blue eyes, that there might be some tension of a sexual nature between them after all. And then attending that convention together in Los Angeles, the black-tie dinner, the closing ceremonies, him in his tuxedo, Lesha wearing a blue evening gown that matched her turquoise eyes, and how sorry he had felt at the end of the evening when she had gone to her room with a curious line of regret etched across her brow, and he had gone to his. No. He couldn't deny it. The best discoveries were usually the most obvious. Even her last-minute application for Stradivari, once she had found out he would head the project, was an indication she felt something for him. He only wished he had figured it out sooner.

Without knowing how, he found himself on the lunar surface again. On his hands and knees. And Lesha was there, hand on his shoulder, the touch electric through his pressure suit. Globules of the entity shimmered like magic on the ground beneath him, silver, reflective, plasmalike. He knew that they had been left there on purpose by Alpha Vehicle. He once again saw an opportunity, and had the presence of mind to take it. He unhooked a sampler from his belt and pressed the intake button. He collected his samples and stood up.

Cam looked up at Lesha. Then at Alpha Vehicle.

And realized it was a misnomer.

It was so much more than just a vehicle.

Johnsie Dunlap, the nurse practitioner, assessed his condition once he returned to Gettysburg. She was a black woman in her early fifties, hair cropped closely to her head, eyes big, shaded with gold makeup.

Her eyes narrowed when he told her about the biomonitors.

"No brain activity either?" she asked.

"No. Everything was flat-lined." And he had to admit, he was as flummoxed as she was, and found it extremely odd that Alpha Vehicle had singled him out this way.

"Yet you remained conscious."

"I remember everything. Most of all, I remember how I felt. At peace. And detached. It was as if I saw things from an entirely different perspective. I don't know how Alpha Vehicle did it. How could it drag me up there? How could it get inside my head?"

"We haven't the diagnostic instruments at Gettysburg to make that determination."

"Yes, but why me?"

"Why not? Maybe they recognize something in

you. You're an accomplished scientist. You're not a run-of-the-mill layman. If they're going to choose anybody, they might as well choose someone with a wide understanding."

"I'm not as smart as all that. I really didn't get what they were trying to say to me."

Johnsie paused. "You saw the solar system?"

"Yes."

"And the universe?"

"Yes."

By this time, she had wires attached. She checked the readouts. "Pulse is normal. Blood pressure and heartbeat are normal. But you say you've got this headache now."

"Yes."

"And it's not going away?"

Cam remembered the purple speck of light touching his brow. That's exactly when his headache started. "It's not so bad."

"You look tired. Maybe you should take a rest."

"I'm fine."

"I'm not so sure. Something happened to you."

"Nothing that's medically significant."

She conceded the point. "That's true, but still."

He could see she had plans for him now. "If you're going to ask me to give up this new research, forget it."

"Maybe you should let Renate take over."

"I'm under orders from Colonel Pittman. She isn't."

"Let's look at your eyes." She shone a small flashlight into his eyes. "Your pupils aren't particularly reactive. Sit up and take a look at the eye chart."

She had him read the chart, first with one eye, then the other. "I take it you wear eyeglasses."

"I started last year."

"And you're sure you feel fine?"

"Yes. Just a little bewildered."

"Do you know the five warning signs of stroke?" This caught him off guard. "Why?"

She pressed her lips together. "Your father had a stroke." She motioned at his chart. "It's in your medical history."

"That's ridiculous. I'm perfectly healthy. You think the doctors at NASA would have cleared me for Stradivari if I wasn't?"

She looked away. "No. I guess not."

"I just have a slight headache. That's all. And a headache's not going to kill me."

And then, to get off the subject, he asked, "How's Jesus?"

Johnsie looked away. "If we had the EEV . . ."

"Is he going to make it?"

She thought about it. "Put it this way. On Earth, yes. Up here, I can't say."

5

Cam got his first Earth-Lunar linkup with Colonel
Timothy Pittman the next day. Cam sat in the Gettysburg Control Tower with Lesha, Renate, Bruxner, and
various other team members. Pittman, whose face
loomed large on the screen, was a rugged-looking
man in his midfifties, with close-cropped silver hair,
a neatly trimmed silver goatee, and penetrating blue
eyes. He wore a gray Orbops T-shirt, the organiza-
tion's blue logo on the left breast. He had bulky bi-
ceps. Military dog tags dangled around his neck.

"And he died when?" asked Pittman. They were
talking about Jesus Cavalet.

Cam studied Pittman. "Yesterday evening."

The colonel looked to one side, his face like sheet
metal, his eyes widening, his brow leveling. "I've reviewed the new rover tapes." Pittman paused. "You
were abducted against your will, Dr. Conrad."

Cam regretted this interpretation. "I wasn't abducted."

"You were forcibly lifted from the ground and confined."

"I wasn't confined. I was welcomed."

Pittman was insistent. "You got close to it, and it responded with a defensive mechanism."

"There's no evidence to support that particular assessment, Colonel. Don't let the accidental death of one man cloud your judgment. We have an opportunity here. We can learn a lot."

"It's destroyed eighteen billion dollars' worth of property, stranded fifteen people, killed Jesus Cavalet, and forcibly confined you. Against your will. I say we've learned enough."

"Let me stress again: the stranding, the damage, and the death were accidental."

"Then it's my job to prevent future accidents." Pittman glanced down at his waferscreen. "I see from your report that you've postulated an advanced intelligence."

"Yes."

Pittman looked up. "How advanced?"

Cam struggled for terms Pittman might understand. "We've conducted several experiments on the samples we've obtained, and over and above its protoplasmic ability to mutate from one element to another, we've also registered brief flashes of what in my own field we've recently taken to calling hyperdimensionality, with energy readings showing the existence of a fifth and sixth dimension. Current Earth science can only extrapolate with generalized theorems to explain how these hyperdimensions are created, though at Brookhaven we've had some success in creating for short periods a fifth dimension by bombarding gold nuclei with high-energy particles. The entity creates this hyperdimensionality naturally in what we believe is a practical application. This evidence has allowed me to extrapolate an advanced intelligence. Extremely advanced."

"I don't get that. Hyperdimensionality. What exactly is it?"

Cam nodded, encouraged that the man was at least asking questions. "Width, length, and depth are the first three dimensions, correct?"

"I would agree. I'm a backyard carpenter."

"And time is the fourth?"

"Okay." Less sure.

"But it's now been discovered that time has a spiral nature. Picture time not as a straight line but as a corkscrew or a rotini noodle. A spiral. Ordinary time is when we travel sequentially and step by step along the spiral, like climbing a staircase in a lighthouse. But when we travel the diameter of the spiral, say leaping from banister to banister in a lighthouse, we get the fifth dimension, what at Brookhaven we call temporal radius. In this way, time can be manipulated, so that we don't have to travel it second by second, but can leap over vast stretches of it. The sixth dimension is a more extreme form of acrobatics around the spiral, not jumping from banister to banister, but up and down entire flights, and this we call sequential drop. It's through these fifth and sixth dimensions that time travel is conceivably possible. We have evidence of nine attainable dimensions, all created through the manipulation of time and space such as I've just outlined, but believe there may be as many as twenty-six, ones we think humans are unlikely ever to observe, much less conceive. You see, Colonel, time and space are critically interlinked, and it's in Alpha Vehicle's manipulation of curved space-time that I hypothesize an extremely advanced intelligence, possessing what to us is currently an impossible engineering platform. My own work on anti-Ostrander space is just starting to scratch the surface of hyperdimensionality."

Pittman paused for several seconds as he thought it through. Cam saw intelligence in the man's eyes that at least attempted to grapple with some of these esoteric concepts. But then he said, "Alpha Vehicle is starting to scare me." Like hyperdimensionality couldn't be trusted at all. "We've got four dimensions. They've got six. Which in my book is an arms race."

"You're generalizing, Colonel."

"How does our scientific know-how measure up to theirs?"

What analogy would the colonel possibly understand? "As ants are to humans, so humans are to the sentients behind Alpha Vehicle."

Everyone in the tower grew still. The colonel shifted, and as he once again glanced at his waferscreen, the muscles around his lips bunched, and the skin turned white as the blood was squeezed away.

"So in other words, they can squash us like bugs."

"If they can bend time and space, the wholesale elimination of a species like our own is certainly within their reach. But I don't think that's their intent. There's no evidence of that at all."

"What about military capability? Does Alpha Vehicle have any?"

Cam raised his eyebrows. He remembered his visit inside the entity, particularly that sublime moment when it had revealed something of its nature, how it was a blank waiting for an impression, a mission waiting for its purpose. "Alpha Vehicle I believe is what I term a proto-form. It gave me this impression when I was inside it. It's nothing yet. It's like a stem cell. Stem cells are the base coinage of all cells. They can take on many different cytological profiles. A stem cell can become a brain cell, a kidney cell, a blood cell—but as a stem cell, it remains a blank. That's what Alpha Vehicle is right now. A blank. One, I think, with mutational properties."

"So you think it's going to mutate?"

"One would infer the likelihood of a future mutation, since that's what it's designed to do."

"Is it within the realm of possibility that it might mutate into a weapon?"

"I don't have enough information to draw any conclusions about that." He added pointedly, "And neither do you."

"Any idea where it came from?"

Cam said, "I've been transmitting Greenhow System imagery and radio data to an astronomer friend of mind, Dr. Nolan Pratt. He's affiliated with the University of Hawaii and assistant director of the W. M. Keck Observatory in Mauna Kea. He's one of the most brilliant astronomers I know. He's uplinked to the Next Generation Space Telescope. You've heard of the NGST, haven't you? The one that came after Hubble?"

"Yes. A research toy, isn't it? I'm of course more familiar with the Greenhow ring, as I was one of the military advisers on the project."

Cam raised his index finger. "*That's* where I've heard your name."

"So, what's Dr. Pratt discovered?"

"He's confirmed that Alpha Vehicle originates from outside the solar system."

Pittman took the news soberly, nodding in a preoccupied manner. "So we're definitely talking aliens."

"I'm glad to say that this particular fact has been established."

Something happened to Pittman. An odd smile came to his face. His chest expanded, and he looked positively elated. "So this is historical."

"Yes." And was glad the colonel recognized the fact.

"And you and I . . ."

Cam got his drift immediately, that they were in the middle of it all. "Yes." Pittman's giddiness unsettled Cam. "Which is why it's so crucial we don't make any mistakes in how we proceed."

Pittman's elation vanished and he got back to business. "So . . . has your friend . . . Dr. Pratt . . . has he figured out exactly *where* Alpha Vehicle comes from?"

Cam nodded. "By using the Greenhow System, as well as the NGST, he's been successful in identifying a series of entity-created transit points, and he's tracked these back a good long ways. He's determined that Alpha Vehicle not only comes from a different solar system, but that it comes from a different galaxy as well, one so far away we haven't even named it yet. It's got a catalogue number only, NGC4945. It's twelve million light-years away. Normal observation of NGC4945 captures light that is twelve million years old. Observation through the transit points captures light that is generated today. Dr. Pratt has determined, based on past observation, the age difference between the normally observed light from NGC4945 and the transit-point light."

"And it amounts to twelve million years?"

"Correct. In other words, the light that reaches us through the transit points is a sample of light leaving NGC4945 . . . well . . . right now. Viewed another way, the light coming through the transit points doesn't take twelve million years to reach us. It reaches us instantaneously. Which means Alpha Vehicle traveled twelve million light-years *instantaneously*. Which is why I believe the sentients behind Alpha Vehicle are stupendously advanced, and why I believe we have to proceed cautiously."

The colonel's lips pursed. "So, when you were inside this thing . . . you say in your report it tried talking to you."

Cam thought about his experience inside Alpha Vehicle. "It showed me the universe, but it also showed me my own life, in microcosm."

Pittman's stare hardened. "I don't see any of those specifics in your report. Why?"

"It was personal." This part of his contact with Alpha Vehicle still flummoxed Cam, and he didn't know what to make of it.

"Dr. Conrad, if, as you say, we have to be careful about how we proceed—"

"It primarily showed me the death of my parents."

This was one of the things that was making him nervous about Alpha Vehicle. Why would it select—and indeed, how could it select—the single most painful event in his life, and make him relive it like a speeded-up film?

"In other words, it made you suffer."

He paused. He felt the anguish of his parents' death as a block in his throat. "I suffered, but my suffering was incidental to what Alpha Vehicle was trying to do."

"And what was it trying to do?"

"If I had to guess, I would say it was trying to know who and what I was."

"In other words, it was probing."

"Not in the military sense. It was curious. It wasn't threatening. It welcomed me. I'm just as mystified as you are by the whole thing, but if you want to know the truth, I believe Alpha Vehicle intrinsically represents a benign force. Even a positive one. Don't ask me how I know this. I can hardly begin to understand it myself. Call it a gut feeling."

Pittman frowned. "Doctor, we have to at least consider the possibility that Alpha Vehicle might be hostile. The Pentagon pays and trains people like me to dream up worst-case scenarios."

"I don't think this is a worst-case scenario, Colonel Pittman."

Pittman paused, then tapped the table a few times. "Do you think Alpha Vehicle has possibly influenced the way you think?"

His eyes narrowed. It was true, sometimes he questioned the need he seemed to have to protect Alpha Vehicle, but he honestly didn't think the entity had in any way brainwashed him. "No." And immediately he couldn't help wondering if that particular answer was too cut-and-dry.

"You were inside it. For two and a half hours, according to Dr. Weeks's report. Even though your own subjective experience calculated the absence in minutes. If this thing's so advanced . . . if it can outthink us a million to one, maybe it's made you one of its spies. You can see why I might be suspicious of everything you say, Dr. Conrad. Maybe it's fooled you. Maybe you're not even you anymore. Maybe you're it."

He gained a new respect for Pittman, for he had certainly run this Descartes-style conundrum by himself a number of times: *I think, therefore I'm it.* But he was not yet willing to deny the continued existence of his own personality. "All I've got is my own subjective experience to go on, but I don't feel any different. And by the way, I have no idea why the thing seems to have chosen me."

"Did it show you anything else, either about yourself or about what it plans to do?"

Cam looked away. "No."

Pittman sighed. "You're lying."

"I'm not lying."

"Dr. Tennant, you're taking over this project. Dr. Conrad's been compromised."

"All right, all right," said Cam. Then, in a softer voice: "It showed me Lesha."

On the other side of the tower, Lesha straightened.

"Lesha?" said Pittman. "Dr. Weeks?"

"Yes."

"Why would it show you Dr. Weeks?"

He frowned. "I really don't think this is pertinent to our investigation."

"Dr. Conrad . . ."

He hesitated, then said, "It showed me Lesha because it turns out . . ."

He told them, and sure, it was embarrassing, but in the greater context of what was going on, it was a small thing, a human thing, an attraction he wasn't ashamed of but which was nonetheless still awkward under the circumstances.

After a few moments, Mark Fuller broke the tension by saying he didn't think Lesha was half-bad-looking either; and Lesha laughed, and didn't seem embarrassed, and even seemed somewhat encouraged, because hadn't she had that longing in her eyes the night they had gone to their separate hotel rooms in Los Angeles? And of course they were all professionals, and they quickly digested the new information, and drew useful conclusions. Specifically, that Alpha Vehicle could probe the human mind. Pittman shook his head, even as a chaotic discussion ensued. Cam lost his focus. Pittman shifted in an agitated manner.

When the discussion finally settled down, the colonel stared at Cam. "Dr. Conrad, for the time being, continue to head the research effort. If you feel things aren't entirely right, or if others observe in you a change, or an unusual tendency to defend Alpha Vehicle—and that's not to say you can't advocate for an unbiased scientific study—but if it becomes apparent to other team members that Alpha Vehicle has in fact manipulated you, I'm going to ask you to step down. Dr. Tennant will take your place. In the meantime, all efforts will focus on why, after a journey of twelve million light-years, Alpha Vehicle has come to our system in the first place. Why, out of all the billions of moons in the Milky Way, did it choose ours, and what is it planning to do now that it's here? That should be your primary thrust, Dr. Conrad, and any extraneous scientific findings should be secondary."

6

The next day, Alpha Vehicle started moving west at a rate of 13.7 kilometers per hour, remaining two to three meters above the ground.

Cam and his team followed in Rover 1.

Rover 2 trailed a short distance behind.

Lesha sat beside him. She gave him a glance. He remembered last evening. The talk they had had. Of the Los Angeles thing. And her admission that she had come to the Moon simply because she couldn't stand the thought of him being so far away. The rover hit a particularly deep pothole and lurched to the side. Their shoulders touched. But touched in a different way. The tuning of things had changed between them. The possibility of a new intimacy, though not yet realized, had at last surfaced.

Renate rode in the back holding a monitoring device, one she had designed and made herself in the tech shop.

Alpha Vehicle looked like a gargantuan silver beach ball rolling over the desert-gray wastes of the Moon.

Renate said, "Dr. Conrad, I'm reading blips of atypical subatomic activity in and around Alpha Vehicle."

Five seconds later, the sky above Alpha Vehicle shifted, whirled, and a vortex—as insubstantial, fleeting, and miragelike as retina burn—appeared. Then disappeared. At first he thought he was seeing things because the green and smoky smudge had come and gone quickly. But when he glanced at Lesha and saw her looking at the same spot, he knew he wasn't mistaken.

"Renate, you got that?"

"It's recorded."

As Alpha Vehicle rolled across the Moon, several such green smudges appeared in the sky over the next half hour.

"Is there any relationship between Alpha Vehicle's sudden movement and this subatomic activity we're seeing?" he asked. "And what about the green vortexes? They didn't appear until Alpha Vehicle started moving. The only other one was when it first arrived."

"Let me make some further observations," said Renate.

They followed Alpha Vehicle for twenty-five kilometers. That's when its speed decreased. Its bulk was such that it reminded Cam of an ocean liner. It veered toward a crater a kilometer away. The crater's rim was a hundred meters high. Any suspicion of random behavior on the part of Alpha Vehicle could now be dismissed—it rolled unwaveringly toward this crater. The dichromatic vista—gray moon, black sky—was demarcated sharply by the rise of the crater's rim. As Cam got closer, the area became strewn with ejecta, and he had to turn the rover to avoid some larger rocks.

In ten minutes they reached the crater.

Alpha Vehicle rolled up the slope, maintaining a two-meter height above the lunar surface, etching a small concave trail in the dust, an effect of its gravitational "push." It balanced on the rim's peak, then rolled down the other side, the impression that of a small setting sun, only this sun was silver, and reflected everything around it with mirrorlike brilliance. It disappeared from view inside the crater. That the alien construct should now be out of sight distressed Cam. Why was it doing this? And why had it chosen this particular crater? And why did he seem to be having this fit of separation anxiety?

"We'll park at the crater's base and climb."

The rovers swung to a stop. Cam glanced at the tracks they'd left behind. They looked lonely—the first human impressions made in this area. He saw Earth, blue and white, hovering above the gray-brown horizon, and found it inspiring.

Everyone got off the rovers.

Renate pointed her monitoring device toward the sky. "Interesting."

"What?" said Cam.

"I'm detecting a subgravitational surge."

"Over and above the usual push?"

"Yes. It's right off the scale in terms of negative g-force."

"Anything else?"

"Each subgravitational surge seems to be encoded

with . . ." She glanced up at him, looking surprised. "Binary language."

Cam bounced over and investigated Renate's screen. Through the rigid format of digital and pixilated imagery, Renate's software had interpreted the binary energy coming from the subgravitational surge as a series of dots and dashes, nothing else, and these dots and dashes spilled over the screen with intense rapidity, so fast that they were nearly a blur. The hypothesis of binary language seemed to be a sound one.

"Communications?" he postulated.

"Possibly. Maybe remote commands from NGC-4945?"

Over the next five minutes, the team climbed the crater's rim. At first the slope was gentle, but as they neared the apex, it got steeper. Loose soil slid from under Cam's feet. Lesha fell and he helped her up. She glanced at him as he took her arm. She clutched his hand. The squeeze was a brief one, but enough to be revealing again of what they had spoken of last night. The attraction had long been brewing, but until this past day, never acknowledged.

A minute later, they reached the top.

The crater had to be two kilometers across. Alpha Vehicle had positioned itself exactly in the center; this in itself was a sign of intelligence—the thing had a sense of geometrical fitness. The sun shone from a forty-five-degree angle off to the left, a glaring white ball illuminating the Moon's surface with caustic brilliance. For several seconds, the team stood there watching Alpha Vehicle.

Then Mark pointed. "Look."

A new phenomenon became apparent to Cam a few seconds later. Using his visor magnification, he observed an odd puckering on Alpha Vehicle's surface, a dimpling at the thing's north pole. A thin filament grew from this flattened section. The weblike streak caught and amplified the sun's light. The filament rose to a height equal to Alpha Vehicle. A second filament rose next to the first one. For several seconds, the two filaments balanced there, reminding him of rabbit-ear antennae. But then they braided together; and as they twined, they fused into a single thicker filament. Then another filament shot out of Alpha Vehicle, and this third one was equal in thickness to the first two combined. After a moment, it melded with the others, creating an even thicker structure.

This operation repeated itself for the next few minutes. The combined filaments at last squared off at the corners to form a solid oblong, one that was equal in volume to Alpha Vehicle and, according to Renate's readouts, equal to its mass as well. Yet Alpha Vehicle showed no diminution of its own mass and volume. The whole process reminded Cam of a great mitosis. He glanced around at his team. Blaine and Mark stared in wonder. Lewis and Lesha set up cameras. Renate was down on her knees rigging up equipment.

He turned to Alpha Vehicle just in time to see the oblong launch itself. One second it was there, the next it was gone, a silver streak traveling so fast, arcing over the far horizon of the Moon, he could hardly see it.

"Did everybody catch that?"

Affirmatives came from Lesha and Mark, then everybody else. The strange, momentary, and elusive launch had the effect of rendering everyone mute for the next several seconds. A rush of adrenaline quivered through his body. The thing was actually *doing* something now? What? That it could throw thirty-story structures around with such lightning velocity made him think of Pittman's query, whether it could mutate into a weapon. For the act was aggressive in nature, and he wondered what the colonel's possible reactions might be to this worrisome development. Where had the new oblong gone? Was it headed for Earth? And how could Alpha Vehicle produce an object of mass and volume equal to itself without depleting its own mass and volume?

Before he could even begin to answer these questions, he saw rising out of Alpha Vehicle another weblike filament. A second quickly joined it, and the two twined together.

The process started again.

By the end of ten minutes, another thirty-story oblong flew off into the darkness, so quickly that it was gone over the Moon's horizon in the blink of an eye.

No sooner was it gone than another filament appeared.

So began a long afternoon.

The destination of the oblongs became apparent only after careful study of Greenhow satellite photographs of the Moon.

Cam and Lesha sat in front of the screen in Gettysburg Tower. He clicked to a higher magnification, stopping when it was the equivalent of two kilometers above the lunar surface, and saw the first of them, clean lines, flat surfaces, right angles startling and unmistakable against the chaotic airless terrain, an alien-created tower rising from the gray pitted regolith like a high-rise apartment. It reminded him of a huge domino. Only, bizarrely, it cast no shadow.

He clicked the magnification to one hundred meters. He looked for activity but saw none. He saved the image, then asked Greenhow software to find like or similar structures.

The camera zoomed out, and he and Lesha saw the curve of the Moon. Then the Moon rotated, and the camera zoomed in. Soon they were looking at another tower.

The camera repeated this a number of times.

It took them close to an hour before all current towers were accounted for, seventy-five so far, spaced equidistance from each other around the Moon's equator.

"Let's switch back to Alpha Vehicle," he said.

He keyed in the parameters, the camera zoomed back, then closed in.

Soon he discerned the principal module showing a slower pace of activity—only two towers had been built in the last three hours, hardly comparable to the frenetic pace of the first five hours. He was baffled. He couldn't begin to guess what Alpha Vehicle was up to.

He sat back and breathed a sigh of frustration. Lesha turned to him. She put her hand on his arm. He placed his hand over hers.

"What do we do?" she asked.

"Observe. And visit each and every one of these towers, if we can."

"That's a major undertaking."

"We would have to retool two rovers into robotic carriers. Just the oxygen requirements alone would use up the space of one rover. Then there's the food and water requirements. It's too bad all the vehicles in the SMCP are wrecked. One of these towers is all the way on the other side of the Moon."

"Would I be coming with you?"

Something in the way she said it.

He turned to her.

And knew it had to happen. The potentiality of the thing had been building all day.

Their lips met.

They kissed—softly, gently, for fifteen seconds, and were still kissing when Renate came into the room.

Cam and Lesha disengaged. Renate glanced at Lesha. Then at Cam. Not that she was embarrassed, but there were a few awkward moments.

"I've got some new findings," said Renate.

Cam, breaking the tension, swung his chair around from the screen and pulled it up to his desk. "Great."

She gave him a circumspect nod and advanced into the room. The tall, austere Dr. Tennant took a waferscreen from under her arm, opened it, and placed it on the table. The screen lit up with a diagrammatic representation of the transit points through which Alpha Vehicle had traveled to get to Earth, as outlined by Dr. Nolan Pratt, Cam's astronomer friend in Hawaii. But now superimposed directly behind these transit points was a map of the dark green vortexes they had discovered warping the sky above Alpha

Vehicle earlier in the day. She leaned over and pointed.

"I've used your own Stradivari software to figure some of this out, as it's good at extrapolating and defining hyperdimensional phenomena. As you can see by this diagram, I've charted Dr. Pratt's transit points. If you set the diagram in motion, it will take you all the way, theoretically, to NGC4945. But that's not what I'm here to show you. These dark green disturbances behind the transit points have been my focus. I'm now calling them relay points. I've been able to determine, using your software, as well as elements of the Next Generation Space Telescope, that these relay points consist primarily of so-called boundary particles, and these particles are in close contact with the more regular quark constituents Alpha Vehicle is generating. Within this space of interaction, we see the formation of gluon chains, and we further observe that these chains behave like the strings in string theory. As a communications specialist I've done much experimentation in trying to transmit messages through different forms of space in the hope of accelerating messages beyond light speed. The friction between these boundary particles and the more standard quarks have allowed these gluons the ability to form strings. And the strings in turn then create this hyperdimensionality that you've written about in your various papers. Through what you've described as temporal radius and sequential drop, the subgravitational surges, or packets as I'm now calling them, can travel much faster than light. As these packets are encoded with binary language, I think our communications theory can stand."

"So in other words, they've created a secondary instantaneous pipeline back to their own galaxy, only for communications?"

"The evidence certainly suggests it."

"And the Builders are using it regularly to communicate with NGC4945?"

"The Builders?"

"Just a name I've given them, since building towers seems to be their primary activity."

She nodded. "It's in place, and in regular use, you're right. With Dr. Pratt's transit points, the . . . the Builders have created an intergalactic highway. With the relay points, they've created a telegraph line. It seems the two systems are needed, each designed for its separate and different tasks, and the properties of each vary accordingly."

He was stupendously impressed. And awed. The Builders were sending messages twelve million light-years to NGC4945, and doing it *instantaneously.*

Renate continued. "As for breaking the actual code in the packets and figuring out what it means, I've had no luck."

He raised his eyebrows and rubbed the top of his desk in a preoccupied way. "Have you quantified the number of subgravitational packets they've sent so far?"

She nodded. "I've counted thirty-one."

"And is there any way we can utilize these relay points to send our own message?"

Her eyes narrowed, and her lips pursed. "I hadn't thought of that."

"Because I think the most important thing we can do right now is try to talk to them. I was on the link to Pittman earlier. He wants us to try and find out what these Moon towers mean." He took a deep breath and sat up straighter. "They're a bit troubling."

Renate nodded. "It might take some work."

"Then I want you to make it a priority. Let's send a message to them. Nothing complicated. We don't want to overwhelm them with cultural overlay. The initial thrust should be at establishing a common language. Let's find out if we even think the same way."

"What would you suggest?"

"As we hypothesize that they understand complex mathematics, I think our first message should consist solely of the first hundred prime numbers. Everything I've seen so far tells me that they're vastly different from us. Since such is the case, to communicate to them in anything else but numbers might scare them away, or worse, elicit an aggressive response. Numbers are pure. Numbers can't be misinterpreted. To send them the prime numbers, one of the fundamental sequences, will illustrate our own higher intelligence. We have to convince them that we're more than just bipedal fauna of no particular consequence before we can actually get them to talk to us in any meaningful or understandable way."

7

Through a live feed, Pittman, Blunt, Goldvogel, and Fye watched Conrad's team investigate one of the so-called Moon towers, this one twenty-five kilometers from Alpha Vehicle. On the screen, the Moon tower rose, geometrically precise, dwarfing the moonwalkers, who took its measurements.

Conrad's voice came over the link. "This tower, like the others, is seventy-five by twenty-two by ten meters. It's emitting electromagnetic energy. Temperature fluctuates from minus–one hundred and sixty Celsius to plus-seventy Celsius. Our team has yet to account for this wild fluctuation in temperature."

Pittman turned to Fye. "Oren, what about the media?"

Fye sighed in his all-is-lost way. "It's been their top story in all formats since we broke it yesterday. It's the Builders, and the Moon towers, and Alpha Vehicle."

"General, the White House?"

Blunt's eyes narrowed. "If we think a preemptive strike is necessary, the president's willing to go for it." He motioned at the screen. "Though he would like some intelligence about the possibility of retaliation."

Pittman said, "I'm leaning toward a preemptive strike myself. Inform the president I think that the building of the Moon towers represents an extremely ominous development."

And, as if these were trigger words, there came a great flash from the monitor at the end of the room, so bright it whited out the screen for several seconds. Audio became a scramble of confused, panicked voices. Pittman heard Dr. Conrad's voice asking for visuals, demanding visuals, ordering all assets to remain in place. Pittman was impressed. Cameron Conrad was turning out to be a soldier.

The burnout on the screen dimmed and the image resolved. The camera lurched dizzily upward. At the edges of the screen Pittman saw the demarcation between the gray landscape and the black sky. The landscape quickly sank from view as the camera rose farther. In a moment, all Pittman saw was a bright blue light rising into the sky, getting smaller and smaller as it got farther away. Now the *towers* were launching things? Whoever operated the camera had the good sense to filter the lens—resolution sharpened.

The launched object was a bird's nest of curving thunderbolts whirling in a continuous eddy of fluctuating light. As the object moved farther away, Pittman got a better view of its underside, and saw that it was donut-shaped. A shimmering film of turquoise plasma coated the object.

"Let's get Greenhow online. I want Peaceshield

scrambled, as well as all available suborbital aircraft.''

It was like a drug. It invaded his body. Combat.
Engagement. The scorpion at last getting to sting.

He watched the thing grow fainter, smaller, until
finally it was nothing more than a speck.

Goldvogel and Fye got on their special phones and
contacted appropriate commands.

Pittman sat there over the subsequent minutes and
watched new information come in. First came the
Greenhow feeds. The screen divided itself into several different windows, and in each of these he saw
similar launches from several other Moon-tower sites,
sudden flashes from the lunar surface, ninety-two
launches in all, one each from the final number of
Moon towers.

Then the Moon towers grew still.

At first the launched vehicles orbited the Moon
several times, gaining speed with each go-around. By
the third time, they were making the journey in less
than fifteen minutes. After the fifth orbit, the vehicles
broke free one by one and headed for Earth.

Pittman's scorpion elation ebbed. This was starting
to look worse and worse. Peaceshield rotated defense
assets to meet the incoming threat, the screen showing green light after green light as the system's six
hundred and twenty killer satellites armed themselves.

"Can Greenhow extrapolate a comprehensive view
of the combat arena?"

Goldvogel immediately got on the phone, asking
for new visual dynamics. Fye was now in contact
with a variety of commands. Blunt leaned toward his

waferscreen, following the readiness reports that came in one after the other. Pittman saw them on his own screen, all elements of the military responding to this sudden emergency.

He looked up and discovered Greenhow had the combat graphics loaded. Earth showed up blue to the left while the Moon was represented in white to the right. The ninety-two incoming modules appeared as red points, while Peaceshield was a comprehensive blur of green dots. The USAF's suborbital fighters, diagrammed as orange arrows, moved into position. Pittman was glad to see that Earth's assets outnumbered Builder assets by a margin of ten to one.

Yet now he was concerned by how fast the alien modules moved. Even the fastest Earth-Lunar vehicle took just under a day to cover the four hundred thousand kilometers to the Moon. Greenhow sent in speed estimates. Twenty-seven million kilometers per hour, so fast that the gulf between Moon and Earth looked as if it would be breached in minutes. It wouldn't matter if these launched vehicles weren't weaponized. At that speed, even an unweaponized projectile would be a planet killer.

He glanced around the room. Fye's hand, clutching his cell phone, eased away from his ear in an absent manner as he watched this miracle of speed. Blunt and Goldvogel looked as if they were witnessing the Second Coming. To see the ninety-two launch vehicles come so quickly, and to realize that the easily perceptible movement on the small graphic was actually taking place in real time, in real space, confirmed for Pittman yet again the Builders' immense technical prowess. Despite Earth's ten-to-one advantage, Pittman realized they simply didn't have anything fast enough.

He tensed up. "Gentlemen, our defensive capability has just been rendered useless."

Nonetheless, he issued a standard attack-when-in-range order. Peaceshield launched orbital missiles and parked them in various positions around Earth, having them prowl geosynchronously in the shallows of the thermosphere like barracudas, poised to strike when the launch vehicles got close enough.

When things looked hopeless, the alien launch vehicles suddenly formed their own orbits around Earth, far above Peaceshield's barracudas.

"There's no evidence of braking," said Goldvogel. "No emissions or thrust signature. They've just stopped."

And it was true: all ninety-two vehicles stopped and right-angled into orbits around Earth—instantaneously—breaking all known rules of physics.

They stayed like this.

Orbiting Earth, doing nothing.

Just beyond Peaceshield's range.

Pittman could only guess what their next move might be.

A few hours later, with the stalemate still unchanged, Pittman and the Orbops crew eavesdropped on a conversation between Conrad and Dr. Nolan Pratt, his old astronomer friend from the university. This was courtesy of Oren Fye, their intelligence man.

Sound quality wasn't the best—voices were raspy, nasal, and long pauses after each transmission punctuated the exchange, the time it took the signal to travel the four hundred thousand kilometers to the Moon. Despite this, the meaning was clear, startling, and portentous.

Dr. Pratt spoke in a faltering way, as if he felt he had to apologize to Dr. Conrad for what he had to say. There was news. About Tau Ceti, one of the sun's closer neighbors.

"Tau Ceti's a main-sequence star, like our own," said Pratt. "I'm afraid something's happened to it. An anomaly. And while I believe it's probably unrelated to what's going on up on the Moon, Cam, I thought I'd let you in on our findings, just in case."

A crackling long pause.

"And what are your findings?"

There came another long pause; Pittman and the Orbops team heard nothing but static. Then Pratt's voice came on again.

"Tau Ceti was supposed to burn as a main-sequence star for the next three billion years. But it's unexpectedly entered its red giant phase early and we can't explain why."

Pittman now felt out of his depth because he really didn't know what a red giant was, and knew they would have to do some digging. What bothered him was the tone in Pratt's voice. Tentative. Unsure. Scared. Most of all, perplexed.

Pratt said, "In order for Tau Ceti to enter its red giant phase, it would have to use all its hydrogen fuel. I'm not sure how it could burn three billion years' worth of fuel so quickly, especially when there's no astronomical evidence of any cataclysmic event. But the analysis of the light coming from Tau

Ceti indicates that it's definitely gone into its red giant phase."

"Anybody know what a red giant is?" asked Pittman.

Fye shook his head and sighed. "I'm looking."

Cam Conrad spoke. "I'm not sure why you think it would have anything to do with what's going on up here."

"I'm not sure that it does. But in the interests of thoroughness, I thought I'd better report it to you. It's a major astronomical event, and a huge mystery. There's no evident cause for this . . . this sudden hydrogen depletion."

"But Tau Ceti's got to be what, three parsecs away?"

"Closer to four."

"Not exactly our neck of the woods."

"Neither is NGC4945."

In the boardroom, Fye spoke up. "A red giant is what happens to a main-sequence star when it dies."

"So, what's your theory?" Cam asked Pratt, and Pittman now noted a slight edge to Cam's voice.

"I don't have a theory. I'm studying the problem. That's all."

"But you felt the need to contact me."

"Merely to report an anomalous observation that may or may not have some bearing on what you're doing up there."

"You think the Builders may have caused this red giant?"

"Builders?"

"That's what we're calling them." Conrad paused.

"Nolan, come on. The light you're seeing from this red giant, it was generated eleven years ago? Correct?"

"Eleven-point-three."

"And the Builders arrived on the Moon last month."

"Yes."

"So that means there's a separation of eleven-point-three years between the two events."

"Correct."

"And you're still supposing a connection?"

"Cam . . . what I'm witnessing—and believe me, I've conferred with my colleagues—what I'm observing is theoretically impossible. Tau Ceti, according to all previous estimates, should have burned as a main-sequence star for the next three billion years. What we're recording here is a new phenomenon, one that's never been seen before. It could be a completely natural phenomenon. Then again, it could be an artificially created one. And because in the annals of both ancient and modern astronomy there's never been anything like it, the artificially created explanation seems reasonable. And if it's created by some sentient force, the engineering involved is extremely advanced compared to anything we have. You probably recognize these last words from the report you sent me a few days ago. The hydrogen depletion in Tau Ceti represents a major achievement, if in fact it was engineered. Now the Builders have commenced this tower project on the Moon. We have no idea if the two are related. And we don't know what all these Moon towers are going to be used for. But it certainly stands to reason that they might be designed to create a hydrogen bleed in our own sun."

A good long pause, and Pittman thought the transmission might be at an end. But then Dr. Conrad spoke. "You're aware of the launch? It happened just a few hours ago. You got my e-mail?"

"Yes. What are they?"

"Energy cells of some kind."

"Has NASA sent a probe?"

"It has."

"That was fast."

"Colonel Pittman knows how to get things done."

"Any useful intelligence?"

"Unfortunately, no. When the probe got within fifty kilometers, its systems died. Without explanation. It's nothing more than space junk now."

"The Builders disabled it?"

"It would appear so."

"Are you going to tell Orbops about Tau Ceti?" asked Pratt.

Now a long pause as interlunar static scratched through the speakers. Pittman glanced around the room, his eyes finally alighting on Blunt. Blunt's face had turned pink.

Dr. Conrad gave no immediate answer. "The red giant perplexes me, Nolan. Why would the Builders do something like that? Why would they come twelve million light-years specifically to turn Tau Ceti into a red giant? You think they would have more immediate local concerns. Colonel Pittman is just itching for a chance to launch a preemptive strike against them, so I'm going to put off telling him for the time being. I need more time to study things. Have you observed any other anomalous red giants?"

"A complete sweep is taking place as we speak."

"Good. I've got Dr. Tennant working on the communications angle. It's important we make ourselves heard. If we can speak up and let them know we're here, then we'll be that much closer to a dialogue with them. And dialogue is what prevents war."

At the end of the transmission, Pittman felt let down by Cam Conrad. That Conrad saw fit to suppress information, even if that information seemed currently extraneous, galled him; he would have thought seriously about dismissing him as team leader if he weren't producing a steady stream of useful results. Still, it was worrisome, and he voiced his concerns to the group. "I'm really beginning to think that thing has turned him somehow."

"We'll certainly have to watch him closely," said Blunt.

"He doesn't understand chain of command."

"He's a civilian. What do you expect?"

"I'm going to have to give him a dressing down. I don't want to go around being suspicious of him all the time."

By the end of the hour, Fye had a report on what would happen to Earth if the sun accelerated into its red giant phase, for the sun also was a main-sequence star.

"As the sun depletes its hydrogen supply, its nuclear furnace would no longer burn with the same degree or force, and so the sun would slowly begin to collapse under the force of its own gravity. Its mass would naturally become denser because of this collapse, and the pressure would then reignite the sun to such a degree that it would become a red giant. During the initial collapse we would experience a significant cooldown on Earth, with temperatures dropping drastically. But then when the red giant phase came, things would heat up to unsurvivable levels. The sun would actually grow to envelop Earth, and that of course would be the end of us.''

8

Cam was investigating another Moon tower fifty-five kilometers away from Gettysburg the next day when blinding pain shot through his head. For a brief instant, he saw the inside of Alpha Vehicle again, the universe all mapped out for him; then he fell to the Moon's gray-brown regolith, bouncing once in the low lunar gravity before he settled on his side. He couldn't breathe. It was as though the entirety of his brain, even the sections responsible for automatic functions like breathing, had been momentarily rerouted to another purpose, and didn't have the capacity to keep his body alive. He clawed his wristpad—which would send an emergency signal to his coworkers—with mounting panic, then called up visuals on his biomonitor, saw his heart flatline, his respiration taper to a standstill, and his pulse flicker into nonexistence.

The Moon tower next to him reversed its customary gravitational push, and now fluxed with a gravitational pull.

It drew him in; he felt funneled by a vacuum.

Unlike Alpha Vehicle, the tower didn't pull him right inside, only to its east wall, so that he was pressed flat against it, caught like a fly on flypaper. His brain tingled, and strangely, unexpectedly, his panic ebbed, and he didn't feel so frightened anymore. He had the sense that the Builders were trying to read him again. He felt precariously balanced on the precipice of existence. Then he sensed a lessening of his head pain, and a moment later his breathing grew easier and his heartbeat came back.

He experienced a mirage. Written figures and symbols danced before him, unlike any he had ever seen before. Were they trying to communicate with him, then, in written form?

Maybe not, because a moment later, the tower pushed him away, reversing gravitational flux so that he toppled to the ground.

He was surprised by the rebuff. And a little hurt. He gazed at the Moon tower in mystification, wondering if the thing had saved his life. Or conversely, had nearly murdered him. He heard Lesha calling him through her radio, but it was as if her voice came from a great distance. He thought of the mishmash of symbols in the mirage, but even as he pictured them, he couldn't remember them anymore. He got up and brushed moondust off his arms.

Lesha now stood beside him. "What happened?"

"I had a . . . a weird episode. I couldn't breathe. And the tower pulled me in."

"Are you all right?"

"I am now."

She motioned at the tower. "The thing reversed flux, according to the instrument readings." She was out of breath, her voice anxious, and she rubbed his arm repeatedly as if she had to convince herself that he was still alive.

He looked at the tower, saw his own reflection in its glimmering surface, the surrounding moonscape, and the black line of the horizon far to the rear. "Everything seized up on me, my heart, lungs, and limbs, like when I was inside Alpha Vehicle, only it was painful this time, and I thought I was going to die." He looked up at the tower mistrustfully. "And when the thing pulled me in, I had this odd hallucination. I saw symbols."

She grew still. "What kind of symbols?"

"Like writing. Or mathematical symbols."

"Can you remember any of them?"

"No. They're gone now."

"But you're okay?"

He brushed himself off. "I seem to be."

Lesha looked at the tower. "I don't like these towers. They're starting to scare me."

"I think I better sit down. My heart's pounding. Why would it try to hurt me?"

"Cam, you're pushing yourself too hard. Maybe you should take a day off."

"I can't take a day off. I've got to prove to Pittman that Alpha Vehicle means no harm or he's going to blow it up. I had no idea he would be eavesdropping on my radio transmissions."

"Just sit here and try and get your breathing under control."

"I didn't like the way he lectured me about my conversation with Nolan."

"Maybe you should have told him about the red giant thing right away."

"He's suspicious of me now. And you know what? I'm suspicious of him."

"You're getting yourself upset."

He got up. "We should start working again."

"Cam, just sit."

But he couldn't. He felt that time was running out. "He's automatically assumed a connection between Tau Ceti and the Builders. And that's just the kind of excuse he needs to get trigger-happy with Alpha Vehicle. I'm not going to let that happen. I'm going to protect Alpha Vehicle any way I can."

She was looking at him now through her yellow visor. "You're starting to sound like a convert. And that might make him get trigger-happy as well."

Johnsie Dunlap, the nurse practitioner, wanted to assess him when he got back at the end of the day. She went over his symptoms one at a time, the bluish light of the clinic lamp burnishing her dark face with a violet penumbra.

"So, sharp head pain?" she asked.

"Yes."

"That's what it started with?"

"Yes."

"And then what?"

"I couldn't breathe."

"So, shortness of breath."

"I wasn't short of breath," he said. "I had no breath at all."

"Any visual disturbances?"

He looked away. He had to be careful here. He could tell she was just waiting to push him off the research team. Yet at the same time he felt he had to tell her the truth. "I had this . . . this vision, I guess you'd call it."

Her eyes widened. "What kind of vision?"

"I saw these symbols. Like writing."

"Writing? What kind of writing?"

He shook his head, now feeling bewildered. "I don't know. I've never seen it before."

"But you're sure it was writing."

"Definitely."

She paused for a long time after that, thinking, then typed a quick entry into her chart. "And you saw these hallucinations while you were pressed against the side of the tower?"

"I wouldn't call them hallucinations. I firmly believe the thing was trying to communicate with me in some way."

She observed him quietly for a few seconds. "You've described several symptoms of transient ischemic attack."

"What kind of attack?"

"Transient ischemic attack. It's like a ministroke. And considering your family history—"

"It wasn't a ministroke. Johnsie, please, listen to me. Colonel Pittman's going to be here any day now. He's not going to play games with Alpha Vehicle. I read up on some of his involvement in the PRNC War. And while I admit he was instrumental in getting the North Chinese to stand down, he was absolutely brutal in the way he went about things. He's eager to fight because that's what he does best, and he's good at what he does, and the country needs men like him, but in this particular case, things might get bad quickly if he declares war against Alpha Vehicle. So please, there's no need to tell him about this little attack I had. Or how I saw these symbols. At least not until we understand the significance of what's happened to me. If you tell him about my attack, he might end up shooting first and asking questions later, and that's the last thing we want."

That night, while he was asleep, the alarm sounded.

He sat up in his bunk. His intercom light flashed. He pushed the button.

"Yes?"

"Dr. Conrad?" It was Lamar Bruxner.

"Yes."

"We're picking up the approach of several space vehicles. Seventeen in all. It looks like the expeditionary force is here two days early. I thought you might want to know."

It didn't surprise him that Pittman was here two days early—the colonel was that kind of man. "I'm on my way."

Cam clicked off, got out of bed, and put on his coveralls. He left his quarters and bounce-shuffled down corridor 2 to the hub. He climbed the companionway and went up through the hatchway into the tower.

The phases of the Moon had reached the point where the sun was hidden behind the horizon. The blackness outside was like a vat of tar. Only a few tracking lights in the SMCP, ones that hadn't been destroyed during Alpha Vehicle's moonfall, illuminated small pools of lunar landscape. The Sumter Module and Command Port was mostly in shadow.

Bruxner and his assistant, Laborde, sat hunched over the tracking screens. Bruxner turned as Cam emerged from the companionway. "They're coming this way. We've hailed them. They haven't responded." Bruxner turned back to his console. The blue light coming from the screens illuminated his wide face.

Cam went over and looked.

In the graphics, the Moon was at the center, and the seventeen vehicles, marked in red, were closing in with tightening orbits toward the curve of the lunar surface. Compared to the Builder energy cells, these vehicles moved at a conventional speed, heading westward at just over fifteen thousand kilometers per hour.

Cam initiated a spectrographic overlay on the screen. "It's them all right. The burn signature is unmistakable."

"Why didn't he tell us he was coming early?"

Cam lifted his chin. "Because he wanted to maintain radio silence. He's under the impression that security is still an issue. He forgets Alpha Vehicle can probe the human mind."

The three watched for the next several moments.

Then Bruxner, with a nervous reach of his arm, toggled the communications apparatus. "This is Gettysburg One. Gettysburg One to incoming vessels. Identify yourself. Repeat, identify yourself."

Nothing.

Cam pictured Alpha Vehicle sitting in Crater Cavalet—for they had named the crater after their dead friend—staring up at the lunar heavens like a big silver eye, watching the approach of the seventeen vessels the way a large and predatory fish might watch seventeen minnows.

Over the course of the next twenty minutes, graphics showed the vehicles descending.

Laborde was the first to make a naked-eye sighting through the tower windows, and pointed to the dark sky. "Look."

They watched seven vehicles approach from maybe forty kilometers up, nothing more than chalky smudges at first.

Then the spectrometer graphics showed sudden burns—the vehicles braking.

At last Cam saw seven ships over Shenandoah Valley. "I wonder what happened to the other ten?"

The vehicles came down one by one, shining their spotlights on the ground, kicking up dust with reverse thrusters. The craft were beetle-shaped—head, thorax, and abdomen. Each had six landing legs. They descended silently, as they must in the vacuum. They were painted in a camouflage pattern of gray, black, and taupe—Moon colors. The other ten vehicles seemed to be landing out there.

Unexpectedly, the Crater Cavalet alarm sounded. The monitors blinked to views of Cavalet. Unlike Shenandoah, the crater was bright with permanent floodlights now.

Alpha Vehicle shimmered like a giant crystal ball in the center. Laborde remote-commanded the cameras to swivel away from Alpha Vehicle and fix on the new arrivals.

Beyond the crater's rim the other ten vehicles sank; these vehicles were much larger than the ones landing in Shenandoah. While still beetle-shaped, several weapons sconces could be seen, appearing as angular shadows at various points along the stout fuselages. The ten craft surrounded the crater.

The vehicles didn't simply land, but burrowed as well. Rotary scoops shot dirt into the sky. As trenches deepened, the vehicles sank from view. The scene was chilling, bizarre, and worrying. Loosened particulate drifted around the crater, sometimes obscuring vehicle activity—until all such activity stopped, and the Moon once again regained its eons-old stillness.

Movement now became noticeable out in Shenandoah. The rover access bays on the seven spacecraft opened and an armored vehicle emerged from each. Headlamps shone from these vehicles. They snaked in a column toward Gettysburg. Because of the vacuum, Cam couldn't hear the vehicles, but as they rounded the eastern edge of the SMCP, he could feel them—the tower vibrated gently.

The radio blared into life, and the images on the screens were overpowered by a visual hail coming from the lead vehicle. A moment later, Cam saw Colonel Timothy Pittman on the screen, goggles over his eyes, a military helmet on his head patterned with the same gray, black, and taupe, and a massive energy-pulse rifle in his hands.

"Operation Moonstone to Gettysburg, this is Colonel Timothy Pittman, Orbital Operations Team Commander. Please acknowledge and make ready for fourteen new billets. I repeat, make ready for fourteen new billets. Activate Air Lock One immediately." Then a pause as the man's face settled like freshly poured concrete. "We're taking over."

9

Cam felt like a civilian in a besieged city as he watched soldiers march through the main air lock. By this time a number of the other scientists were up as well, including Lesha. In their armored suits, the troops looked like big black robots. They weren't tidy about their movements, but clumped down the hall with the belligerence of warriors preparing to go to battle.

Cam, Lesha, and Bruxner trailed a few steps behind Pittman.

A lieutenant named Haydn, like the famous old composer, accompanied Pittman. So did a smaller man, Newlove, who was loaded with gear.

Events in the next ten minutes unfolded at a rapid pace.

Pittman and his troops went into the common room. Pittman said, "Haydn, have the troops conduct an electronic sweep. Newlove, get the field unit going in the corner. I want linkups to our positions around Crater Cavalet, and target-acquisition visuals on Alpha Vehicle as quickly as possible." Haydn and

Newlove went about their tasks. "Wake the others," Pittman told Bruxner. "We're having a briefing."

Bruxner went to the intercom, unable to hide the ill grace on his face, and sent a general hail through the public address. "All personnel, please report to the common room, repeat, please report to common room immediately."

In a few minutes, Newlove had his equipment up and running, including a large monitor that showed various views from the emplacements around Crater Cavalet. At the center of Newlove's gridded screen sat Alpha Vehicle, serene, inscrutable, like a giant pearl in a gray dusty shell.

Other Stradivari Team members now came into the common room—Mark Fuller, Blaine Berkheimer, Lewis Hirleman, campus types, with long hair and brutally intelligent eyes.

Support staff member Harland Law followed.

Renate Tennant came a few minutes later with the Princeton Team—Peggy Wilson, Silke Forbes, and Maribeth Finck.

At last came Johnsie Dunlap. She looked around at the new arrivals with deep misgiving, then glanced at Cam, as if acknowledging that his concerns about Pittman shooting first and asking questions later might be legitimate after all.

One by one, as the soldiers finished their security scans, they came to relay their findings to Haydn, who in turn reported them to Pittman. The colonel slung his weapon to his shoulder and clasped his hands behind his back. He looked around the room. Cam surveyed the room as well. On one side were nine academics in pajamas. On the other stood fourteen soldiers in black armor. The contrast couldn't have been greater.

Pittman addressed the group. "As you've probably guessed, from this point on, Gettysburg is under my command. My command consists primarily of Marine Corps enlisted personnel operating under the Orbops umbrella, and they are trained specifically for hard-vac, high-rad, low-grav missions. They are here to help you. And protect you. At the same time they will have authority over you. That's not to say I'll be imposing martial law. I understand we have a respected and responsible group of scientific and support staff here, and under the circumstances, I don't think martial law will be necessary. But I may, from time to time, issue directives, and I'll expect them to be followed to the letter."

Then something approaching a grin came to the colonel's hard face.

"I'm pleased to say that your own civilian rescue shuttles are scheduled to reach lunar orbit in the next eight days." There came sudden murmurs of approval, and even a little applause from the Princeton group. "But we are urging all of you to stay on the Moon for the duration, as your research efforts have been invaluable to us." The applause immediately died down. "In particular, we are asking Dr. Cameron Conrad, Dr. Lesha Weeks, and Dr. Renate Tennant to stay, and I even have presidential orders to that effect. The rest of you won't be compelled to stay, but we hope that you will volunteer to stay. You are now conducting your research under the auspices of Operation Moonstone. For those of you who want to be taken back to Earth, we urge you to continue your research there. You'll be given funding to study Alpha Vehicle. On Earth you'll be answering directly to one of my subordinates, Lieutenant Colonel Oren Fye. You'll be given full contact information for the lieutenant colonel presently, and if you do return to Earth, he'll be expecting daily reports from you. Meanwhile, if you feel the need to speak to me here on the Moon, you may do so through Lieutenant Haydn. In the event of hostile action on the part of the enemy, certain secure military channels will be established—"

"The enemy?" Cam couldn't stop himself. "Why do you call them the enemy?" He could feel Alpha Vehicle prompting him, even more so now that he had had his second episode with one of its Moon towers. "Let's not get carried away, Colonel."

Pittman looked disgruntled by Cam's interruption. "Have I misspoken myself, Dr. Conrad?"

"Let's not characterize the Builders as the enemy. They're anything but."

A forbearing grin came to Pittman's face. "If it'll make you feel any better, we'll call them potential belligerents for now."

Feeling an uncustomary evangelistic zeal, he said, "I happen to believe they're a potential godsend."

"Dr. Conrad, common sense dictates we must exercise caution. Now, please, I don't mean to be rude, or to start off on the wrong foot, but if you could refrain from further interruption?"

Cam let the misbegotten semantics of the thing go.

Pittman went on to describe the kind of consumables he'd brought to support his troops while on the Moon, adding that he in no way wanted to utilize

Gettysburg's obviously limited resources. The more Cam listened to Pittman, the more nervous he got. Newlove's radio continued to erupt with sporadic bursts of chatter, and several times Cam heard references to "the enemy" or "the target" or "the Moonstone objective." By the time Cam finally spoke with Pittman one on one at the end of the briefing, it was in what he thought was a context of looming disaster.

"You're going to mount a preemptive strike, aren't you?"

"I'm not at liberty to discuss our tactical plans, Dr. Conrad."

Lesha, Renate, and Bruxner crowded around to listen.

"If you're not planning a preemptive strike, what's all that armor doing around Alpha Vehicle?"

"Should a response be required, I want elements in place."

"But how do you expect the Builders to take this?" persisted Cam. "You haven't even given Renate the chance to complete her communications effort yet. Why don't we at least try to talk to them first?" He remembered his hallucination of the bizarre and indecipherable written symbols, and added, "At least in terms we can understand."

As if reminded of Renate's communications effort, Pittman turned to her, and with weary impatience, said, "I'll want a full report on your efforts by eighteen hundred hours, Dr. Tennant."

"Of course, Colonel."

"Whatever you do, don't mount a preemptive strike," warned Cam.

"I'll do whatever it takes to protect the United

States. Look at it from the Pentagon's viewpoint, Dr. Conrad. Unknown visitors have breached the territorial sovereignty of the solar system without our welcome."

Cam frowned. "The solar system has territorial sovereignty?"

"Legislation to that effect is being drafted as we speak. And in breaching our sovereignty they've become de facto aggressors. They've landed on our Moon and destroyed, without provocation, our primary lunar module and spaceport, a facility that took three and a half decades to build, and eighteen-point-six billion dollars to finance. They've killed one of your own scientific staff. They've stranded you and your colleagues, necessitating a rescue mission costing American taxpayers millions of dollars. They've forcibly confined you. And while all these things are of grave concern, what worries us most is the way you've been talking to them. Because of that, the senior team and I think you might have been compromised in some way. We discussed this possibility extensively after we learned you hid the red giant anomaly in Tau Ceti from us, and the outcome of our discussion is that we've decided to take extra precautions with you once you return to Earth. Our plan is to run some diagnostic tests on you to see if anything has changed inside your brain, anything that might possibly influence the way you're thinking about this whole thing."

"What?"

"Since such is the case, when you return to Earth, you'll be put under the direct care of Dr. Jeffrey Ochoa, one of our staff physicians. We feel this is a reasonable course of action. He'll be responsible for running these tests on you."

Cam was alarmed. "Why?"

"Surely you don't object to this. Dr. Ochoa has extensive knowledge of brainwashing techniques. He's also well seasoned in various medical strategies that help obtain the truth. We want to find out what they've been saying to you. In fact, it's *essential* we find out what they've been saying to you."

"Nothing I can figure out. Which is why it's so important we wait until Dr. Tennant's efforts yield some results. Let's attempt a meaningful dialogue with them before we start shooting, or picking my brain apart strand by strand. Forget this Dr. Ochoa. He's just going to end up muddling the whole process."

"Command personnel of Operation Moonstone have deemed it necessary that you be put under his care once you're no longer needed here on the Moon. He's going to help us get to the bottom of what they might have been saying to you."

"In other words, he's an interrogation specialist."

"He's a fully trained practicing physician."

"This is ridiculous. You don't need to do this to me. Alpha Vehicle is not a threat."

"What about the construction of all the Moon towers, the launching of the energy cells, and the transformation of one of the solar system's closest neighbors into a red giant?" He tapped his head. "You're not right up here if you think that's not threatening. And that's why Dr. Ochoa needs to take a look at you."

*   *   *

Later that day, when Cam was suiting up to investigate another Moon tower, the mood in the air lock was grim.

Lesha came up to him and put her hand on his arm. "You shouldn't be coming out with us today."

"I'll be fine."

She stood on her toes and kissed his cheek. "Pittman's a study, isn't he?"

He shook his head. "I went to this bar once, and there was this guy, and he staggered from patron to patron looking for a fight. Fighting was his idea of a good time. There didn't have to be a reason for it. Fighting was what he did. That's the sense I get from Pittman."

"This Dr. Ochoa worries me. Can they do that to you? I mean legally?"

He raised his eyebrows. "Apparently so." He shook his head. "But what bothers me more is how I seem to be the only one stopping Pittman from blowing up Alpha Vehicle."

"You're not. I'm behind you a hundred percent. And so's Johnsie."

His brow rose. "Johnsie is?"

"I was talking to her. She's agreed to suppress her latest assessment of you."

He nodded. "Good."

"But you should stay in Gettysburg today. You don't want to aggravate things. If you get too close to another tower, you might have another attack, and who knows what Pittman will do to Alpha Vehicle if he thinks it's giving you attacks? He'll most likely call it an act of aggression and give the okay to retaliate."

"No. I've got to go out. If I can uncover irrefutable proof that Alpha Vehicle means no harm, then maybe he'll stand down and the human race can get on with the greatest thing that's ever happened in its history. Don't worry. I'll be fine."

And he was fine. For a while. But then he realized he should have taken Lesha's advice.

For as he was in the rover with Lesha and Mark halfway to the Moon tower, his face started to tingle. Then his left eye went blind. Then his head throbbed with such severe pain, he slumped over in his chair and groaned. Lesha leaned over him in alarm. He heard her calling him through his suit radio, and he tried to speak, but couldn't get the words out.

Lesha turned to Mark and cried, "Turn around, turn around! They're at him again."

What was particularly strange as he drifted into a state of semiconsciousness was how he saw, in the vacuum above, the same cryptic written symbols he had seen when drawn against the other Moon tower yesterday.

10

As Colonel Pittman came over and looked at him in the infirmary after they got him back, Cam didn't feel entirely human anymore, but more like a sea creature from the deepest part of the Mariana Trench gazing at the world with weird sightless eyes.

Colonel Pittman came into view as if through a fish-eye lens. All Cam could do was stare.

Lieutenant Haydn stood next to Pittman, his extremely fair complexion and white-blond hair bright in the overhead lights. Cam felt trapped by his own compromised condition, felt confused, was fairly certain the Builders had done this to him, but now couldn't help wondering if something medical had happened to him as well; he kept thinking of the stroke his father had had.

When Johnsie Dunlap came over and talked to Pittman, Cam had to rethink the stroke idea. "Of course, we have no advanced diagnostic equipment on the Moon, and from a clinical perspective, I can't really determine what's happened to him at all. He has a family history of stroke, but a lot of the clinical signs of stroke are missing. There's no left- or right-side weakness. And he's conscious, and his eyes move, and if you look at him, you can see that he's listening to us, and understanding us. But he doesn't seem to be able to move. Or register pain." She poked his arm with a needle, drawing blood, and Cam didn't feel a thing. "The best thing we can do is transfer him to medical care on Earth. And I don't necessarily mean to Dr. Ochoa." This last was said with a certain amount of sternness.

"No. Dr. Ochoa will definitely be his physician." Pittman peered at Cam more closely. "Any chance Alpha Vehicle did it?"

Johnsie looked more closely as well. "I can't say. He was nowhere near Alpha Vehicle, and not really anywhere near one of the towers. But it's certainly not beyond the realm of possibility."

"Ms. Dunlap, you should have told me about the previous Moon tower incident sooner. You want us to start thinking Alpha Vehicle has gotten to you too?"

Johnsie said nothing. Cam felt his heartbeat quicken. She had told Pittman after all?

The colonel said, "You can go now."

Johnsie gave him a sour look and retreated.

Pittman squared his shoulders and stared at him. Haydn was now checking something on his waferscreen.

Under Pittman's fringe of silver mustache, a consoling grin appeared. Yet for all this, Cam knew the colonel wouldn't hesitate when it came to launching a first strike against Alpha Vehicle, especially if he found out the Builders were responsible for his own curious paralysis-like state. He remembered Lesha's words. *He'll most likely call it an act of aggression and give the okay to retaliate.* How could he make Pittman understand?

With superhuman effort he willed the paralysis out of his arm, grabbed Pittman's shirt, and focused his eyes. The grin slipped from the colonel's face. ''Ms. Dunlap?''

Johnsie came back and noted the movement. Her eyes widened but she said nothing.

Pittman's sympathetic expression came back. ''Dr. Conrad, I would ask that you let go. And I just want you to know that Orbops and the United States government are proud of your sacrifice. Believe me, if it turns out Alpha Vehicle is responsible for this attack upon your person, we'll make it pay, and pay dearly.''

Pittman gently clutched Cam's wrist and pulled it away. Johnsie said something to the colonel, but now it wasn't only the paralysis; it was also a strange and entirely unexpected lack of understanding, for she seemed to speak in a foreign language he couldn't decipher, like suddenly they had all decided to speak Greek. Lesha came into view. She focused on Pittman. Cam struggled to make Pittman understand one last time that he should under no circumstances launch a preemptive strike against the Builders, that what the aliens might or might not be doing to him was incidental, and that he really didn't want to be the cause of a war, but all that came out of his mouth was a scraping sound that reminded him of water draining from a tub. At last the effort overwhelmed him and he gave up. Tears came to his eyes. Sweat bathed his forehead.

Pittman backed away, the corners of his lips turned down, his eyes puzzled, as if he were embarrassed by Cam's tears. He smoothed his Orbops camouflage shirt. "Needless to say, Dr. Tennant will be taking over the research end of things from here on in."

Haydn pressed his black earpiece with two fingers, listened, then leaned forward and murmured a few words to Pittman. Cam couldn't hear what he was saying. Pittman nodded.

The two soldiers left.

Cam closed his eyes.

He might have slept.

When next he opened his eyes, he was being wheeled along corridor 9 to the air lock. Lesha leaned over him. She carried his flight bag, and was smiling, even as she struggled to fight back tears. He tried to see who was wheeling him at the foot of the gurney, and caught a glimpse of Laborde.

Lesha said, "Colonel Pittman's agreed to an emergency evac in one of the military spacecraft. He's not such a bad sort after all."

But he couldn't help thinking how he was going to be delivered to Dr. Jeffrey Ochoa, ostensibly for his own medical care, but in fact more for interrogation and study.

He tried to tell her he didn't want to leave, couldn't leave, *mustn't* leave, but the gurney rolled forward until they were at the air-lock pressure door. He heard hissing and clanking. The air lock opened and Laborde raised his hand, signaling to whoever was pushing him from the head of the gurney to stop. Cam glanced up, able to lift his head only marginally, and saw an Orbops pilot, the name Bynum stitched on his uniform. Lesha moved forward from the side of the gurney to say good-bye. She gripped Cam's hand in hers.

"Don't worry. Everything's going to be all right."

He tried to utter something, make one final protest that he should be left on the Moon, but the words simply wouldn't come. The Builders weren't letting him speak. She leaned over and kissed him on the cheek. His skin was so numb he couldn't feel it. She patted his hands, gave him a small wave, and retreated into corridor 9. The air-lock door sank, and he was left alone with Laborde and Bynum.

They wheeled him into the air-lock garage, where another pilot, Laurenzi, waited by a Moonstone rover. The blue lights were on in the garage, indicating sufficient pressure. They pushed him over to the Moonstone rover and got him into the back. Once this was done, Laborde returned to Gettysburg.

Inside the rover, Bynum and Laurenzi clamped his gurney into special medevac braces. They then went to the front, where Cam saw screens, controls, and switches studding the rover wall. The two Moonstone pilots got the vehicle going.

A short while later, the rover did a three-point turn and positioned itself at the surface-access air lock. *No, no, no*, he wanted to cry. He heard hissing from outside. Through the rover's small bubble-shaped skylight, he saw the lights in the air-lock garage change from blue to red. Sounds from outside became muffled, then disappeared as the vacuum took over. They rolled forward. He saw the red light disappear, replaced by black lunar sky.

The launch was uneventful, the g-force relatively mild. He looked at the primary observation screen. He saw the lunar surface recede, change, lose definition. He felt the same way: receding, changing, losing definition.

The module banked, and the sun, now that the Moon was further along in its phases, appeared over the horizon, brightening the spacecraft's skylight.

He was finally engulfed by weightlessness. He felt sick. For the next several hours he traveled in a cloud of nausea. For all this, he had a sense of anticipation, and began to theorize that the Builders, by rendering him helpless this way, were preparing him in some way for a new and heightened attempt at communication. He took a deep breath and tried to relax.

He glanced at the various screens—the Moon behind them, the Earth ahead of them—and there didn't seem to be any change in size in either of them. But the Earth slowly got bigger until it was finally a massive blue orb ahead of them.

He was certain Bynum would brake.

But before any braking occurred, a bang came from the vessel's right side, and the ship shook.

A moment later, the red combat lights came on and the alarm sounded—high tone, low tone, back and forth. The ship rolled sideways, suddenly, violently, as though slammed by a great hand. All but the emergency systems died. The craft drifted.

He heard Bynum and Laurenzi clicking through their crisis procedures, trying to contact Orbops, but the radio was as dead as everything else.

Cam looked out the side window, a small slit of pressurized polycarbonate, and saw several Builder energy cells approach like big blue, glowing jellyfish. As they got closer, their luminosity increased. Cam heard a curious singing in his head, taut, austere, high tones weaving in and out of lower ones, two long and one short, like the original sound parcels from Alpha Vehicle. Was it language? What was the significance of the pattern?

Bynum and Laurenzi ignored him as they struggled to get systems back online.

The energy cells got closer, brainlike in shape, transparent, surrounded by turquoise plasma, dark blue bolts flickering inside. He looked out the opposite window and saw them coming from that side too. As with his visit inside Alpha Vehicle, he now felt an extraordinary peace, and understood that everything he had gone through, the two attacks and so forth, had to be part of his education. The blue glow permeated not only the windows but also the hull. It seemed even to penetrate to the learning centers of his brain, for he felt unusually receptive to everything.

In the cockpit Bynum and Laurenzi barked numbers and codes into the radio, but Cam felt far away from it all.

Then Bynum and Laurenzi abruptly slumped. He looked at them with growing alarm. Were they having attacks like his? And did this particular turn of events herald an attempt to communicate with the pilots, or maybe a wider military attack on Earth?

He steeled himself as the blue light penetrated farther. Then, miracle of miracles, he felt his numbness disappear. He lifted his hand and realized he had regained the ability to move.

He unstrapped his gurney and drifted free.

He tested his ability to speak with his favorite Einstein quote: "The most beautiful thing we can experience is the mysterious." Now he talked fine.

In free fall, he maneuvered to Bynum, held his hand in front of the pilot's nose, and checked for respirations. He was still breathing. He checked Laurenzi as well, and he was breathing too.

He then looked out the window where he saw the energy cells clustering around the spacecraft. He felt infused with energy. Looking down, he saw blue beams intersecting his body at all angles, penetrating but not impaling, skewering but not injuring, just like Alpha Vehicle's silver plasma, only different. Was it more preparation? Or a kind of fertilizer to the purple light that had penetrated his brain while in Alpha Vehicle?

He maneuvered to the cockpit. The odd two-to-one music grew louder. The date on the pilot's control monitor said yesterday, while the date on the copilot's said tomorrow. Bynum and Laurenzi were unconscious. Out the cockpit windows, he saw more energy cells.

Then the energy cells drifted away. The lesser their number, the sicker he felt, so that the numbness returned, and he began to find it increasingly difficult to move.

He maneuvered into the cabin, lay in the gurney, and waited.

Were they again trying to contact him? Probe him? Or, because he was in the vicinity, had the energy cells simply decided to come over and have a look? He glanced out the starboard window and saw five cells drift away. He managed to get himself strapped in—with Pittman already suspicious, he meant to leave no clues about this particular visitation.

Five minutes later, Bynum and Laurenzi awoke.

Neither of them said anything. It was as if nothing had happened.

A moment later, he felt the g-force of routine braking.

Bynum looked back and smiled. "We'll be home soon."

They landed in the Mojave Desert.

An Air Force jet flew him under special military police escort to Baltimore. At the airport an armored truck, called out specifically for his arrival, took him to Johns Hopkins Hospital, where a dedicated wing had been set up for him on the fifth floor.

Orderlies wheeled him to this wing, the back half of the fifth floor, just past the nursing station, where another two military police, assigned to him, stood guard in the corridor. He didn't feel like a patient. He felt like a prisoner. Even an enemy combatant.

By the time they got him cleaned and in fresh pajamas, it was close to midnight, late, but not so late that Dr. Jeffrey Ochoa didn't stop by to pay his patient a first visit.

Dr. Ochoa was around forty, had coppery hair, and a neatly trimmed beard. The expression on his face, if he had one at all, showed a trace of mild professional curiosity. He gazed at Cam for several seconds, like a medical examiner about to make a Y incision in the chest cavity of a cadaver, then turned to the guard.

"Corporal Fountas, you may go."

"Yes, sir." The guard left.

When he was gone, Ochoa walked to the door and closed it. He then came over and stared at Cam for a long time. At last he said, "Can you hear me?"

But Cam couldn't move or speak.

Ochoa finally sighed. "Dr. Conrad, I don't know if you can hear me or not. But we're concerned about you. We know your spacecraft was disabled on the way in. Greenhow picked up the whole visitation with its sector C satellites. So please don't try to hide it from us when and if you come out of this thing, the way you tried to hide Tau Ceti and your Moon tower attack, because that will just further confirm for us that Alpha Vehicle has somehow turned you against us. And don't look so anxious. Rest assured, we're going to do everything we can to help you, at least within the parameters of the military necessities of the situation. But I'll be honest with you. Helping you may sometimes take a backseat to getting information out of you, because we're now faced with an ominous escalation by Alpha Vehicle, what with the building of the Moon towers and the launch of the energy cells. And that means things may have to be accelerated at this end as well. Particularly with you."

He lifted his chin and appraised Cam calmly.

"As you seem to have a special relationship with Alpha Vehicle, the president's task force has assigned me to find out what I can from you, using whatever means I deem necessary. And that means certain chemicals and perhaps even a few surgical techniques that might end up altering the structures of your brain. One of the things we're trying to find out is why the Builders have chosen you in the first place, and not anybody else. I'm sure you're just as puzzled as we are. And it concerns the president greatly that they might plan to use you against us in some way as well. So we have to get to the bottom of it all, and I'm sure that as a scientist you can appreciate that a disciplined investigation is the order of the day. Unfortunately, certain of the chemicals I might use to loosen your tongue could cause permanent brain damage, and I should warn you that you may never be the same again. But that's the price we sometimes have to pay for the sake of our country. When the president is faced with a crisis of this magnitude, he has to decide in favor of saving many lives instead of just one. It's really starting to seem as if the Builders, as you call them, mean to be our enemy. It's believed they wouldn't have mobilized all those energy cells otherwise."

Cam was now in the grip of a mounting terror. His worst fears were coming true. The powers that be were going to characterize the Builders as enemies, no matter how hard he tried to dissuade them.

Dr. Ochoa continued. "For now, we're just going to run some tests on you, starting with a brain scan at seven a.m. tomorrow. We're going to take a conservative approach, at least for a while. We're going to see if we can identify anything useful by employing diagnostic and rehabilitative techniques. If we can get you talking again, that will be a big step.

Once we do that, we'll hear what you have to say. We'll analyze it. And only if we're dissatisfied with the intelligence you give us will we resort to the more drastic measures I just told you about." He raised his index finger. "But just remember this: no hiding things on us anymore. I guarantee, that will just make matters a lot worse for you."

11

Back on the Moon, Lesha attended a special briefing by Dr. Renate Tennant in the common room the next day. The poses of the various individuals gathered, both military and scientific, made her think more of a tribunal than of a briefing. All the chairs had been put in the middle of the room, while the tables had been shoved against the walls. The scientific staff sat in the center and the military personnel stood around the perimeter, brutal-looking in their black armor. One table had been placed at the front, like a judge's bench. Colonel Pittman and Renate Tennant sat at this table, a podium next to them. The faces of the scientific staff—Mark, Blaine, Lewis, Peggy, Silke, and Maribeth—looked drawn.

"Dr. Tennant is here to report on the status of her communications effort with Alpha Vehicle," said Pittman. "Dr. Tennant, go ahead."

Renate got up, tall and skinny, looking debilitated by overwork. She placed her waferscreen on the podium with jittery hands. Her hair looked as if it could use a brushing. She cleared her voice.

"The Moon is bombarded daily by various kinds of radiation," she began. "In fact, radiation has been one of our biggest obstacles in establishing a long-term presence on the Moon. Currently, it's recommended that no lunar mission go beyond ninety days, as radiation absorption becomes critical at that point. But as it turns out the Builders are using this radiation. Specifically, the stripped galactic radiation that comes from all the stars in the Milky Way. When this stripped radiation hits the Moon's surface, it fractures into subatomic particles, and it is these fractured subatomic particles that the Builders are utilizing to construct their subgravitational communications packets. By incorporating some of the salvaged Stradivari particle-accelerating equipment, my team and I have now successfully completed some experiments in rebounding subatomic quanta off the surface of the Moon the moment a Builder relay point opens. With this method, we've effectively instantaneously sent information twelve million light-years to NGC4945 using the established relay points." She turned to Pittman, and added, "This means we're the first research team ever to make something travel faster than the speed of light in any meaningful way outside the laboratory."

"Your accomplishment has been noted, Dr. Tennant, and the proper superiors will be informed."

She glowed at Pittman's acknowledgment, then examined her waferscreen notes with fresh verve. "So far, these subatomic packets have been random constructs, purposely camouflaged as background radiation to hide them from the Builders. But we've now devised a way to piggyback *structured* messages using basic binary code. Evidence suggests the Builders are familiar with binary code. Dr. Conrad wants our first communication to consist of only the first one hundred prime numbers. I believe we have to go further than this. In the first message, I propose sending binary digitized samples of Earth's seven most common languages—a kind of subgravitational Rosetta stone, if you will. To show the Builders that we understand the concept of prime numbers will do nothing to further our goal of establishing a dialogue with them, and considering the urgency of the situation, we have to accelerate things. We have to provide them with the basic materials of our languages in the hope that they might then reveal to us the critical elements of theirs."

Lesha's spine straightened. She smelled disaster looming ahead. She got to her feet and interrupted. "Renate, the whole reason Cam wanted prime numbers in the first place was to avoid the possibility of any dangerous misinterpretation on the part of the Builders. If you send something that tries to explain our various evolved languages, who knows what the Builders are going to make of it? They may take it as a threat, such as Cam has suggested. On the other hand, mathematics can't be misinterpreted. If in return for a prime-number message we get a positive response, Cam has told me that he wants to send *pi* rendered to the hundredth decimal. And if that works, the next step would be a kind of pictographic representation of E equals MC squared. If that's successful, we'll proceed with a dialogue from there. The last thing he wants is to try talking to them right away through the idiosyncratic languages of Earth. We're opening a Pandora's box if we go that route."

Renate's face stiffened. "I don't see any evidence for that."

"You were the one who wanted to hunker down and play it safe when the Builders first got here. You were the one who advocated caution."

"As an isolated contingent on the Moon, we were in no position at that time to do anything at all. Now that we have Orbops here, and a clear direction from the Oval Office, I believe it's essential we establish a meaningful dialogue as soon as possible, especially because of the obvious aggressive gestures the Builders have made toward us recently."

"Aggressive gestures? What aggressive gestures?" Lesha's frustration mounted. "So far, only one human being has died, and there's a fairly convincing argument he was killed inadvertently, simply by being at the wrong place at the wrong time. Other than that, the Builders have been peaceful. I'll admit, we don't know why they're building the Moon towers, and have no idea what the energy cells orbiting Earth are for, but it's not beyond the realm of possibility that rather than constructing a weapon, they might be giving us a gift. First contact between different peoples on Earth during the great age of exploration was symbolized by gift giving. Maybe the Builders are trying to establish goodwill. At the same time, misinterpretation, fear, and lack of communication were the greatest dangers during the age of exploration. All Dr. Conrad wants to do is establish a firm foundation before we proceed with more intricate overtures."

Pittman shook his head. "With the building of the towers, the launch of the energy cells, and Tau Ceti accelerating into its red giant phase, I'm inclined to put a grimmer interpretation on what the Builders are doing. It was the same with the North Chinese. They said their satellites were for peaceful purposes. And we believed them. And look how wrong we were."

Lesha frowned. "Yes, but if the Builders wanted to destroy us, they would have done so long ago. Even you, as a battle tactician, must realize this. They've given away their chief advantage: the element of surprise. Cam's graduated approach is best."

But she was overruled.

Pittman made a special point of coming to her afterward. "I'm sorry we don't agree, Dr. Weeks, but under the circumstances I think we have to talk to them in a meaningful way as soon as we can. And by the way, Dr. Ochoa tells me there's something peculiar going on in Dr. Conrad's brain, now that the Builders have had a go at him."

The sudden worry that came to her was like a knife in her side. Pittman must have seen the change in her face, for his expression became compassionate, and he seemed to understand just what Cam had come to mean to her.

"Why wasn't I told?" she asked.

"I just found out myself."

"And what has Dr. Ochoa discovered?"

"That there's increased electrical activity in a special part of his brain, the sylvan fissure. Dr. Ochoa thinks they're utilizing his sylvan fissure as a way to communicate with him. I'll send you the report once I get back to my quarters."

She reviewed the report later.

She discovered that the sylvan fissure was a unique part of the brain, characterized in at least several recent reports as the mental apparatus for empathy, understanding, and communication. Manipulation of the sylvan fissure might result in a subject's greater ability to detach more easily from previous norms, understand abstract ideas, and communicate more fluently. In certain cases, a flowering of genius was possible.

Using the baseline EEGs NASA had performed prior to the Stradivari mission, and comparing them to the new scan Dr. Ochoa had conducted at Johns Hopkins that morning, the Orbops physician suggested that the change had begun during Cam's initial visit inside Alpha Vehicle, and that his brain had undergone further conditioning at a number of different times since, most notably during the journey to Earth, when another visitation, this one by the energy cells, had taken place.

Lesha watched Renate's communication attempt from the screens in the tower. The cameras at Crater Cavalet recorded the historic event. She sat with Johnsie; she was becoming friends with the nurse practitioner.

On the screen, she saw Alpha Vehicle in the middle of the crater, a big silver eyeball. Dr. Tennant and the other Princeton Team members—Peggy, Maribeth, and Silke—worked in the crater's base, preparing to rebound a communications packet off the lunar surface into the next relay point.

"Any thought on what the Builders are doing to Dr. Conrad?" asked Johnsie.

Lesha's eyes narrowed. "Trying to talk to him, I think." She motioned at the screen. "Maybe all this is for nothing."

The African features of Johnsie's face grew still. "This whole empathy . . . and understanding . . . and the possible flowering of genius. Mind you, I always thought Cam was a genius. To understand all that theoretical physics stuff, you have to have something going for you. Maybe he has the particular kind of intelligence they're looking for, the only kind they can communicate with." They watched Crater Cavalet for a while. Then Johnsie said, "Do you think Tau Ceti has anything to do with it?"

Lesha considered. "I've got this idea about it, and it won't leave me alone."

"What?"

"That we're being tested."

"Tested?"

"And that if we don't pass the test, that's it, the sun goes red giant. I sometimes think the Builders are being mysterious on purpose to further the goals of this test."

"Really?"

"If we can't prove we're worth saving—and Cam and I talked about this—then we don't deserve our place in the Milky Way."

"Wow. That's biblical."

"And to tell you the truth, I think Colonel Pittman's going to make matters worse. If the Builders are preparing to talk to Cam—and I really think that they are—and Pittman starts throwing missiles at them before Cam gets the chance, then that's it, we fail the test. The timing of Cam's evac to Earth makes me climb the walls." She motioned at the screen. "And now Dr. Tennant is trying this risky communications attempt, in direct contradiction to what Cam has advised. It might aggravate the hell out of them."

It was fully another hour before Dr. Tennant reported the opening of a relay point. A dark green swirl became dimly visible above the silver sphere. Colonel Pittman, who had been pacing at the other side of the tower, looked at the screen, his jaw stiffening. Silence enveloped the tower as everyone waited.

Various other screens flipped to the Moonstone emplacements surrounding Alpha Vehicle. On one screen, Lesha saw a soldier in fully pressurized armor on bended knee next to a field cannon. The futility of the military preparations struck her afresh.

She turned to Dr. Tennant's screen. Renate intoned into the microphone, "We're charging the accelerator now. The countdown has begun." The amorphous green net, like a bruise in the sky above Alpha Vehicle, widened as if to receive any messages Renate decided to bounce across the universe.

Lesha didn't expect the Builder reaction to come so swiftly.

Greenhow, two or three minutes after Renate's "send," preempted the various emergency screens and showed fluxing images of the energy cells surrounding Earth. Twenty-three out of the ninety-two—in other words, 25 percent—had broken free of the existing ring and headed toward Earth, on apparent collision courses.

Pittman immediately barked a coded language into the headset. Something with a lot of Greek letters in it.

It was apparently directed at Greenhow command, for a few seconds later Greenhow extrapolated more detailed graphics that showed one of the alien energy cells heading first toward New Delhi, then another to London, then others to Hong Kong, Tokyo, Paris, New York, and Mexico City. Minutes later, it confirmed hits on another sixteen cities, accounting for the entire twenty-three energy cells.

Then, outside on the lunar surface, an aquamarine dawn came. Moments later, over the dark edge of Bunker Hill, she saw a blue and nebulous man-o'-war that could only be another energy cell. This energy cell splashed over Gettysburg like an electric turquoise tide, and seconds later, all the lights went out. The computer screens flickered with a whirling motion.

Bruxner tapped at the main terminal with increasing apprehension, but all he got was a shifting pattern of light so intense and strobelike, Lesha turned away.

"Firebase Alpha, do you read?" cried Pittman, trying to get in contact with his Crater Cavalet Moonstone vehicles. He got no response.

Lesha rose. Johnsie got up as well, her brown face bathed in the blue glow coming in through the windows. Lesha walked to another of the interfaces and tried to establish control.

Bruxner, next to her, attempted a complete reboot. He was speaking into his shoulder unit. "Laborde, get to the server, repeat, get to the server," but all that came over the comlink was strange music—taut, austere, with high tones weaving in and out of lower ones, two long and one short, in the most eerie counterpoint she had ever heard. Singing? Was it a language?

"Firebase Alpha, interdict the enemy immediately."

She tore herself away from the terminal and toggled Pittman's communications dead.

Pittman gripped her wrist as if with an iron claw and yanked her away.

"Dr. Weeks, you're to be confined to your quarters. This has become a military matter now."

"And I'm asking you to stop, Colonel Pittman. This is ridiculous. There's been no attack."

"They've launched. Can't you see that?"

"We're still alive, aren't we?"

Pittman glanced at Haydn and Newlove, and they took a few threatening steps toward her.

She raised her hands. "Listen to that . . . that singing. Does that sound like the music of war to you? Have they blown us up yet? Are we dead yet? That music sounds like angels to me."

They all listened, and the music sweetened, was sad and joyful at the same time. Looking at Pittman, she saw he was fighting with himself, that ordinarily he wasn't a man predisposed to emotion; yet his face now twitched with small spasms, as if in fact he had been affected by the music in some small way as well.

He at last nodded. "All right. And by the way, when I say interdict, it doesn't mean destroy." He issued a command into his shoulder mike. "Firebase Alpha, stand down. Remain on high alert. Do not fire unless fired upon. Repeat. Do not fire." He clicked off his mike. "But let me reiterate, Dr. Weeks. This is a military matter now. And while I might need a direct order from my superiors to outright destroy our enemy, they've given me a free hand in defending Gettysburg any way I must.''

Then the slow and steady hiss of the oxygen vent went silent, and a warning tone dinged over the serene music that was coming from the small speakers.

Pittman's shoulders sank. He turned to Lesha. His face was like granite. "Life support just went offline." He glanced at a monitor. "And I see the heating is gone too. And communications as well. It's like they're trying to degrade our infrastructure before a full-scale attack."

Her brow hardened. "You're looking for any excuse, aren't you? Just like Cam said you would."

His upper lip stiffened under his silver mustache. "In the interests of restraint, I will allow Newlove and Haydn to further assess the current systems malfunctions before we go ahead with any offensive operations." He turned to Bruxner. "Engage the emergency oxygen supply, Mr. Bruxner. Also the heating, but use it sparingly, a few degrees above zero, nothing warmer. Newlove, see if you can raise Orbops command. Find out what they want us to do about this." He glanced around the room. "Looks like we're going to have to hunker down, everybody. At least until we figure this out. I would request that you all return to your quarters immediately. We should keep physical activity to a minimum. Gettysburg is now under round-the-clock curfew to conserve oxygen. No scientific staff members come or go from their quarters without my say-so." He focused on Lesha. "And that goes for you in particular, Dr. Weeks." He turned to his adjunct. "Lieutenant Haydn, escort Dr. Weeks to her quarters."

12

Cam was in his hospital bed in his special set aside wing at Johns Hopkins when through closed eyelids he detected a change in the light coming from outside. Momentarily confused, and still half asleep, he believed the light flickering through his eyelids might be fireworks—he had a rough notion it was July Fourth. He kept his eyes closed because in the quivering light beyond the few millimeters of his pink lids he sensed an uncanny peace, and felt as if the crossed wires of his brain were quietly untangling themselves in the beneficent glow of this mysterious light.

He then heard hospital personnel walking quickly up and down the corridor and knew something wasn't right. His window began to rattle. He opened his eyes. He looked at the television in its T-brace. No picture, just a cascade of shifting color. He peered outside. He'd never seen a sky like that before; it was not blue, but turquoise.

He pushed himself up, found he could do so easily—his recovery was proceeding faster than expected, even as the sense of his own receptivity to the Builders had increased. He shifted his feet out of bed, grabbed his cane, and moved to the window. The glass shook harder, and he heard a jet roar. Close. Too close. And too low. Only where was it? He clutched the windowsill.

Downtown Baltimore stretched to the south. Patterson Park's leafy canopy shifted in the wind across the street. Immediately around the hospital he saw a number of medical buildings. The jet was getting so loud that the window blinds started to vibrate. Down on Jefferson Street, several cars had stalled, with the drivers getting out and opening hoods; he thought it odd that so many cars had stalled at once, and all along this same stretch of Jefferson. Car alarms had gone off, and the neighborhood resounded with their racket. Was that sylvan fissure thing Dr. Ochoa had told him about confusing him again? Because none of this made any sense. Especially the sound of that jet getting louder and louder. Was he on the verge of having another attack? He hoped not because he was recovering so nicely.

He peered at Patterson Park, with its few acres of trees. How odd those trees looked in the turquoise light. Even without his nearly confirmed connection to the Builders, he knew this had to be their doing.

Then the jet screamed by overhead, coming in from behind the hospital, the nose appearing, then the wings, then the tail, so close he saw each individual rivet. Was it coming in for an emergency landing? Where did the pilot think he was going to land? The jet skimmed the roofs of the medical buildings across the street. Everyone on the street looked up as the aircraft continued southward under the bizarre turquoise sky, none of its landing gear deployed. How did the pilot expect to land without wheels?

The jet slammed into Patterson Park. Its fuselage bent so that there was a kink in it, like a partially broken cigar. It was a big jet, of the airbus variety. The aircraft plowed through the trees, thrusting them aside. A huge tear opened in the new kink, passenger seats became detached, and the force of the crash flung people from the aircraft through this tear with a ferocity that made nausea rise in his throat. A moment later he felt the shock wave against the hospital. The aircraft skidded to a stop, its jet fuel got loose, and a moment later flames engulfed all of Patterson Park.

Ten kilometers in the distance, another plane came down. He squinted through the turquoise duskiness. From this far, the aircraft was nothing more than a small cross in the sky. As it careened in a slow and steady arc downward, its left wingtip nicked a roof, and it somersaulted like a ninja star through a residential neighborhood before disintegrating into a fireball farther west. Again he thought that none of this seemed right. Was he hallucinating? Being shown something by the Builders? Was this some kind of threat? Something that might at last prompt him to have a more cooperative attitude toward Jeffrey Ochoa?

A third plane, this one of the regional commuter variety, came down in front of him and skidded along Jefferson, the pavement shearing its underside as the friction threw up sparks.

He moved from the window as if in a daze,

stunned by everything he had just seen, and horribly
shocked that so many people seemed to have lost
their lives outside in multiple plane crashes. Yet he
still didn't trust it. Was it a mirage? A figment of his
sylvan fissure? It was all so bizarre. He looked up at
the television. The screen was still a cascade of color.
Through the tiny speaker he heard the oddest . . .
music. And he recognized it, the same music from
aboard his military evac spacecraft, with the odd
two-to-one rhythm, and a sound not unlike a half
dozen pianos playing all at once. The music moved
him. Momentarily brought tears to his eyes. Was sad.
But also strangely hopeful. The song seemed to be
about life. As well as death.

He hobbled on his cane, opened the door, and
peered outside.

The military police who guarded his special section
were at the far end of the corridor, looking out the
window at all the chaos outside. For the first time
since his arrival he actually felt like a free citizen.
Some nurses and doctors stood around the unit station looking at computer screens, which had the
same fuzzy pattern as his television, while others
were rushing to help in the chaos outside. He wasn't
sure what had happened, but was now fairly convinced, what with that music coming from the television, that it was indeed the Builders. Other patients
farther down the wing beyond his special section, the
majority of them much older, stood at their doors.
He continued down the hall. At the unit station all
the nurses and doctors continued to cluster around
the three computers. On the nearest, he got a better
look at the same cascade of color. He felt invisible.

No one was paying any attention to him. The guards were still at the window with their backs turned. Then the nurse, Malka, spotted him.

At first the small blond woman's face was blank with fear. Two seconds later, her manner changed. She came around the side of the unit station and gripped his arm.

"Dr. Conrad, all patients are to remain in their rooms. Especially you. You know you're a special case. You know that extremely elaborate arrangements have been made for you through the surgeon general's office."

He didn't bother asking her what was going on, because he already had a good idea. And he didn't want to let on that he was getting his facility for speech back, because his apparent muteness was the only thing keeping Dr. Ochoa from filling him full of interrogation drugs. He turned around and shuffled back to his room. Malka quickly abandoned him, too concerned with what was happening at the unit station to bother with him long.

He kept going the other way, past his room, all the way to the opposite bank of elevators. He looked at the indicator lights. All three elevators were going up and down, up and down, none of them stopping at any of the floors.

The vent above was malfunctioning, blasting hot air, even though it was July.

He continued past the elevators to the common room. It was empty. One of the vending machines dispensed one chocolate bar after another—something seemed to be wrong with its internal computer.

The television in the corner showed the same abstract wash of light. He approached the screen. Within the kaleidoscope of spectra, he saw symbols, the same ones he had seen during his encounter with the Moon tower.

And oddly, they now made a mind-bending mathematical sense to him, as if the seeds of understanding planted when he was inside Alpha Vehicle, and perhaps by the energy cells on his trip back to Earth, had at last begun to bear fruit.

He went back to his room and saw the same symbols on his own TV.

He watched them for a long time.

Dr. Ochoa came a few hours later, and under his coppery mustache, Cam saw that his lips were set. Outside, sirens still blared from time to time. A few more jets had crashed in the vicinity. A steady stream of ambulances came and went from Johns Hopkins. Ochoa didn't look too pleased. He came right up to Cam's bed and peered at his patient with unrelenting scrutiny.

"Did you know?"

With no context, Cam wasn't exactly sure what the doctor was talking about, but he could fairly guess that he was referring to the widespread catastrophe that was unfolding outside.

"Was there no way you could have warned us?" pressed the doctor. He squared his shoulders, lifted his head, and looked out the window. "The president had some uncomfortable questions for me. And I kept telling him that you're having a hard time speaking, and reminded him of what we're seeing on your scan, that unidentified shadow near your sylvan fissure. I explained to him that the chemical thumbprint of this shadow is unlike anything we've ever seen before, and that we have to proceed cautiously because we're dealing with an unknown entity. But of course the Oval Office wants results and they expect me to get them. You've regained movement. You can walk. I don't know why you can't talk." He motioned out the window. "I don't know why you can't help us."

Cam lifted his hand and pointed to his mouth, then shook his head. "Talk . . . bit."

Ochoa contemplated him for several seconds. "They did this. You know they did. I might as well start by telling you that. Greenhow, before it was disabled, detected a wave emanating from the Moon, and was able to pinpoint the source of that wave—before the system went down, that is—to Crater Cavalet. Then twenty-three energy cells broke orbit and headed for Earth. It all happened a few moments after Dr. Tennant sent her information packet to NGC4945. We're still trying to sort it all out, whether it was a deliberately aggressive act on the part of Alpha Vehicle, or if, as you so like to characterize things, it was inadvertent. But the upshot of it is, we've had a worldwide computer crash. Systems are off-line everywhere. Jets are falling from the sky. Stocks markets have lost billions. Troops have mobilized everywhere. One of the worst consequences was the Eas Tanura oil refinery in Saudi Arabia. It went up in flames due to a computerized pressure malfunction. PRNC missiles have armed themselves in their silos, and three of them have detonated on-site. Over ten thousand aircraft have gone down. Elevator accidents have happened all over the world. And again, we're baffled by the enemy's intent. What do they want? Have they told you?"

Cam was horrified by all the havoc Ochoa was describing, and he was particularly disturbed by the plane crashes, and by all the innocent people who must have died in them. But what also unsettled him was Ochoa's apparent rush to judgment, and the way he characterized the Builders as the enemy even though he didn't have any reasonable answer about what had happened.

Cam pointed to his mouth again. "Not . . . enemy." Because it was becoming increasingly clear to him, through the new receptivity he was gaining, that the Builders viewed humanity neither as enemy nor friend, but simply as something that wasn't part of the overall equation under which they operated.

In a rueful tone, Ochoa said, "I wish I could believe you, Dr. Conrad. But hundreds of thousands of people have lost their lives in this worldwide crash. And I'm sorry to say that we've lost contact with the Moon. We know you have a growing fondness for Dr. Weeks, and it's our sincere wish that she's okay."

Cam felt a stab of worry. As much as he believed everything was inadvertent on the part of the Builders, he would certainly hold them responsible if their action led to the loss of Lesha's life.

"Have they talked to you at all again?" asked Ochoa, his voice pinched, concerned. "Have they given you any more glimpses?"

Cam fought the strange knee-jerk impulse to protect the Builders, and at last was able to tell Ochoa the truth. "Symbols."

"Symbols?" Ochoa leaned closer. "What kind of symbols?"

He tried to speak, but the words simply wouldn't come, so Ochoa tried to fill it in as best he could. "They've shown you symbols." Cam nodded. "Written symbols?" Cam shook his head, lifted his hand, raised one finger, two fingers, three fingers, counting. "Numbers?" ventured Ochoa. Cam nodded. "Mathematical symbols?" Another nod. Ochoa thought this through. "We're trying to figure out why they've chosen you, and if you're telling me they've shown you mathematical symbols, who better to understand them? You're one of the country's preeminent mathematicians and theoretical scientists." Ochoa thought some more. "Where did they show you these symbols?"

Cam motioned to the corner of the room.

Ochoa looked. "The television?"

Cam nodded.

"Can you remember any of them? Did any of them make sense to you?"

He shook his head.

"But you knew they were mathematical."

Cam felt his new intuitive sense and receptivity again. He nodded.

Ochoa considered. "I really don't want to give you chemicals if I don't have to, particularly because we're dealing with some unknown thumbprints in your brain. The main thing is to get you speaking again so you can communicate with us, and I think

the best approach to that is to bring in a speech therapist. Johns Hopkins offers the best speech therapists
in the country. In fact, they pretty well have the best
of everything, which is why we've chosen to put you
here as a special inpatient. Starting tomorrow, we're
going to get you into some speech sessions."

After the speech therapist, Rhona Lindsay—a
young woman with as much cheerfulness as any one
man could reasonably be expected to take—had him
go through various vowel sounds until his jaw ached,
she at last felt the time was again ripe to try him
with a sentence, even though the most perplexing
thing happened whenever he tried to speak in a complete sentence. All the while he looked at her computer screen, which was now showing its regular
icons. He missed the cascading colors. And the symbols. He thought of Pittman, the Moon, then Lesha,
and worry invaded his soul. The Moon had lost its
voice.

"Let's use a simple phrase now, and I want you
to try to pronounce it as crisply as you can." She
gave him a grin. "And in English. 'Father, I'd like to
know more about our family.' "

He got ready to say the phrase, but the same thing
happened again—it came out in Latin. "*Pater, velim
cognoscere plura de familia nostra.*"

Why was this happening?

Rhona shook her head and smiled. "Try not to
worry about it. The mind is a funny thing. And in
your case, we really don't know what's going on anyway. My own hypothesis is that your academic stud-

ies are obviously surfacing. You did take Latin, didn't you?"

He nodded.

"And the academic transcripts we now have say you were at the top of your class."

He nodded again. But university Latin was over twenty years ago, and he had forgotten most of it. So why was it surfacing now? All this about his sylvan fissure was really starting to worry him. He couldn't get the simplest phrases of English out, but Latin came easily. Were the Builders, when they finally decided to say something comprehensible to him, going to speak Latin?

"It's all right. Let's try another. 'I have flowers in my garden.' "

He was momentarily homesick for his house in Navasota, Texas, and hoped his house-help, Connie and Fernando, were making sure his flowers had plenty of water.

He tried the phrase. "Αποτελέσματα αναζητήσεως."

Rhona's eyes widened. "What was that?"

His worry intensified into perplexed alarm. "I think . . . Greek."

"You know Greek?"

He had the sensation that the floor was shifting beneath him. "No."

"None at all?"

"The . . . usual . . . scientific . . ."

That's all he could get out in English.

After the session, back in his room, he brooded on the Greek for a long time.

Dr. Ochoa came an hour later, and was coolly practical, even though Cam could tell he was professionally excited. He tested Cam on several phrases, Rhona sitting by, and now, mercy of mercies, he often got them out in English. But sometimes they came out in Latin and sometimes in Greek. And a number of times he said them in French, Spanish, and Cantonese, languages he didn't know at all. He was afraid. But also elated.

Dr. Ochoa noticed his elation and asked him to explain.

"It's as if I've . . . let go."

He tried to further define his explanation, but the words wouldn't come. Ochoa theorized. "I can't help thinking that it's more than a coincidence that you're now speaking several of the languages included in Dr. Tennant's expanded communications packet."

Cam went cold. This was the first he'd heard about any expanded communications packet. Expanded from his originally proposed prime number sequence? He tried to voice his protest but the words again wouldn't come.

Ochoa continued. "Have you ever wondered why Alpha Vehicle landed on the Moon in the first place, Dr. Conrad? And why it landed in Shenandoah, only a kilometer away from Gettysburg? If it was going to make Crater Cavalet its final operational base, why didn't it go there first?" He gave him a glance. "Because you were there. That they've modified your sylvan fissure proves they've marked you in some way, and their choice of Gettysburg for their moonfall confirms it. Then you told me about these mathematical symbols they've shown you. Now you're speaking Greek. And Cantonese. And Spanish and French. Languages you don't know."

Later, Dr. Ochoa performed another CAT scan, and it showed further increased activity in his sylvan fissure. When he was done, he said, "I think you should prepare yourself, Dr. Conrad. I think they're getting ready to tell you something. And I think it's going to be big. Something you're going to have to let the Orbops team know about right away."

13

"You have a visitor," said Malka, the nurse, later that evening, when Ochoa had gone.

The nurse left, and in a moment he saw his old astronomer friend from the University of Hawaii, Dr. Nolan Pratt, peering in at him from the door. He was happy to see Nolan, with his perpetual tan, wearing a dark blue blazer, light blue shirt, and white sailor pants. Hadn't seen him in a while. His glasses were new, had horn-rimmed frames. His hair was scrupulously blow-dried, perhaps to hide what appeared to be increasing baldness. Hadn't seen him in . . . four years? That interdisciplinary convention in Boston, yes, that was it, drinks in the bar, always the Bailey's and Kahlua for Nolan, while Cam preferred a glass of Chardonnay.

Nolan came in, hooking his thumb back toward the corridor. "You have the whole wing to yourself. Nice. But those guards are something else."

Cam was surprised to see Nolan in Baltimore. "You're . . . here." And it indeed needed explanation, because why had Nolan come all the way from

Hawaii, especially when flights were so difficult to get post–Worldwide Crash?

"They flew me over," said Nolan, and came over to his bed. "How are you feeling?"

"Getting better. Tire easily." He pointed to his mouth. "Speech."

"Dr. Ochoa was saying."

Cam motioned at the chair. "Sit."

Nolan sat, his eyes now preoccupied, and rubbed his hands together. He glanced out the window, then at Cam's cane, and finally at the pitcher of water on Cam's bedside table. "Have they talked to you today? Blunt and the others? I was at the Pentagon this morning."

"Ochoa . . . that's all." He pointed at his mouth again. "For speech."

"Ah. Right. Your speech."

"It's better than it was."

"General Blunt's an interesting man."

"We haven't . . . met."

"No, he said you hadn't." Nolan leaned forward, put his elbows on his knees, and rubbed his right fist in his left palm. "I think they might be coming to see you. The whole lot of them. Blunt. Oren Fye. Brian Goldvogel. I thought I'd give you a heads-up."

"Good . . . good . . ." Because he now felt desperate to participate.

"I thought I'd come here first. To explain some of my more recent findings. Because Blunt may report them with a certain coloration."

"You have new findings?"

Nolan stopped rubbing his fist in his palm, lifted his chin in a manner that was quick and resolute, and examined Cam with the fatalism of a Buddhist monk. "Centauri A went red giant."

The image that came to Cam's mind was a field of white clover, and in the middle of it all, a single pink clover, Centauri A, the sun's neighboring star, swelling on them.

"Why?" And then, as if it really mattered, "How?"

"How? Just like Tau Ceti. A massive hydrogen bleed. As to why?" Nolan shook his head, a scientist at last baffled by the nature of the universe. "I have no idea. Centauri A was supposed to burn as a main-sequence star for the next few billion years, just like Tau Ceti." His eyes widened. "But Blunt and the rest of his team are blaming the Builders." A look of resignation came to his face. "And they're coming to see you about it. You're the closest thing to a Builder spokesperson. And to tell you the truth, they're a little mad about that."

General Morris Blunt came with Oren Fye, Brian Goldvogel, and Dr. Ochoa the following day. General Blunt was a man in a blue Air Force dress uniform, but instead of Air Force insignia, he had Orbops insignia. His appearance and manner were that of a kindly grandfather. He had a round pink face, and a white goatee. His features were elfin, and reminded Cam of Santa Claus. Oren Fye was twenty years younger, a man battling a weight problem. He was bald. He had small eyes screwed into his pudgy face, and his forehead was moist with perspiration, even though the air-conditioning in Johns Hopkins Hospital was now operating normally after the crash. Goldvogel, a man roughly Fye's age, had startlingly blond hair that looked laminated in place. It was Goldvogel who for some reason came and held him steady, like they were going to extract a bullet from his stomach without anesthetic. That's when Ochoa came around Goldvogel with a hypodermic needle poised in his right hand.

"Don't worry, Dr. Conrad. This is perfectly safe. It's just going to help you talk."

His body tensed, and Goldvogel held him tighter, and before he could struggle further, Ochoa shoved the needle in his leg. He sighed. Seconds later, he felt jittery, full of energy.

General Blunt, in a voice filled with nothing but goodwill, explained to him that the Worldwide Crash, as the media had called it, had been a curious phenomenon indeed. And while he viewed the change in Alpha Centauri A with grim suspicion, and in fact told him it was the reason Dr. Ochoa had shoved the needle in his leg—time seemed to be of the essence—Blunt took a more lenient view toward the Worldwide Crash. "You'll be pleased to hear that we've decided it's an attempt by the Builders to communicate with us, and not an overt act of aggression. Our computer analysts have now begun decoding what appears to be a dump of some kind. It's become apparent that the Builders have provided us with a vast system of symbols. Many of these symbols, now that the Builders have rifled through our databases, have been correlated in superscript to some of the more difficult mathematical symbols we use here on Earth to describe the kind of work you're pioneering in hyperdimensionality. Dr. Ochoa tells us they've shown you some of their symbols." Blunt pointed up to the corner of the room. "On the television. Our Pentagon mathematicians, while they understand part of them, don't understand all of them, and so have drawn up a short list of world-renowned mathematicians to help them. You, of course, are at the top of that list, Dr. Conrad, which doesn't surprise us at all, as it seems they've targeted you specifically for your mathematical ability."

Cam now grew intensely curious, but it was a curiosity he didn't entirely trust because it seemed to be compelled from somewhere outside himself, a Builder-instigated interest. "You have . . . samples?"

Blunt gave Fye a kindly glance. Fye opened a large briefcase and, sighing, took out a custom-made computer.

Meanwhile, Cam's mind raced more and more. He had to wonder what drug Dr. Ochoa had given him, whether it was designed to momentarily suppress the more sluggish effects of that strange shadow clouding his sylvan fissure, or if it had methamphetamine in it.

Fye put the computer on his dinner trolley, wheeled it over, and booted up the rugged-looking unit.

The computer didn't default to a desktop but went right into a galaxy of strange symbols, a lot like the ones he had seen while in contact with the Moon tower, and on the television here in the hospital, but slightly misrepresented because of the way they had to be re-created on the screen, pixel by pixel.

In superscript above various sections of this code, he saw several phrases of human mathematical language. He was surprised to see that some Builder

equations mirrored a few of his own rough but in-
complete ideas about hyperdimensionality. There
was a shorthand description of anti-Ostrander space,
something he usually used pages and pages to describe, but which in this instance had been rendered
deftly in a terse sprinkling of quantum mechanical
cuneiform. As he studied it more and more, he felt
a growing excitement. And he got the sense, through
the heightened features of his modified sylvan fea-
ture, that the Builders were indeed trying to tell him
something important. Something big, as Ochoa
phrased it. It was, in a sense, somewhat like the
prime number sequence he had tried to send, for
there appeared to be a definite and deliberate effort
to establish a common language and shared terms of
reference, only on such an advanced level, it was at
first hard for him to follow.

There was a mathematical description of time, how
time was like a coil after all, and how you could
detour past the linear route by jumping from each
individual turn of the coil, something described as a
sixth dimension, the so-called sequential drop, and
which he himself had described in a number of arti-
cles using a cumbersome mathematical language that
took columns and columns to render, but which here,
in the new and natural framework of the hyperdimensionality in which the Builders seemed to exist,
was sketched in quickly, with all the complex terms
of reference implied. And the strangest thing of all
about reading this particular equation was that it
wasn't only an intellectual equation but an emotional
one as well, as if once one entered the realm of hyperdimensionality one had to use all one's intellectual

and emotional power to truly comprehend it, or at least to feel all the implied hyperdimensional terms of reference. That quantum physics could have an emotional component struck him as one of the craziest theories he had ever heard. Yet he remembered what Niels Bohr had always said: It wasn't that a theory was crazy, but that it wasn't crazy enough. The Builder description of time wasn't like reading a mathematical equation but like a line of poetry.

He was instantly transported. He felt a shivering weakness through his body. He was hypnotized by what he was reading, and only dimly perceived the kafuffle that was now taking place in the room around him—Dr. Ochoa racing forward because of his shivering, examining him, checking his blood pressure, his pulse, and Oren Fye mopping his brow in a sudden excess of nervous energy. It was, in a sense, like having another attack, and he could feel the Builders buzzing through his body like low-voltage electricity. He also had the distinct feeling that he was now on a runaway train, that even if he wanted to stop ciphering this mystical mathematical language, he was locked in, a prisoner, attached to the rails of its idiomatic, intrinsic, but ultimately alien logic.

He moved on. Past the terms-of-reference section—that section where it seemed as if the Builders were trying to test him, to see if, as a three-dimensional creature he might, like those prehistoric fish that first crawled out of the sea millions of years ago, be able to breathe the air of hyperdimensionality. Left that section and went on to a more specific section.

And that's when one particular equation caught his eye.

It stabbed him like the point of an arrow, and it at last revealed to him the true danger of their situation. He didn't want to believe it. Didn't want to admit that the Builders could be so indifferent to the human race. Especially after they had made such overtures toward him. Didn't want to accept that they could go ahead and do something like this, especially when they were putting out such intense mathematical feelers. But he couldn't deny it. And he hated to think Colonel Pittman might be right about them after all.

He tapped the segment, and he looked at Blunt through the welter of his growing apprehension. He tried to express to the general in clear English what they were up against, but the Latin and Greek got all mixed up in his mind again, and what emerged from his alien-bedazzled mind was a hybrid of the two.

"Omega Sol."

The words, though soft, were fraught with fear. He tried again, wanted desperately to explain to them that what the Builders had done to Tau Ceti and Centauri A they were now about to do to their own sun.

"Omega Sol!"

This time with an exclamation mark.

He didn't know why, he didn't know when, but it was now a certainty that their hyperdimensional visitors were going to bleed the hydrogen out of their own sun. They were going to take away its fuel so the sun would implode. And when its gravity reached a critical point, it would turn into a red giant, and consume the Earth. He had no idea why. The intermittent mental snippets he received from the Builders told him only that the destruction of the human race wouldn't be an aggressive act but simply an *inadvertent* one, like cutting down a rain forest to put through a superhighway.

Omega Sol. Something that didn't concern humans, but which would end by destroying them.

He was more mystified—and frightened—by the Builders than ever.

PART TWO

Nuclear Vox

14

Pittman walked along corridor 6 on patrol, letting everyone but Haydn take in a bit of early-morning rest, the guide lights on either side of his helmet casting beams through the darkness. He liked walking around in curfew conditions, making sure the scientists didn't stray from their dormitories, enjoyed in a serious but satisfying way maintaining order during this emergency situation. Haydn walked beside him. He glanced at his adjunct. Haydn was like having his own human pit bull, smart in the areas he had to be smart in, a fierce fighter, and absolutely loyal.

"Carbon dioxide levels are reaching critical, sir. Permission to suggest our breathers."

Pittman grinned in the cold. He liked the way Haydn phrased things. *Permission to suggest our breathers.* He was a soldier through and through.

"Dr. Weeks might need a breather, Gunther." He was feeling philosophical, and whenever he felt this way, he liked to address Haydn by his first name. "And so might the others. But we don't. Did I ever tell you I climbed Mount Baker once? The air's really thin up there. In thin air, the mind starts to go. You get altitude sickness. And then this cold, too. Reminds me a lot of Mount Baker. We lost a man during the climb. Froze to death. The helicopter couldn't make it in time. The snow was thick. Worst blizzard Mount Baker had seen in years. Eighty centimeters of snow. We tried to sled him down the south face. I did most of the pulling. Everybody else was too bagged from the thin air."

The lieutenant jerked his head oddly and held his hand to his ear. "It's just that . . . remember this ringing I told you about, sir? This thrumming I have in my ears?"

"You still have that? I thought when we wrapped things up in Beijing it was as good as gone."

"It's come back, sir. And the cold seems to bother it. Also the thin air."

Pittman frowned. "Blame Alpha Vehicle, son." He considered. "I don't think we're ready for breathers just yet, Gunther. We can't show them we're weak."

"No, sir, we can't."

"And you can stand a little thrumming in your ears, can't you?"

"Yes, sir, I can."

They walked a bit.

He pondered the situation. "I think there can be no doubt about it now."

By this time, they had reached corridor 9 and were on their way to the tower.

"No doubt about what, sir?"

"That the Builders are anything but our friends. I think I've shown admirable restraint. Enough to demonstrate to Dr. Weeks that I'm taking her seriously. But this is starting to go on a bit long. Are they going to make us live in the dark forever?''

Then, to his great frustration, and as if to make him eat crow, the lights came back on. After three days in this glorious bloodcurdling darkness; after telling everybody, including the painfully alluring but irritatingly proper Dr. Lesha Weeks, that the Builders were monsters from Planet Evil and not superintelligent and godlike hyperdimensional beings from NGC4945—after all that, the Builders were flinging it in his face by turning the lights back on. The air vent hummed as well, and the stale atmosphere inside Gettysburg sweetened like the desert after a rainstorm. He also felt heat.

The comlink strapped to his wristpad vibrated, and glancing down, he saw he had full access to the Moonstone mainframe once more. He heard the hubbub of voices—scientists leaving their rooms.

"Do you remember Die Zwei Hunde, that tavern in Germany when we were stationed there before the first deployment?" he asked Haydn.

"I do, sir."

"And how you lost that money?"

"Yes, sir."

"It was three-card monte, wasn't it, Haydn?"

"I didn't know that particular con at the time, sir."

"That's what the Builders are doing now. Playing three-card monte. Remember the patter? The black for me, the red for you? Ten gets you twenty. And twenty gets you forty. Just keep your eye on the lady?"

"My eyes weren't fast enough, sir."

"Mine are."

*　　*　　*

They got to the hub. They climbed into the tower. The lights were on. The emergency lights out in the Sumter Module and Command Port were on as well. All the computer screens glowed, defaulted to their regular desktops.

The first thing he did was engage the communications console and establish links with his various emplacements around Alpha Vehicle.

Pittman spoke to Merryman, Newman, and Weisgarber, and was relieved to learn that they had all survived the shutdown, and that, as with Gettysburg, their systems were all coming back online one by one. He spoke to Wain, Kalp, and Christner, all good men, tough soldiers, officers who would easily have made it down from Mount Baker in the middle of the century's worst blizzard. They were all up and running again as well.

So began what turned into a long morning. Status reports. Damage and readiness reports. And finally Greenhow came back online and they got views of various areas around Earth—but primarily he focused on Saudi Arabia, the huge plume coming out of the Eas Tanura oil refinery, because he didn't like the look of that at all. The military couldn't do without oil.

"Can we magnify?"

Newlove magnified and they saw the entire refinery engulfed in flames, the plume drifting westward in the prevailing winds like a black thumb over the Indian Ocean. Were the Builders tough military strategists after all? Because this was one of the first installations Pittman would have taken out as well.

They saw other satellite evidence of catastrophe.

The wreckage of over two thousand airplanes. And thousands upon thousands of house fires. All in grainy satellite imagery, the only thing they had to go on until they at last reestablished communications with Arlington.

General Morris Blunt said, "Three hundred and twenty five thousand dead."

"General, we have to launch against them. Those deaths have to be avenged."

"I'm afraid all those deaths may have been inadvertent, Colonel."

Inadvertent. The word now galled him.

The general recounted the strange tale of the Worldwide Crash, with its bizarre dénouement featuring Dr. Cameron Conrad as its central character, and its even stranger catchphrase of *Omega Sol.* It seemed Dr. Conrad was talking to the enemy after all, which didn't surprise Pittman in the least.

"As I say, the deaths from the Worldwide Crash were inadvertent. But this Omega Sol business doesn't seem inadvertent at all. I've told the president that I view it as a deliberate act of aggression, and he's now weighing his options. It doesn't look good, Tim. First Tau Ceti. Then Centauri A. Now the sun? Dr. Conrad was able to understand the figures as plain as day. The equations are all there. They've told us what they mean to do. They're throwing it in our face. It's their damned arrogance I can't stand. What gives them the right to come here and do this to our sun? I don't like the way they're simply ignoring us while they go ahead and exterminate us."

"So, what exactly did Dr. Conrad say about the equations?"

"His speech is still a little bit of a problem, and we've had to get our speech therapist to help him a lot, but he says that according to the Builder numbers, the whole red-giant process will happen at an accelerated rate, in a matter of months. In a mathematical subset, they've even outlined what will happen to each and every planet in the solar system, as if the whole thing is just some kind of great experiment or hypothesis they're trying to prove."

"So what can we expect on Earth?"

The general now outlined that particular part of the equation for Pittman. "As the Builders bleed the sun's hydrogen away, Earth will experience an initial cooldown. Like Oren told us when we first found out about the Tau Ceti thing. For two or three weeks, we'll go into a deep freeze. This deep freeze will wreak havoc on customary weather patterns. Multiple major hurricanes will brew in the equatorial latitudes of both oceans, but once these hurricanes move north and hit the deep freeze, they'll turn into major snowstorms. Then as the sun begins to collapse through the force of its own gravity, it will heat up again, as Oren explained to us as well, and Earth will go from a deep freeze to a blast furnace. What I don't get is why they would tell us what they plan to do. Why would they deliberately reveal their attack plans to us? It doesn't make military sense."

This perplexed Pittman as well. "Has the president decided anything?"

"Not yet. But rest assured, Tim, I've advised him to launch against Alpha Vehicle. I understand that the Builders might be trying to communicate with us, and that we might even learn a lot from them, but what about Omega Sol? That's what I've asked the president to base his decision on. He's talking to Russia. And the PRNC."

"The PRNC? Why does he want to talk to Po Pin-Yen? He's a lying son of a bitch."

"Tim, you have to moderate your views on the North Chinese. They're a major power now. Which means nothing can be done about Alpha Vehicle unless we touch base with them first."

The president must have got the go-ahead from the PRNC and Russia quickly, because he decided to launch the next day.

Pittman felt the thrill of combat surge through his blood. He was approaching Crater Cavalet in Moonstone 5 with Merryman, Newlove, and Weisgarber. Having crawled out of their emplacement moments ago like a half-buried beetle, they rolled across the lunar plain, moving from their defensive position on the outside of the crater, to their offensive one on the inside. The scientists had gone back to Earth in one of his own Moonstone shuttles—NASA's planned civilian rescue had now been canceled, as it wouldn't be here soon enough to get the Stradivari and Princeton Team members out of harm's way. He had taken the position of forward gunner, was up in the battle bubble, and had a full three-sixty view.

The other hard-vacuum vehicles made their own approaches toward the outside rim of Crater Cavalet. Their treads turned and turned, scarring the Moon's gray-brown dust. Moonstone 5's shock absorbers gave as the vehicle hit the first upward curve of the crater's rim. The clarity of it all was like a moment with God—the sun shining with a diamond glare, the Moon lit up as if from within by neon gas, black sky that was as impenetrable as a swath of sable velvet, and Moonstones 4 and 6 to his left and right, their own shock absorbers shifting in the fluid pull of the Moon's weak gravity.

As Moonstone 5 climbed Crater Cavalet's rim, the treads dug deeper. Looking behind, Pittman saw huge clouds of dust—but not clouds like he made with his pickup on desert roads back home, because this dust settled quickly, didn't have the resistance of air to stop its fall. It was like a shower of gray sequins in the sun, as heavy as lead, plummeting toward the dry surface.

At last Moonstone 5 reached the top of the crater. Its weight crumpled the rim, and as the vehicle lurched forward, Pittman bashed his face against the bubble's pressure glass. He didn't wince. He went into battle and afterward he had bruises, cuts, and scrapes he couldn't account for, tattoos he was always proud of. They churned down the inside of the crater.

To actually go inside Crater Cavalet was to gain an appreciation of its true size—at least two kilometers across and one kilometer deep, with the eastern edge of the rim casting a deep round shadow. Through this shadow he saw Moonstones 7, 8, and 9. Cloaked in darkness, the hard-vac war vehicles revealed themselves only by their red running lights. Along the western rim he saw Moonstones 10, 11, and 12, fully lit by the sun, but still hard to see because of their gray, brown, and black camouflage. On the south side, discernible only by the dust they kicked up, were the remaining Moonstones.

In the middle of the crater sat the *thing*.

Why wasn't it trying to protect itself? A perfect sphere, and more reflective than the most polished mirror, it reminded him of a Christmas ornament. Why would it just float there two meters off the ground and not do anything when it obviously knew they were approaching? Not for the first time did he feel the strangeness and unreachablility of the alien construct.

He contacted his units.

"This is Moonstone Five. Repeat, this is Moonstone Five. Do you copy?"

All the other Moonstones copied.

"Commence emplacement and prepare to engage."

The shovels to his rear revved and Moonstone 5 dug its way backward into Crater Cavalet's slope. The crater reminded Pittman of the Roman Colosseum. Alpha Vehicle stared at him—the thing was looking at him the way a human might at a bug under a magnifying glass.

On the arching interior of the crater's rim he saw the other Moonstone hard-vac battle vehicles dig in. After five minutes, everybody was in place. His men ran system checks and reported in.

He then intoned the words that as far as he was concerned were the only words in the world that mattered: "Fire at will."

He had his hand on the joystick, and his thumb on the firing button. The button was hard red plastic, had a hairline crack on one side, and responded beautifully, with a hair-trigger quickness to the first slight pressure of his thumb. The Moonstone's big guns mounted left and right spit their ordnance, and his first volley arced like two flying stars toward Alpha Vehicle.

Thirty-six other flying stars from the other Moonstones flew toward the sphere, and it was just too easy, didn't make sense, was, at least for Alpha Vehicle, the battlefield equivalent of suicide. The thing had the viscosity of egg yolk, according to all reasonable testing, and was going to splatter like a balloon filled with strawberry jam.

As the flying stars got closer and closer, he saw their reflection in Alpha Vehicle's convex surface, like sparklers in a fun-house mirror, the images foreshortened. And in those few instances before the ordnance hit, there seemed to come to the battlefield an atmosphere of bated breath, of seconds lasting an eternity.

But when the ordnance struck Alpha Vehicle and penetrated its shimmering membrane, it simply disappeared without so much as a ripple.

No explosions, detonations, or rending of that perfect sphere, no final shutting of that awful silver eye. Alpha Vehicle *ignored* Moonstone's best conventional effort. Had they dropped stones into the deepest part of the ocean, the result would have been the same—obscure and momentary.

"Fire again!" came his words, but this time they were uttered in the telltale emasculated tone of the defeated.

He thumbed the cracked red button, and more flying stars jumped from his twin guns.

Over the coming minutes, the Moonstones fired

enough ordnance to level a major city, but Alpha
Vehicle retained its placid perfection. Pittman remembered his son's terrible temper in the days before he and Sheila had split up, and how Tom, not
getting his way, would come at him, red-faced with
fury; Tom would swing at him, and Pittman would
simply put his hand on Tom's forehead to keep him
away. Alpha Vehicle was doing the same thing now:
Cognizant of its far greater power, the thing chose
to ignore, or at least tolerate, them. It galled Pittman.
Rankled his military ego. For Alpha Vehicle, quite
simply, was *above* engaging Moonstone.

"Cease fire! Cease fire!"

The firing stopped.

He stared at the thing. Perspiration etched its way
over his temple under his helmet. He didn't know
what to do. He began to regret getting rid of all the
scientists. He thought of Dr. Conrad. If anybody understood Alpha Vehicle, he did. He sensed his whole
team waiting.

"Men, I know you'll be disappointed, but until
we . . ."

A Greenhow prompt came to his strategic screen.
He opened the incoming prompt and saw the little
red emergency horn in the corner flashing on and off.

Moments later he had a visual of Tower 47—for
they had numbered the towers now. Tower 47 had
launched another energy cell. Further little red horns
appeared all in a row, each one rigged to a specific
Moon tower. He pressed the ENTER key repeatedly,
and got successive visuals of various Moon towers,
and each one was launching its own energy cell. He
feared the energy cells might converge on their posi-

tion. But it soon became apparent the energy cells were leaving the Moon.

After a minute, he saw that they were in fact heading toward Earth.

A few hours later, Pittman and Haydn, up in Gettysburg Tower, watched the incoming reports. Ninety-two additional energy cells—and why ninety-two, why not a hundred? It didn't make sense to Pittman, but little about the Builders did—had established orbit around Earth with the preexisting ninety-two, making a total of one hundred and eighty-four, now equal to the number of towers.

A short while later, a delicate pinging came from the Greenhow prompt on the screen. Pittman got up and leaned over Newlove's shoulder.

"Report."

Newlove double-checked the incoming data. "The blue hawks are leaving the poultry yard."

Greenhow showed the energy cells breaking away from Earth orbit.

An hour later it was confirmed by Orbops that all one hundred and eighty-four cells were sinking sunward at a rate of ten million kilometers per hour.

Ten hours later, Moonstone got the news from Orbops that all had impacted into the sun's surface. Why would the cells dive into the sun?

He knew the answer only all to well.

The following day, Orbops established that a hydrogen bleed had indeed begun in the sun.

Omega Sol had become a reality.

15

Lesha walked toward the Johns Hopkins Physiotherapy Department a few days after the energy cells had plummeted into the sun. A freshly pressed man's business suit hung from her fingers. The president's voice had sounded different in person. She felt suspended in a world that had become inordinately unreal to her. A week ago she had been on the Moon. Now she was taking a suit to Cam so he could meet with the president.

She rounded the corner to the Physiotherapy Department and saw Cam walking on a treadmill in running shoes that looked too big for his legs. Whatever the Builders had done to him was slowly letting go. He was coming round a bit more each day. His hip gave slightly each time he put his left foot down, as if he had a pain there. She paused in the doorway and watched him. His eyes were intent above the broad planes of his prominent cheeks, and his brow was like a rock. The outline of his strong chin was thrust forward. Despite his forty-five years, his body had a youthful trim.

He at last noticed her. His face lit up with a smile. He continued to walk because he had no choice—the treadmill was still on. He reached quickly—and a tad awkwardly—for the switch. And when he had turned the contraption off, he used the support bars to swing himself around.

As if propelled by a magnetic force, she hurried toward him. She let the new suit drop to the floor. She felt giddy. They embraced and, comically, he lost his balance, and she lost hers because she was still newly returned from the Moon and didn't have her Earth legs back yet. They gripped each other so they wouldn't fall, and kissed.

"Are you ready for the president?" she said.

He nodded. "I'm just glad you're coming with me. I'm so happy you're back."

She motioned at the door. "A car's waiting."

"What did the president have to say this morning?"

Her brow rose. "He wasn't too happy about the whole thing, particularly because Po Pin-Yen has suggested Omega Sol is our fault. He's just glad you're sufficiently recovered to have a sit-down with him. And he understands that you want me there. In case your speech gets bad again. He wonders if Omega Sol is retaliation for Pittman's attack against Alpha Vehicle."

He shook his head. "I think Omega Sol is incidental to Pittman's attack. But there seems to be an ominous development with myself in regard to Pittman's attack."

She looked at him with sudden concern. "What?"

"I can't speak Greek anymore. Not that there's a

definitive link, but I can't help thinking that it's more than a coincidence I lost the ability to speak Greek just a few hours after Pittman launched against Alpha Vehicle. It could mean any number of things, but I fear it might mean they've given up on me because of the attack. In fact, I'm afraid they might have given up on all of us. We've failed whatever test they've set for us. It's the first overt act of violence we've committed against Alpha Vehicle. Maybe they've learned all they need to know, and have now shut down any and all communications attempts with us. It's too bad, because just before Pittman launched, I thought I seemed to be making a breakthrough with them."

She grew still, peered at him more closely. "You had another episode?"

He nodded. "A few hours before Pittman's strike. The symbols were on the wall this time. I was reading them. Remember how I was telling you there was an emotional component to them?"

"Yes."

"I felt this odd kind of . . . of pity from them. It was as if they were trying to probe my intelligence, but when they saw that I couldn't think in for what lack of a better phrase I'm calling hyperdimensional logic—or at least not think in it as fluently as they could—they more or less dismissed me. And that's when I felt pity from them."

"The failed test idea?"

"Maybe."

She helped him dress, as he still lacked some coordination. She held his pants and he slid his legs in. He couldn't manage his tie, and she tracked down a staff physician to produce a sturdy Windsor for them.

The president's chief of staff, John Gielgud, called her while she was helping Cam with his shoes. "The president's waiting."

She hurried as best she could, but it was difficult because despite Cam's great progress, he still wasn't fully recovered; and though he insisted on walking to the elevator, she finally convinced him into a wheelchair and pushed him quickly down the corridor. They couldn't keep the president waiting.

The elevator doors opened and she squeezed in next to a janitor who was taking a large gray cart full of bagged garbage to the receiving bay. The janitor, an older black man with a saggy face, kept glancing at Cam, as if he knew perfectly well who Cam was, the special inpatient up on 5-East who was all tied up with this Omega Sol thing that was going on in the sun—for the energy cell impact had been reported widely in various media.

It was the same on the ground floor as they passed the volunteers in the information kiosk, kindly old ladies from the purple-rinse set who gazed at Cam with the numbing blankness of individuals who feared they were doomed.

Lesha pushed him quickly out the front door. The chauffeur, seeing them from his parking spot at the end of the drive-through, pulled up to the front door and got out. He wore dark sunglasses, but took them off to get a better look at Cam, as if even this government employee had to take his own measure of Dr. Cameron Conrad, the only man who had talked to the Builders, and who might be able to talk to them again if the right hyperdimensional conditions were fostered, and tell them to stop playing dangerous games with the sun. The chauffeur's plea was implicit in his narrowed eyes—*maybe if you just talk to them, reason with them, tell them that we're not so bad after all*. The big man, who had a granite physique and a communications earpiece, opened the rear door. He tried to help Cam out of his wheelchair, but Cam grunted and got out of the chair himself. He pulled his Builder-compromised body into the back of the limousine. Lesha got in after him and the chauffeur shut the door.

Once they were moving, she said, "The president wants to hear your ideas."

"They're not my ideas. They're the Builders'. And really, they're not even the Builders' ideas. They're absolutes. Only absolutes from a different plane than the one we're used to operating on."

"Your speech is a little rough. I'm having a hard time understanding you." She glanced out the tinted window as they drove along Jefferson.

"I'll just have to talk slower, then."

They came to Northern Parkway and turned west. They followed the highway in silence for a while. She glanced at Cam. He slouched on the supple leather upholstery, his hands folded over his cane, and stared straight ahead, deep in thought. She couldn't help thinking he looked lonely. Or at least not so much lonely as alone.

She said, "If you can outline some of your preliminary ideas. About how we might fix all this. Or at least tell me what you think they've been saying to you, and how you've been interpreting it so we have

a clearer idea of where we stand when we're in front
of the president."

So that's what he did.

Over the next twenty minutes, as they headed
south on the Baltimore-Washington Expressway to
the airport, Cam sketched in his rough notions about
what and who the Builders were, what they were
saying to him, how they regarded the human race,
what they were up to, and what the president might
possibly do about them. "They more or less revealed
a lot of this to me in the few hours before Pittman's strike."

"And it's a test after all?"

"In a manner of speaking, yes. But it's more like
they're trying to determine where we fit into the
overall hyperdimensional scheme of things. If we
pass their criteria, they might let us live. If not,
who knows?"

While they walked from the limousine to the waiting military helicopter, she decided the air had become distinctly chilly. They said the sun was going
to cool first before it heated up. She was sorely
tempted to glance at the sun, risk the retina burn,
see if it had changed, but she experienced a sudden
irrational fear. The sun—*her* sun, the same old sun
she had tanned under as a girl growing up in
California—wasn't the same anymore. The Builders
had filled it with the stellar equivalent of amphet-
amines, and now it was going to rush through its
life cycle like a Roman candle. She found she
couldn't bring herself to look at it at all.

"Why do you think they're doing it?"

Cam's eyes narrowed. "I wish I knew."

The helicopter was black, had a white roof, and its rotor turned slowly as the aircraft idled on the tarmac. A short run of boarding steps hung from its side, like a corrugated metal tongue. A young female intern in a snappy business suit clutching a folded waferscreen, and an older, more senior member of the Secret Service, waited for them. These two ushered Lesha and Cam aboard. The Secret Service man made a call and said, "Navasota is secure and on the way." The intern gave them security passes; she was young, and reminded Lesha of a wedding planner trying to get everybody organized.

A few seconds later the helicopter lifted into the smog-filled Baltimore morning.

"What about the symbols?" Lesha asked.

He nodded. "They simplified them before they turned them off. I was understanding more of them."

"And the music?"

"Not since Pittman's strike. Just like the Greek."

"So you really think they've given up on us?"

He considered the question for several seconds. "Before I lost my sense of them, I got the feeling they were grappling with . . . greater concerns. They're really not that interested in us. They're frying bigger fish."

Her eyes narrowed. She felt slightly ill. "So it's like you say. We're incidental."

"Exactly."

She brooded on that. Incidental. She looked out the window at the pollution-blurred urban sprawl below— Baltimore and Washington, one big megalopolis— and resumed an old nervous habit, nibbling her thumbnail. *Ignored.* The word Pittman had used in his report. *Target ignored our assault.* The word struck with chilling implication. And greater concerns? Out there in the wider universe? What was going on out there that the Builders should have to accelerate one main-sequence star after another into red giants? How big was the fish they had to fry, and why did they have to wipe out the human race in order to fry it?

"Do you think another launch against Alpha Vehicle might help? Or maybe one against the Moon towers, since Alpha Vehicle didn't work? The president was asking."

"We don't know how they'll respond. Until we have a better understanding of the way they think, any further military action is really pointless, and could end up being disastrous."

Lesha saw the White House a short while later. The helicopter descended to the South Lawn, and two Marines in dress uniforms greeted her and Cam with crisp salutes.

Lesha showed her pass smartly while Cam fumbled with his. She helped Cam up the steps into the building and they followed one of the Marines down a long corridor to the west part of 1600 Pennsylvania. They were shown into the waiting room outside the Oval Office.

Chief of Staff John Gielgud came out and got them a few minutes later.

Having missed Gielgud on her previous visit to the White House that morning, Lesha was meeting the man for the first time. He had a broad but close-lipped smile, and his head, bald, of average size, with the pink color of a cooked ham, was as spherical as Alpha Vehicle. Like the president, he was of below average height. He walked quickly.

"Dr. Weeks. Dr. Conrad. Right this way. President Langdon is waiting. He's so happy to know you're feeling better, Dr. Conrad."

Lesha helped Cam to his feet and they followed the chief of staff into the Oval Office.

A number of people were already assembled there, waiting for them. Secretary of Defense Leroy Congdon stood by the fireplace, his black face set, his brow an unrevealing line, the coppery planes of his cheeks like twin battlements. Brian Goldvogel, of Orbops, sat on a yellow sofa trying to look poised, but came across more like a nervous bunny in a boa constrictor's terrarium. General Morris Blunt was admiring one of the paintings, hands clasped behind his back, looking desperately tired, his usual pink face now the color of an old paper bag. Dr. Jeffrey Ochoa was there as well, a smile frozen to his face, standing at the end of the yellow sofa. Oren Fye sat in a Queen Anne chair next to him, his substantial bulk looking precariously supported in the delicate old piece.

Most surprising of all was Dr. Renate Tennant. Lesha found it strange to see her out of her Gettysburg coveralls and in a standard business suit.

President Ray Langdon was a short stocky man, barrel-chested, with thick limbs and short hair. An aging drill sergeant, thought Lesha. And so unbelievably tiny. Even smaller than Gielgud. So that as he came out from behind his desk to shake hands with her for the second time that day, Lesha was again surprised by how far she had to incline her head. "So good of you to come again," he said. He didn't move with Gielgud's same quickness but with a deliberate step, toes pointed outward as he walked toward Cam, soles of his oxfords sinking with casual and assured ownership into the thick pile of the flag-blue rug. "And, Dr. Conrad. How are you feeling?"

Lesha glanced at Cam apprehensively, fearing his speech would misbehave.

"Better. Much better."

His second word came out like "mush," and Lesha watched the president glance at Dr. Ochoa. Dr. Ochoa's eyebrows rose.

The president turned back to Cam. "Good, good. I'm glad to hear it. I trust you know these others."

Langdon quickly went through everybody. Only the secretary of defense came forward to shake Cam's hand, then hers, as he hadn't met them previously. "Why don't we get started?" said the president. "Dr. Weeks, did you have a chance to talk to Dr. Conrad on the way down?"

"Yes. And I've got news. He tells me he had another major episode with the Builders just before Colonel Pittman launched his attack against Alpha Vehicle."

The president's brow rose. "Really? And have they changed their position on Omega Sol at all?"

"Not exactly. But they seem to have revealed more of their nature."

"Let's have it, then. Dr. Conrad's agreed to let you be his spokesperson under the circumstances?"

"Yes."

"So, what did the Builders say this time?" asked the president.

"Dr. Conrad says that in his most recent contact with him they seem to have expressed pity for us."

"Pity?" said Congdon. "Why?"

"Perhaps because we are unable to think the same way they do."

Blunt turned to Congdon. "You see what I mean by nerve? And arrogance?"

Lesha pushed on. "Dr. Conrad spoke quite extensively about the Builders on the way down."

The president said, "And what does he make of them, now that he's had time to reflect in Johns Hopkins? What about the Worldwide Crash? Have they explained that at all? We still haven't got Dr. Conrad's opinion on that."

"Dr. Conrad believes the Worldwide Crash is a direct result of the unnecessarily complex message Dr. Tennant sent to the Builders."

Renate stiffened. "We have no proof of that."

Lesha gave Renate a patient glance, then continued. "The Builders received Dr. Tennant's message, and Dr. Conrad believes they were so puzzled by it, particularly by all its complex cultural overlay, that in their search for greater context they rifled through all the world's computers—the Moon's as well—and inadvertently shut them down."

"Inadvertently," said the president. He glanced at the secretary of defense. "There's that word again." He turned back to Lesha. "Go ahead, Dr. Weeks."

"Dr. Tennant sent samples of seven different languages: English, Latin, Greek, French, Spanish, Cantonese, and Arabic. But with no easily understandable referents, the Builders launched twenty-three energy cells to Earth, and two to the Moon. By searching through our databases for referents, they derailed all normal programming in an attempt to piece together some kind of understanding. In such a computer-dependent world, it caused major chaos and widespread fatalities.''

"Yes, but think of what we've gained," protested Renate. "If it weren't for me, we wouldn't know about Omega Sol. It was embedded in part of their information dump, and the information dump happened as a direct result of my communications attempt."

"Perhaps. But there are three hundred and twenty-five thousand dead, Renate."

"Ladies, let's not talk casualties," said Gielgud. "Dr. Tennant's decision to send an expanded communications packet was sanctioned by the highest levels of government. And Dr. Tennant's right. It seems likely that if it weren't for her communication attempt, we never would have found out about Omega Sol."

"But then you responded to Omega Sol with an attack against Alpha Vehicle, and this has just made things worse. Dr. Conrad can't hear them anymore. That's the real import of his latest episode with them. They've more or less said good-bye to him."

Dr. Ochoa stepped forward, looking concerned. "Is this true?"

"Yes. He can't speak Greek. He doesn't hear the music. He hasn't seen the symbols since the colonel's launch. He believes that because of the colonel's launch, they've abandoned him."

Ochoa glanced at the president, who in turn looked at the secretary of defense. Congdon said, "That's unfortunate, and it certainly lessens the possibility of reaching some kind of peace accord with them. But I think our bigger concern is Omega Sol."

"Yes, but don't you see? The colonel's attack has escalated things."

"The logical tactical response to the Omega Sol equation was to launch against Alpha Vehicle. We had to stop what they wanted to do to our sun. Unfortunately the mission seems to have failed."

"Logical tactical responses aren't going to work with the Builders. We've shown a fantastically advanced class of intelligence that we respond like animals. Dr. Conrad believes that they might have been willing to give us the benefit of the doubt, and that their possible careful probing of his own mind might have been the first overtures in establishing a meaningful dialogue with them. You've read Rhona Lindsay's reports? Dr. Conrad woke up one day understanding all seven languages included in Dr. Tennant's subgravitational 'send.' And as much as we don't agree with the unnecessarily complex and even dangerous communications packet Dr. Tennant transmitted, we believe they were getting ready to talk to him using those languages. Then came Colonel Pittman's overt military action against Alpha Vehicle, and now it's all gone. Dr. Conrad thinks that after the Moonstone attack on Alpha Vehicle, the Builders had all the answers they needed about us, weren't going to put out any more feelers, and withdrew those few probes already in place."

Dr. Ochoa interrupted. "I'd like to run some tests

on him. If what he's saying is true, it represents a medical change, and it should be investigated."

"Dr. Conrad I'm sure has your willing consent," said the president.

Cam nodded. "If it will . . . prove to you . . . that I've been deserted."

The president leaned forward. "Does Dr. Conrad think the Omega Sol energy cell impacts into the sun are a direct result of Colonel Pittman's attack on Alpha Vehicle?"

"No," said Lesha. "He believes they would have gone ahead one way or the other."

The secretary of defense spoke up. "Dr. Conrad, it's now been theorized by some of our leading strategists and scientists that the Moon towers might be more vulnerable than Alpha Vehicle, and that together with the energy cells they could be driving the incremental changes we're seeing in our sun. Do you have any idea of what we might do to take these towers down?" Cam turned red with exasperation at this suggestion. Congdon continued. "Even as we speak, I'm amassing significant forces on the Moon to put at Colonel Pittman's disposal. If you're telling us that negotiations are at an end with them anyway, then I feel I must defend the United States using whatever means necessary. As the Moon towers don't seem to have the same structure as Alpha Vehicle itself . . ."

Cam's face turned redder. He raised his hands and shook his head. "That will just . . . ex . . . exacerbate . . ." He sounded drunk. Cam turned to Lesha in frustration. "Dr. Weeks . . . please explain. . . ."

She put a reassuring hand on his knee. "We spoke about this on the way over as well. Dr. Conrad feels that further military action against the Builders might be potentially disastrous. They may have ignored Colonel Pittman's first attack, at least in the way of any direct counteroffensive, but that doesn't mean they won't respond aggressively if you go ahead with a second one. You have to remember, these are beings, or entities, who have traveled twelve million light-years through a series of space-time way stations that have brought them to our system instantaneously. Based on everything Dr. Conrad's seen, documented, and learned from the Builders, he contends they could exterminate us instantly if that was their ultimate goal. And so to throw more missiles at them would be pointless. Dr. Conrad believes the only way to move forward is to again try to establish communications with the Builders, and to do it through the universal language of physics."

"Physics?" said the secretary of defense, as if he had never heard of the field.

"Yes. And it has to be frontier physics, as Dr. Conrad feels the Builders have shown a specific interest in our ability to understand these more abstract concepts. Let's not forget, the Builders are masters of curved space and bent time, fully comprehend the multidimensional intricacies of membrane theory, and are experts in the true essence of the universe, right down to its mysterious string-theory particles. Humans have barely scratched the surface of these subparticle phenomena."

The president spoke up. "As a matter of fact, we were just talking about another communications attempt with the Builders before the two of you arrived. As an alternative to an attack on the Moon towers, Dr. Tennant thinks we should send a second even more expanded packet. It will give us a good chance to ask them why they're targeting us for extermination.''

Cam groaned and turned to Lesha a second time. ''Tell them . . . that . . . we have . . . nothing to do with it.''

She nodded. ''While the administration might believe the Builders, by instigating a red-giant process in the sun, are launching an unprovoked attack against the human race, Dr. Conrad thinks the human race has nothing to do with it, and that the Builders are turning the sun into a red giant for reasons we can't begin to comprehend. After all, the Builders didn't specifically target the sun. Tau Ceti and Alpha Centauri A have also experienced the same activity. Dr. Conrad thinks the Builders have much bigger things at stake, and that the human race is a side issue to their larger goals.''

The room grew quiet. Then the president said, ''In other words, we're *incidental*.''

''Precisely.''

''What could they possibly have at stake?'' Leroy Congdon asked, in his deep baritone.

''Dr. Conrad doesn't know. Only that it stands to reason that if they've turned Tau Ceti and Centauri A into red giants, the sun's red-giant process is part of a much larger project.''

The president's face quivered into a mask of puzzlement. ''I don't understand why they would hopscotch from star to star, turning them into red giants.

And frankly, I don't care. My main concern is how to stop them."

Lesha watched Cam lean forward with mounting agitation. He spoke but it was with a strained effort. "If we can assume . . . that before Moonstone . . . they were investigating us . . . trying to determine our intelligence . . . and everything I went through in Alpha Vehicle tells me this . . ." He grew frustrated with his inability to get the words out. As the Builders couldn't seem to communicate with humans, so the man she loved couldn't either. "Would you find it . . . strange . . . if you were confronted by two-dimensional beings?"

Cam glanced at Lesha with a pleading in his eyes, and the reference to two-dimensional beings jogged her into her next explanation.

"What he means is that a two-dimensional being would have height and width, but no depth. A stick figure drawn on a piece of paper. In a metaphorical sense, can such a figure have intelligence? Dr. Conrad theorizes that the Builders operate on various hyperdimensional planes, and as hard as it might be for some of you to grasp five, six, seven, and even up to twenty-six dimensions, this is the kind of physics Dr. Conrad deals with every day. The work we were doing on the Moon, Stradivari Project, was all about generating, for a measurable amount of time, a sizable hyperdimensional field known as anti-Ostrander space. With the production of this field, Dr. Conrad hoped to prove the existence of these higher planes. To put it simply, we as stick figures have to get up off the page and communicate with the Builders, let them understand that we compre-

hend at least some of the principles of the universe
the way they do, and that we share the same terms
of reference. The understanding of hyperdimensionality is the yardstick by which they measure intelligence, and maybe if we can show them we're
intelligent according to their own criteria, they might
think we're worth saving."

"There's that arrogance again," said Blunt.

"It's not arrogance. It's simply an obstacle that we
patiently have to overcome. We have to establish
some commonality between the four dimensions of
our own existence—I include time—and the hyperdimensionality of theirs. Dr. Conrad's begging you to
let him lead the effort."

The president and his chief of staff glanced at each
other, then looked at the secretary of defense. Congdon gave his head a curt shake, just once, a quick
twitch of his massive chin to the right. This was followed by a swiveling of his dark eyes on Cam.

Langdon said, "I think the consensus of everybody
here is that you aren't well enough at present to lead
an effort this crucial. Plus we don't really know
whether you've been compromised by the Builders
and might just end up working against us. As much
as we admire your zeal, commitment, and patriotism,
Dr. Conrad, I believe at this point we have to consider other options. According to your analysis of the
Omega Sol equation, we haven't got more than three
months at the sun's current rate of change before
radiation levels become harmful to life on Earth. In
other words, if we're going to try to open diplomatic
channels to the Builders again, our schedule would
necessarily have to be tight. And as Dr. Tennant is

our expert on communications—and, unlike yourself, in good health—I feel more comfortable appointing her as our leader on this extremely critical project. Considering everything she's learned from her first 'send,' I think she's well positioned to transmit a second one, especially because there's evidence that they actually understand us now."

Cam groaned as if in pain. "But what's the good of . . . a second conventional 'send'? Somehow . . . we have to tell them . . . that we understand their plane."

"Dr. Conrad, unless you can immediately offer us a way to stop the hydrogen drain in the sun," said Langdon, his voice hardening, "I think it only makes sense to allow Dr. Tennant to use all the masses of data we recorded from the first 'send' and have another go. Especially because you yourself are trying to dissuade us from a strike against the towers. Isn't that compromise enough for you? The technology's in place. We have experience with it. And when it comes right down to it, Dr. Conrad, do you have any better suggestions?"

Lesha watched Cam, saddened by how painfully obvious the Builder-induced genius was now gone, and how the man was casting around for any straw. "Let me try to talk to them again."

"Nothing would make us happier if you could do that, Dr. Conrad. But you yourself have said they have deserted you."

"Perhaps if I were in a setting more conducive."

"Like where?"

"Navasota. I want to go home. Maybe they'll come . . . back to me in a setting like that."

The president glanced toward Dr. Ochoa. "Can we

discharge him yet, Doctor? And do you think letting him go home might help things along?''

Dr. Ochoa thought for a moment, then nodded. ''It's certainly worth a try.''

16

As Pittman rode in Moonstone 5 to Crater Cavalet
again, he felt sorry for Dr. Tennant. Now that she
was back on the Moon, he could see she was driven
by demons she would never admit to, just like he
was. She stared out Moonstone 5's front window,
and the alabaster light of the lunar surface reflected
dimly in her pale blue eyes. Her hand rested on the
back of Newlove's chair, and she had to dip to see
because the carrier section of the hard-vac fighting
vehicle was higher than the driving area. Her lips
were clamped, and she surveyed the track-torn surface of the Moon around Crater Cavalet with apprehensive eyes. She must have sensed him staring, for
she glanced at him, and her brow arched. He didn't
say anything, just watched.

They reached the crater's rim, and the hard-vac
vehicle gave under the upward strain. He saw the
black lunar sky. And floating through the sky was
the gold band, what had come to be known as the
Bleed. It was all the hydrogen drifting away from the
sun as the Builders depleted the star's fuel prepara-

tory to igniting it into a red giant. His face stiffened as he watched the Bleed; it was like a cloud of platinum sequins, a nearly magical phenomenon that was a constant reminder of how the Builders were getting away with things, no matter how hard he tried to stop them.

"And so the linkup should be an easier thing this time?" he asked, because this was all he had taken away from her exhaustive briefing in the common room this morning.

"They gave me much more computing power." As if it were a prize she had won.

"But Rembrandt? And Michelangelo?"

"The rationale is to send a bit of everything."

"And plans for a nuclear bomb?"

"They have to understand that we're ready to defend ourselves. They have to know we understand how things work."

As they reached the rim's crest, Pittman couldn't help predicting failure. "I've been out several times. I've stared at it. And it's stared back. Have you ever stared at something a long time? You can learn a lot by just staring. It's a trick I learned in the desert."

"And what have you learned about Alpha Vehicle?"

Pittman's face hardened. "That I have to kill it. Or die trying." As Moonstone 5 headed down the crater's inner rim, the headlights casting two stark beams over the track-chewed terrain, he saw the *thing* in the crater's center. "As a matter of fact, Alpha Vehicle talks to me. Not the way it talks to Dr. Conrad. But I come out here alone sometimes. I walk right up to it. I see my reflection in it. All bent and curved like a fun-house mirror. And I feel something from it."

"Like a . . . a peace?"

"No, nothing like that." How could he put this? "Do you know anything about the martial arts?"

"I took karate as a girl."

"It's like that. We know we're enemies, but that doesn't mean we're going to dishonor each other. We respect each other. We understand each other. As warriors. And we both know that the showdown will have to come."

The quality of the ride in Moonstone 5 changed as they reached the bottom of the crater. Here, moondust had been blasted clear in the meteorite's initial strike millions of years ago, leaving only the underlying bedrock. It was so smooth they could have been driving down I-95.

They stopped a hundred meters from Alpha Vehicle. Moonstones 4 and 6 appeared to the left and right.

Pittman put himself in the background—Dr. Tennant was in charge now.

Once out on the surface with her team, she was a precise technocrat. He watched her move with divine competence, never showing weakness, setting up the new relays and accelerator conduits quickly. Maribeth, Silke, and Peggy assisted her as needed, running cables, calibrating angles, and fine-tuning the codes.

At last she was ready.

She looked at him through the yellow visor of her helmet. "I'd prefer it if you and the other Moonstones retreat a safe distance. Just in case."

So he left Dr. Tennant and her team in the scarred gabbroid basalt of Crater Cavalet and retreated in Moonstone 5 until he was at the rim's ragged summit. He told Haydn to get out of the shotgun seat so he could watch. He strapped himself in. He punched a command into his wristpad. His visor magnified Crater Cavalet to the fifth power.

They had to wait three hours before an amorphous green vortex formed above Alpha Vehicle—now that the sun's transformation had been set in motion, relay points appeared less often.

"Commencing acceleration." Dr. Tennant's voice was steady.

All the new data seemed to be making a difference, because the subgravitational packet shimmered easily through the black, reminding him of heat filming off the desert highway outside his home. And something new happened to the relay point this time. It brightened, began to spin, and threw off sparks like a pinwheel on the Fourth of July. He checked Moonstone 5's systems, glancing quickly at the status screens, and the quality and character of the usual background radiation changed, registered an ever-growing number of electrons, as if the usual stripped galactic nucleotides were fighting for cohesion, stability, and meaning.

He glanced through Moonstone 5's windshield just in time to see a tendril of green plasma stretch down through the vortex, straining like an attenuated digit toward the dust-free basalt, illuminating the figures of the communications team so that their shadows reached far.

"Do you hear it?" Dr. Tennant's voice came through his radio in a wash of static.

"Hear what?"

More static, then, "Music." The word was uttered in fearful yet joyful anticipation.

Then, like a moray eel lunging for prey, the sparkling fluid digit struck quickly, encircling the women, absconding with them through the olive relay point, leaving behind the impression of four separate screams bursting through the static of Pittman's helmet radio with bloodcurdling intensity.

The relay point closed and the women were gone.

17

Cam heard a truck come down the country road outside his place in Navasota, Texas, and knew it had to be Lesha, back from her weekly jaunt to Washington.

He lifted his cane, gripped the edge of the table, and carefully rose from his chair. His red setter, Roosevelt, got up from the hearth. Cam glanced out the sliding glass door into his gentleman's acreage, watched the wind weave patterns over the wild grass, worried that in the middle of August the Texas sky should be so cloudy all the time, with temperatures ten to fifteen degrees below normal as the sun went into its preexpansion chill phase.

He maneuvered around the table into his open-concept living-dining area. As he passed the CenCon—the house's Central Control Console—it asked him if he wanted to adjust the thermostat, and he said yes; then it told him that solar power storage was nearing depletion, and offered him a choice, his independent generator or the grid.

"Put me on the grid," he said.

"Acknowledged," said the CenCon.

He crossed the living room, cautious as he made the transition from the carpet to tiles, his Builder episodes still affecting his motor skills, though not nearly to the same degree as before. He gripped the doorknob, gave it a gentle twist, opened the door, and walked to the stoop.

Lesha came up the long hickory-lined drive in her truck, the cab a dove gray shell over her head, her hands at ten and two o'clock, driving manually because automatic feeds ended at Conroe. She took a dip in the drive, and the shock absorbers gave. Then it was up a small incline and past the side door. She waved and headed to the small lot at the rear.

Cam negotiated the three risers down to the drive and ambled toward her. Two barns rose at the end of the lot, one a gray relic from the past, the other an aluminum Quonset. Lesha swung left and brought the truck to a stop next to his. She got out.

It was strange to see her in a camel-hair jacket at this time of year when ordinarily it was so hot. She wore knee-high boots over beige cords, and had added gold highlights to her hair—he could readily imagine the California blond of years ago. She dug behind her seat, pulled out her computer gear and other electronics, swung them over her shoulder, slammed the door, and came toward him with a purposeful stride.

"Have you seen the news?" she called.

"Not since last night."

"The PRNC Pacific Fleet has gone on maneuvers." She reached him and gave him a kiss. "Congdon characterizes the move as provocative. Po Pin-Yen claims the maneuvers are routine, and have been scheduled for a long time.''

"Has the U.S. responded?''

"Not yet.'' She motioned toward the south. "And Hurricane Delilah has shifted. It's expected to make landfall on the Texas Gulf Coast instead of Mississippi.''

"You're rattled.''

"A week of Washington does that.''

"I've got coffee brewing. Are you hungry?''

"How are your nights? Are they getting better?''

"I haven't slept in forty-eight hours. Yet I don't feel tired at all.''

"I've got the results of your scan.''

"And?''

She leaned over and kissed him. "Your sylvan fissure remains enlarged, but there's no atypical electrical activity anymore. And the shadow is gone. Maybe you should tell Dr. Ochoa about the insomnia.''

He shook his head. "Until I have definitive contact with the Builders again, I'd sooner be left alone. Do you realize Goldvogel actually had the nerve to suggest a guard platoon? I told him to buzz off. The point of coming out here is solitude. Solitude is more conducive to getting in contact with the Builders than having a guard platoon as company. Come to the kitchen. I'll make a sandwich for you.''

She slipped her hand through his elbow and they walked to the house. She pulled back and watched his legs. "You've really improved.''

"Roosevelt and I walk to the spring each day.''

"And your speech." They climbed the steps and went inside. "It comes more quickly."

In the kitchen, he got tomatoes, cheese, and romaine lettuce, and sliced some whole grain bread. Lesha reacquainted herself with Roosevelt, taking the setter's chin in her hands, scratching his neck, telling him he was a good dog, her long hair falling past either side of her face, her brown knee-high boots making her legs look alluring. He had the oddest feeling, one he hadn't felt in a long time. He was happy. And he couldn't help regretting that the Builders were cooking the sun into oblivion just as he had discovered this unexpected Nirvana with Lesha.

The knife sliced through the tomato. Lesha put her stuff on the wicker chair next to the sliding glass doors, looked out at the pool, then walked over to the entertainment unit and turned on the TV. It was already tuned to the news channel.

A cute chickadee of an anchorwoman cheerfully delivered the latest developments in the renewed tension between the U.S. and the PRNC. The USS *Terpsichore* and USS *Rondon* had been given new orders, were leaving the Indian Ocean, and chugging toward the Pacific to "observe" the maneuvers of the PRNC fleet.

"And Hurricane Delilah has strengthened to the strongest category-five hurricane on record. What has meteorologists particularly worried is how far south the jet stream has moved. Due to the sun's recent cooling, a massive cold front has moved down from Canada, as far south as Texas."

At this point a weather map appeared. It showed

frigid Arctic air covering most of the contiguous United States. Underneath this mass, in the Gulf States, the area was entirely red, with temperatures well above normal. Hurricane Delilah fed on these record-breaking highs.

The anchorwoman said meteorologists were worried by this unusual convergence of cold and hot air masses, feared this new possibility everyone was talking about, the superblizzard. "Experts say that if this occurs, it won't last long but that damage could be extensive." She then continued with a few details. Sustained winds of three hundred and eighty-five kilometers per hour. Snow, hail, and freezing rain. All thanks to what the Builders were doing to the sun. The storm was now expected to make landfall at Freeport, rip through Houston, and continue north over Navasota.

At the mention of Navasota, Cam put the knife down and turned to the television.

Lesha was now sitting on one of the stools staring at the TV intently. She turned to him. Their eyes met, held for several seconds as the anchorwoman described how the storm was three hundred kilometers across, and how all of eastern Texas would be affected.

"Highway Forty-five from Houston to Conroe was packed," said Lesha.

"These windows are hurricane-proof."

"So we're going to ride it out here?"

"We'll hope the cold front doesn't move too far south."

"How far inland are we?"

"Two hundred klicks."

"You think we'll be okay?"

"It'll be a rough night, but we should make it."

Over lunch, Lesha briefed him on the latest Operation Moonstone developments. "Dr. Tennant has been up there getting things ready. The new 'send' is scheduled for today. The administration has installed buffer software on all critical systems to guard against another Worldwide Crash."

"Have they released the contents of the new 'send'?"

"I have it here on my wafer. Not that there's anything you can do about it now." She glanced at her watch. "In fact, I think they might have already gone ahead." She offered her wafer. "But Blunt thought you might want a look."

Over the coming hours, as the sky got darker, and the wind strengthened, Cam and Lesha reviewed the new "send" materials.

They included an overview of Newtonian physics, a recording of Mozart's Fortieth Symphony in G Minor, a thousand visual images, Einstein's theories, and at last, Cam's own rough equations that groped toward an understanding of hyperdimensionality.

"It was Blunt who insisted we include your equations."

Cam remained skeptical. "I'm flattered, but my own equations remain unproven." And here the loss of Stradivari haunted him like the ghost of a dearly departed friend. "I mean, yes, I agree. Here in this packet are the most profound examples of human thought. Yet I intuit in the Builders a species so advanced, a race so well beyond the envelope of human knowledge, I can't reasonably anticipate this fresh message will move them in any way. It may show the Builders music and pictures, and outline my own unproven and possibly erroneous equations regarding the more esoteric subatomic features of the universe, but I don't think it will be enough to convince them to stop doing what they're doing. We can't *tell* them that we're smart. We have to *show* them that we're smart."

And there it was, the thing that Cam had been looking for, what had eluded him ever since his meeting with the president. They had to show the Builders with a demonstration. But a demonstration of what? He glanced outside. And saw snow. Snow in August. In Texas. They had to illustrate to the Builders that they knew about strings. About hyperdimensions, interdimensions, and even antidimensions, the whole gambit of unproven, highly speculative, and counterintuitively reasoned physics, where gluons met quarks, space met time, science met faith, and where the universe turned out to be far stranger than anybody could imagine.

"If we could demonstrate, even for a few seconds, that we can swim in the same waters they do, breathe the same air, give them some notion of Stradivari . . ."

Lesha sighed. "Yes, but with the Stradivari equipment destroyed . . ."

"Can you ask Blunt for new equipment?"

An apprehensive hardening came to her brow. "What? Right now?"

"Call Blunt on your cell."

She hesitated. But then took out her cell and called Blunt.

She had to hold for five minutes, but at last she got through.

Cam watched her. She explained his idea cogently. But then the corners of her lips turned downward, and her delicate nostrils twitched, and she gave him a worried glance, and said, "I see," every now and again for the next two minutes. At last she said good-bye and folded her phone.

"He characterizes your proposed demonstration as a laboratory experiment, and says that they need more than laboratory experiments at this point. They need something definitive, a gesture that's going to diffuse the situation. Especially now that the PRNC fleet is on maneuvers. We have to show the rest of the world that we have the Builder situation under control. And we particularly have to show the PRNC."

"So it's politics now?" His voice grew sullen. "We're going to be slow-boiled in our own atmosphere all because they want to play politics?"

"He also mentioned resources."

"Five hundred million at most. Particle accelerators have really come down in price."

"And he questions your motives."

"*My* motives?"

"It's your life's work. You lost it all. He thinks you're exploiting the situation to get a second chance."

"That's ridiculous."

"Unless you can guarantee a concrete return—"

"We're dealing with what we think are hyperdimensional beings who operate on a completely different plane than we do. How can I guarantee anything?"

"His exact words were 'concrete strategic and political return.' And then he told me that if Renate's second 'send' doesn't yield a strategic and political return, they may have no choice but to attack the towers."

Cam shook his head. "And this time the Builders might not choose to ignore us. This time they might wipe us out completely."

The storm came in a series of stronger waves over the next hour. Cam was embroiled with his own inner storm. He hardly noticed when the CenCon told him it had no choice but to switch to his independent generator—the utility grid was down, and most of eastern Texas was blacked out.

At one point, hailstones the size of eggs slammed into the windows, but the special hurricane glass held, even as the whole house shook under their onslaught. Blunt called them again to make sure they were okay, suggested that it was too late to airlift them out, and that they should hunker down and stay put. "Delilah's wreaking havoc over the entire southeastern United States. Nothing can move anywhere. It's going to be bad."

"Don't worry, we'll be fine. Cam says this house has been here for over a hundred years."

Sometime around midnight, they heard a loud crash outside, like a bunker-buster bomb.

"The old barn?" said Lesha, her voice strained.

"Maybe you'll feel more comfortable in the cellar."
They moved downstairs.

They sat on garden chairs and fecklessly played chess as a way to keep their minds off the biggest and most destructive blizzard the world had ever seen. Roosevelt kept whimpering in the corner.

The noise around the house doubled in decibels over the next three minutes, going from something they could bear to something that was intolerable, the wind so strong that Cam now heard a weird creaking from above, then three loud crashes in a row. Thirty seconds later water trickled under the cellar door. The door rattled in its jamb. With the rain coming into the basement, he knew the house, or at least part of it, had to be gone. Roosevelt leaped to his feet, hurried to the stairs, and barked at the door.

They gave up on chess. They moved the table against the cellar wall and shored it up on either side with the washing machine and dryer. They crawled underneath. He put his arm around her.

It got ferociously cold, and in a matter of ten minutes the water on the steps glazed over into a thin sheet of feathery ice.

The lights went out. Cam felt his way to the emergency cabinet, retrieved candles, matches, a flashlight, and blankets. They made a nest as the storm raged above what was left of his house.

For the next several hours, Cam forgot about a strategic and political return because he feared the hurricane would pull the floor away and suck them into the maelstrom. He had a lot he wanted to say to Lesha, how he was a new man because of her, but it was like miners' blasting outside, and the explosive weather made it too hard to talk.

At three o'clock in the morning the storm lessened. He tried 911 but got nothing. The calm thickened above them.

"The eye?" she said.

"I think so. Let's go up and have a look."

They climbed the stairs with care because the risers were covered with ice.

When Cam reached the top, he pushed the door open. At first it wouldn't give. He put his shoulder to it. He shone the flashlight out the crack and discovered accumulated snow blocking it. Flakes meandered by his flashlight. He pushed a little harder.

Lesha came upstairs behind him. "Is it bad?"

"My house is gone. And we're buried in snow."

He lifted his leg and stepped into the snow. The snow was wet and heavy. Only parts of his house were left standing. His kitchen counter was there. So was the island. But the rest of the house looked like a gigantic game of pick-up sticks. He fought to control his distress. Shining the flashlight farther afield he saw that the old barn and Quonset were gone. As for trucks, his was still upright, coated in a half meter of snow, but Lesha's had been blown on its side.

"Look!" said Lesha.

She pointed straight up. He saw stars. But also a hypnotic shimmering gold band. He stared for several seconds—and quickly came to the realization that this was the Builder-created hydrogen spill from the sun, the so-called Bleed.

When the winds came again—this time from the reverse direction—they weren't as strong or as noisy.

Cam and Lesha were back downstairs, dozing under the blankets. While he dozed, his mind sorted out his plan for the Builders. By the time the winds finally stopped, and the two of them were again climbing the stairs to check things, his ideas coalesced. He had to talk to the Builders in some way, that's all there was to it, and he was becoming more and more convinced that it had to be through a demonstration, even though Blunt had initially given them a no-go on that plan. He had to figure out a way around Orbops intransigence. For wouldn't it be marvelous to hear that music again, and be touched by the infinite wisdom of the Builders once more? Wouldn't it be wonderful to understand those mystical and sweetly emotional mathematical symbols? And wouldn't it be a godsend to at last comprehend the true nature of the universe? He felt this was what was at stake, nothing less.

He pushed the door open. Snowflakes fell. Behind the snowflakes he saw the sun. Sunshine and snowflakes. At the same time. The new world order. His truck was buried. He tried 911 and discovered cell phone service was still dead.

But he was hardly even thinking of that.

"I always knew there had to be a simpler explanation. And a more intuitive one."

"An explanation for what?" she asked.

"For the universe. And I think the Builders were trying to give it to me before we got them mad."

"They were going to tell you the meaning of the universe?"

"Yes. All my life I've been devising these complex equations to explain it."

"Hyperdimensionality?"

"That's certainly part of it. But I think what the Builders want to tell me goes beyond even that. They want to give me the answer to the question everybody asks."

"Which is?"

"Simple, really. Why are we here, and what does it mean?"

18

Pittman and his Orbops team investigated the scene of the Princeton Team disappearance thoroughly. As they waited for the Builders to respond to the expanded message, Pittman had to ask himself why these particular disappearances bothered him so much when during the days of the PRNC War he had dealt with MIAs all the time.

The crater bedrock had hundreds of runnels in it now, blasted into the Moon by the flywheel sparks coming off the vortex immediately after the disappearance, parallel to each other, each ten centimeters wide, some straight, some curved, a gray-brown mural, beautiful in an alien way, like artwork, but daunting in its implications. Was this the only response they were going to get, these runnels, and could they actually mean something in the way of a communication?

Confirmation of death for at least one of the Princeton Team members came when they found a human mandible in a runnel; a check of dental records showed it belonged to Silke Forbes. Of the others, no remains were found. Missing in action. There was no worse fate for a soldier, as far as Pittman was concerned. And it was further provocation. He believed a definitive second attack was now warranted, and he only hoped that Blunt would agree, and agree soon.

Yet Blunt continued to tell Moonstone to hold off on a second offensive. Nothing would have given Pittman greater pleasure than to use his fifty-three new hard-vac assault vehicles that Defense Secretary Congdon had recently sent, and attack the Moon towers—it was generally agreed that the Moon towers would be their next target. Additionally, he had a nuclear warhead now orbiting the Moon, and could call down a strike whenever he wanted. So to have to wait, especially when he had all his elements in place, was frustrating for Pittman.

In a transmission around noon the same day, General Blunt explained it this way. "Communication is all about exchange. It's about coinage and the use of proper currency." Blunt, dim blue in the oblong of Pittman's waferscreen, smiled sadly. "Some in our think tank believe the disappearance of Dr. Tennant and her team was just an effort by Alpha Vehicle to communicate with us again. Like the Worldwide Crash."

"In other words, you're considering her possible death *inadvertent*," said Pittman, and was deeply dissatisfied with this.

"Just be patient, Tim. You have to give the diplomats time to come to what to us are obvious conclusions."

So the afternoon passed as they waited for an additional Builder response over and above the runnels. All the soldiers on the Moon tried to keep themselves busy with pointless polishing, exercise drills, and weapons cleaning. The Moon, with its perpetual grayness, and its eternally black sky, bred in them a stupefying ennui, occasionally mitigated by the quiet terror they all felt in the presence of that unblinking silver eye in Crater Cavalet.

Late in the afternoon, to alleviate boredom, Pittman found himself following the fly. This common blue housefly had made its appearance on the Moon seven days ago, along with the new hard-vac vehicles, and had immediately become a celebrity of sorts, the only example of wildlife anywhere in Gettysburg. It was now an endless source of speculation to many of the men because it was one of the few things in Gettysburg that reminded them of Earth. As Pittman followed the creature down corridor 4 to the exercise room, he recalled the endless arguments the men had had about the insect. They debated about its mode of arrival, whether it was immune to all the extra rads the men were being exposed to on a daily basis because of increased solar radiation from the Bleed; whether its flight patterns had changed because of the weaker gravity. They argued about whether it would lay eggs. How long it could survive in a vacuum if it should be caught in one of the air locks during decompression. How it was getting its food.

Whether they should kill it. Or let it live.

This last debate was perhaps the most hotly contested. As the small creature entered the exercise area and landed on a treadmill control panel, Pittman recalled how the fly had finally become a symbol. Was this what the Builders saw when they looked at human beings? An animal so stupid and inconsequential it was no better than a housefly, and deserved to be killed?

With no overt or readily understandable reply from the Builders, think-tank personnel on Earth did indeed begin to believe that the new runnels engraved on Cavalet's stone floor might constitute the only response they were going to get. Blunt ordered Pittman and his men to photograph, measure, and map the entire area. They spent a good part of the evening doing this. The pictures and other data were then transmitted to scientists everywhere. Pending a conclusion about the runnels, Pittman was ordered to stand by for a potential attack against the Moon towers.

This contingency of course elated Pittman, and he felt himself going into scorpion mode.

But before he got an okay on the attack, he received other disturbing news just before midnight, and he broke this news to his men in an emergency briefing.

"Another three local stars have gone into their red giant phases." He looked around at his soldiers. "So if there was ever any doubt about the Builder agenda, that doubt is now put to rest. Also, three new naked-eye supernovae in the Milky Way have appeared, all in the same vicinity. The scientists tell me a supernova is the kind of end-stage sequence a larger star—much larger than the Earth's sun—will have. What's strange about it is that naked-eye supernovae appear on average once every four hundred years. To have three appear at the same time, all in the same vicinity, suggests outside manipulation. So we have to assume that the Builders are firing up these bigger stars as well. Of course, we have to ask ourselves, why are they doing this? The scientists tell me that maybe the Builders are doing something on a galactic scale, and that whatever it is doesn't include us. Fine. We don't have to be included. But we wouldn't be soldiers if we didn't try to stop it."

Blunt gave the order to attack and destroy the Moon towers at four o'clock that morning.

Pittman was glad the order came when it did, because the increased radiation from the sun's Builder-instigated hydrogen Bleed was starting to disrupt their communications from Earth. In fact, Earth had to try repeatedly with the logistics transmissions that followed, and even then not everything got through. It seemed that because of the sun's increased radiation—radiation that was slowly withering the Earth's magnetosphere—Moonstone was finding itself trapped behind an ever-thickening wall of radio silence, and because of this difficulty, they didn't get under way until a little past noon.

Pittman, Haydn, and Newlove, now commanding Moonstone 32, reached Tower 48 within two hours and prepared to attack. The Moon had phased so that the sun had reached the horizon and was ready to sink any time. The Earth was in the east.

From a distance, Tower 48 looked like a high-rise building made out of reflective glass. With the sun shining low from the west, it glowed with diamondlike intensity. It rested on a slope. It didn't follow normal architectural load theory but was built level to the gradient of the slope, so that it rose at an angle, like the Leaning Tower of Pisa, a strange sight because such a tower built on such an angle would ordinarily collapse immediately. This one stayed aloft, like a rectangular helium balloon, another indication that the Builders employed far-fringe physics that had nothing to do with Newtonian principles.

The three soldiers dug in.

And eventually, when all the other vehicles were in place, Pittman once again gave the only order that mattered: "Fire at will."

The ordnance arced through the air. But as with Alpha Vehicle, the tower simply absorbed the shots, like throwing pebbles into the ocean again.

Reports of the same disappointing result came from the other vehicles.

Then they got a Mayday from vehicle 52, some shouting, some yelling, then radio silence.

About the same time, Haydn reported a temperature rise inside Moonstone 32, from twenty to thirty degrees Celsius—then just as quickly to sixty.

Pittman didn't stop to think about it; he depressurized Moonstone 32 quickly, climbed out, and jumped to the ground as the vehicle's armor started to glow. Haydn got out too. Newlove tried, but the heat inside reached the conflagration point, and the soldier burst into flames, the oxygen from his pressure suit feeding the fire so that he was burned alive, his screams so loud Pittman turned down his radio, even as he recoiled in horror from the sight.

Moonstone 32 turned orange, then white, and finally got so hot it melted—melted till all that was left was a puddle of steel, plastic, and other space-age materials, hardening quickly on the Moon's surface into the equivalent of a giant Rorschach ink blot.

Haydn was about to bounce over to Newlove in an effort to help him, but Pittman grabbed him by the shoulder and yanked him back. He voiced his guess about what was going on, and it came out as a terse military command. "Take cover."

The two men ran toward a crater about the size of a car, their movements hampered by lunar gravity, yet also counterbalanced by their armor's weight. With Newlove incinerated, Pittman became apprehensively aware of the temperature readouts coming from the tiny screen in the upper left corner of his visor. Fortunately, temperature remained stable at twenty-two degrees Celsius. He continued to run.

The ground gave underneath his feet with a crunch, and the closer he got to the small crater, the more the surface became pitted with ejecta. He jumped, rising a meter off the ground, and sank feet first into the crater, then scrambled around.

He saw Haydn loping toward him with the curious slow-motion movements the Moon's gravity forced. Through his radio, Pittman heard several Maydays; he had to assume similar emergencies were happening with other Moonstone teams all over the combat theater, and that they were indeed at last under attack. At the same time he was assessing the situation as calmly as he could. He heard his own breathing. He heard Haydn's breathing. And a few screams. Some gagging. Some prayers.

Despite this, he continued to assess. Having held a dozen Moonstones in reserve at Gettysburg for possible rescue operations, he now tried to contact the installation, but radiation from the agitated sun blocked his signal, and he couldn't get through. And if everyone else was under attack, and all Moonstones were being destroyed, that might mean they would have to get to Gettysburg by foot. Which wasn't a good thing, because further compounding the danger was limited personal life support. He watched Haydn running. Haydn jumped into the crater next to him and turned around. The problem continued to nag at Pittman. Their suits had only so much air. Which meant they had only so much time to get back to Gettysburg before their air ran out.

He surveyed Tower 48. Any further attacks for the moment now seemed suspended.

"Looks like they've stopped, sir," said Haydn.

"For now," said Pittman. "But I always knew they were just an enemy waiting to happen."

He keyed in the appropriate command on his wristpad and checked his life-support stats. With refill capability from Moonstone 32 no longer available, only nine hours of personal air remained. They were one hundred and three kilometers from Gettysburg. If they had to walk, they would never make it.

"Looks like we're in a bit of trouble, Gunther."

"What kind of trouble, sir?"

"With our life support."

Haydn assessed his own readouts. "Oh."

"Exactly."

Pittman tried to raise a number of Moonstones again, but all he got was scrambled, panicked snippets. About the only bright spot was a mechanical and systems green light with the Moonstone that

Hawker and Callison commanded; but while the vehicle seemed to be intact, that didn't necessarily guarantee that the two soldiers were still alive. He radioed them but couldn't raise them. He checked the field reports coming in over his visor screen. "I'm losing one Moonstone after another, Gunther. About the only one still operational is the one Hawker and Callison are commanding, but I can't raise them, nor is Greenhow letting me plot exactly where they are because of all the haywire radiation. So that essentially means no Moonstones. And without the Moonstones, no one's going to have enough air to get back to Gettysburg."

"What about the twelve reserve rescue vehicles back at Gettysburg? They can come and get us."

"Only I can't get through to Gettysburg either, so have no idea of the status back at base. We don't know if the attack included those twelve reserve vehicles."

"Yes, but maybe they're already on their way. Maybe Greenhow transmitted data about the attacks."

"Gunther, didn't you hear what I just said? Greenhow is up against major interference."

"Yes, but, sir, if the reserve commands think something is wrong, they should be on their way."

"We can't count on that, Gunther. Too many battles have been lost in the history of warfare by the front line assuming their rear echelon is intact. Gettysburg could be destroyed, and frankly, it's the only safe tactical assumption we can make. Which means we're on our own. And that's bad, because someone's got to make it back to Gettysburg to continue this mission. The strategic system is bunkered, and will still be intact, no matter what. Hawker and Callison are closest, but it seems they have their Moonstone running on automatic systems, which means they could be dead, and we can't count on them making it back safely. We can't raise anybody else. So that means it's up to us."

"But, sir, how can we make it back if we don't have enough air?"

"If we pool our oxygen, maybe one of us can make it back. And one is all we need. We need to retract the sinkholed strategic system and have one more go at Alpha Vehicle before it's too late. But it poses us with a bit of a problem, doesn't it, Lieutenant? Which one of us is to give up his oxygen for the other? Which one of us is to make the ultimate sacrifice? Say you were the president, and you had to make this decision? Say you had to decide which one of us was expendable. Would you choose the commanding officer of Moonstone? Or would you choose his lieutenant?"

Haydn grew still. "Sir, I don't want to die."

"I know you don't, son. But for the sake of your country, I think you might have to."

"But I'm only twenty-seven, sir."

"That wouldn't be a factor in any decision the president would make about our situation. You see, son, what I'm worried about is this growing radio communications problem. We're becoming increasingly cut off. It might come to the point where we might actually have to make our own decisions unilaterally about Operation Moonstone. You see that, don't you? And from an operational standpoint you simply don't have the experience to make the kinds of decisions that might have to be made about the Builders, particularly if it comes down to the nuclear option."

Haydn looked up at him, alarmed. "You might use the nuclear option, sir?"

"That's what I mean when I say we have to retract the strategic system from its bunker."

"Yes, but, sir, maybe we can both make it back. Or maybe if we put out a hail to Hawker and Callison."

"Son, we're getting nothing personally from Hawker and Callison, even though we're getting a read on their vehicle, just barely."

He peered through Haydn's yellow visor at the young man's face. Never was there a clearer picture of distress, with the corners of his lips drawn back, his eyes wide, and his nostrils flared. Pittman couldn't blame him. He was distressed himself. All those units down. His options nearly gone. And all those fine young men dead. But he was seasoned. He understood combat. Meanwhile, Haydn began to hyperventilate. As much as Pittman hated to make soldiers lay down their lives, there were certain inalterable equations when it came to war, and one of them was to sacrifice the troops at the expense of maintaining viable leadership, for without viable leadership, they all went down.

"I was hoping I'd get home for Christmas."

"I'll make sure you receive full honors, Gunther."

"But I don't want to die, sir."

"None of us does, son. But sometimes we're called upon to make that sacrifice. You have enough morphine in your automatic med-pak to go out peacefully. I'll make a nice marker for you. I'll personally travel to Blossburg and tell your parents how brave you were. You have an opportunity to be a major hero in this war, Gunther. When the historians come to write about Earth's first intergalactic conflict, your name will be synonymous with noble sacrifice."

"But, sir, I've got a girl back home."

"Do you have a message for her? I'll make sure she gets it."

Haydn was growing more and more restless, moving from side to side, as unsettled as could be. "I guess you could tell her that . . . I love her . . . and that I was planning to marry her . . . and that I had my eye on a little white house on Vine, just near where the bridge is." He became even more agitated. "And I guess you could tell my parents that I love them as well, and that I thank them for raising me, and that I—" His restlessness now reached fevered levels, and before he said anything else he was up and out of the small crater and running toward the far rise.

Pittman sighed. He reached for his sidearm and took careful aim, right at the man's back. He didn't want to do this. But military expedience made it necessary. He didn't blame Haydn for running, yet was somewhat disappointed that the man didn't have a little more courage. He then did what a scorpion did best. He stung, squeezing the trigger ever so gently. The ordnance penetrated Gunther's suit, and the man went down, arms outstretched, falling face-first into the loose regolith of the Moon, skidding a bit in the weak gravity before he came to a rest. Pittman surveyed the scene: dead soldier in a space suit at the bottom of a treeless sun-blasted rise that stopped ruler-straight at the perpetually black sky twenty meters up. So be it. He felt sad. But also as if he had accomplished something. When he went to tell Gunther's parents, he would rewrite things, at least a bit. For Gunther had still made a sacrifice, and though his fear had gotten the better of him at the last minute, Pittman would always consider him a brave young man.

The StopGap sputtered green and sticky into the suit's breach, stopping catastrophic oxygen loss. Pittman got up and went over. He disengaged Haydn's oxygen supply, then turned the soldier over. Gunther was dead, his face a faint blue. Pittman raised his hand in a salute. It was a sublime moment. For nothing was more inspirational in fighting an enemy than the death of a fellow officer, and it gave him further determination to stop the Builders using whatever means necessary, even if he had to unilaterally drop a nuclear bomb on Alpha Vehicle.

19

Pittman thought he might bury Haydn, but then decided the extra exertion would tax his already limited oxygen supply, now timed to a combined twelve hours and twenty-five minutes. So instead he drew a cross in the dirt above Haydn's head, knowing that a memorial scratched in lunar soil was more permanent than any marker on Earth, wrote the Marine's name, the date, and the words *Semper Fidelis* below his feet.

He then set off over the airless surface.

He wondered if in the annals of lunar history such a hike had ever been attempted. He found the darkness a bit much. He tried to get in touch with Gettysburg as well as his Moonstones, but the Moonstones weren't responding, and because Gettysburg was still so far away, radiation from the destabilized sun interrupted his signal.

He got hungry three hours later, so ate some nutrition paste. His guide lights picked out dirt, pebbles, and rock. He felt he was walking on top of hardpacked snow. He hated the treelessness of the place, the lack of any vegetation anywhere, because even the desert back home had vegetation—creosote, sage-brush, cacti, and various tough grasses.

He thought of powdered cement. It was as if a cement company had come to the Moon and made the whole place its dumping yard. The darkness—especially with that black sky all the time—was like the impenetrable murk of a graveyard at night. Not for first time he felt something supernaturally horrifying about the Moon's darkness. And all this emptiness, as with the desert back home, made him *think*—and thinking was often like a slow poison to him.

He thought of Haydn. Was it right to sacrifice the Marine? At the time it had made perfect military sense, but now he couldn't help second-guessing himself.

After he got done thinking about Haydn, he thought of his ex-wife and children.

His ex-wife, Sheila, who had never got the hang of military life, couldn't understand it was a culture unto its own, that sacrifices had to be made, and attitude adjustments rigorously maintained. He loved her, but hated her, yet loved her, and regretted that the PRNC War had finally driven them apart.

He thought of his daughter, Becky, who had turned thirteen just before he got the call from Blunt to fight the North Chinese, goddamn their souls to hell. Becky, shy, silent, and loving, but so horrified that her father had to go to war.

And Tom. Ten years old at the outbreak of PRNC hostilities. An *oops* child, but who, in a way, had become his best friend, his hope and inspiration, so much like his father, good at sports, competitive, wanting to win at any cost.

He fretted over his family for the next three hours. He knew he shouldn't let the acid mind-blowing regret of losing his family hurt him this way, but he couldn't help it. And he grieved for Haydn. He thought of Haydn's parents, who lived in Blossburg, Pennsylvania, not far from Philadelphia, where he had made his home with Sheila and the kids for the longest time. When he got back to the desert he would drive up to Pennsylvania, make a point of visiting not only Blossburg but also Philadelphia. It was about time he saw his kids.

He stopped. He looked around. The Moon was now brown in his twin guide lights, like powdered cocoa. Standing here in this immense blackness all by himself, he had a terrifying notion of just how insignificant he was.

He saw the Earth, little more than half-full, a blue and white balloon. He wanted the sight to somehow change him, transform him, because even the earliest Moon explorers had recounted transformative experiences when viewing the Earth from the Moon. But the Earth just made Pittman feel sad, and caused him to think of Haydn again, and how Haydn wouldn't be going home for Christmas.

He turned away from the Earth and continued walking.

Over the next two hours he tried, via the Greenhow System, to contact Orbops Command in Arlington. He wanted to urge them to exercise the nuclear option after all, didn't want to take the definitive step by himself if he didn't have to. But the immense amounts of radiation coming from the sun made communication impossible. He couldn't get through. So he finally decided that he was going to have to go solo. Make a command decision. Because whatever came to pass, he wasn't going to let Alpha Vehicle win, not after what it had done to all his Moonstone soldiers. Not after Haydn's sacrifice.

An hour later, he switched to Haydn's oxygen. On Earth he could make out the dim brown continent of North America, the eastern half in morning daylight, the western half still in shadow.

Five hours later, wanting to keep marching but now beginning to realize that even with Haydn's extra oxygen he wasn't going to reach Gettysburg, he stopped. He was in the middle of a large crater, not as large as Crater Cavalet, but still at least two football fields across, not particularly deep, but flat. He felt like he was standing in the middle of a gigantic pie crust.

He bounce-walked until he was as close to dead center as he could get. A good place to die. He radioed Gettysburg and discovered he was now close enough to get through all the radiation.

"Gettysburg responding, it's good to hear your voice, Colonel." Lamar Bruxner sounded tired but deeply relieved.

"Mr. Brunxer, we've been attacked. Send immediate rescue."

"Rescue?" said the support chief, sounding confused. "Rescue in what?"

"The twelve reserve Moonstones at Gettysburg."

"But they've all been destroyed, Colonel. They . . . all melted. It was the oddest thing I'd ever seen."

"And the men inside?"

"Dead."

Pittman momentarily grieved for his fallen soldiers and even for the destroyed vehicles. "What about Gettysburg? Has it been attacked?"

"No. I've been trying to raise you for the longest time."

"Have Hawker and Callison returned to base?" Because he still hoped Hawker and Callison might make it back to Gettysburg. "Have you heard from them?"

Bruxner was surprised. "You're the only one to call in yet, Colonel. Radio interference has been getting worse and worse. I was lucky to get a last call to Earth. They're sending a rescue vehicle. For the support staff only, though. I thought all of you were dead. They'll be taking six returnees only."

"Listen to me, Bruxner. Our mission has failed. Which means we go to our fallback. It's up to you now."

"Up to me?"

"We have to destroy Alpha Vehicle. I want you to retract the strategic attack system from its sinkhole beneath the tower hub, access the military command software, and commence targeting procedures with our nuclear asset. We have one warhead orbiting the Moon, and this warhead is Earth's last chance." He paused. His words sounded bizarrely grandiloquent. Ten years ago, stationed in Germany, Sheila insisted he accompany her to a performance of Wagner's *Götterdämmerung*. His words were like that, Wagnerian, operatic in the grand-gesture and larger-than-life sense of the word; and standing in the middle of this shallow crater he indeed had the sense that he was on a stage, and that he was about to perform this one last heroic act before succumbing to his death. "Here are the codes. I'm transmitting now."

What wrecked it was the way Bruxner argued with him, saying that he didn't want to be responsible for a nuclear launch against the Builders, that he was just chief of support at Gettysburg.

"Bruxner, listen to me. If you don't do this—if you don't get a grip on yourself—then everybody on Earth dies. I tried to make it back, but I don't have the oxygen. I thought Hawker and Callison might make it back, but they haven't. So it all comes down to you. You can go down in history as the man who saved the world. Or you can be remembered as the world's biggest coward."

It seemed as if Bruxner didn't understand the meaning of the word *glory*, at least not in the way Pittman did, and Pittman had to argue with him for many minutes until Bruxner finally revealed he had a young family in Cleveland.

"Do you want them all to die, Bruxner? The oceans are going to boil. That means the atmosphere is going to fill with superheated steam. Now picture your family scalded alive in this steam. Is that something you want?"

When he had only twenty-five minutes of oxygen left, he finally convinced Bruxner to go through with it.

At the twenty-minute mark, he saw a bright flash on the western horizon. It filled him with such joy, he sank to his knees, because he knew Alpha Vehicle must have taken a direct nuclear strike.

At the seventeen-minute mark, he stiffened in ter-

ror because another bright flash came from the western horizon, this one substantially closer, and
seconds later it rained rocks. Gettysburg? A nuclear
strike from Alpha Vehicle in retaliation?

At the ten-minute mark, he looked up at Earth,
and saw six tiny flashes sparkle over the eastern
United States. With an overwhelming sense of dread
he realized that maybe he hadn't taken out Alpha
Vehicle after all, and that, as such, he might have
precipitated a nuclear exchange. Had one of those
sparkles been Philadelphia? From his knees, he sank
to the seat of his pants, and his operatic sense of the
moment disappeared.

At the five-minute mark, he was getting ready to
make peace with a med-pak overdose when, over the
rim of his nameless-piecrust-of-crater, a Moonstone
appeared, the big knobby tires out front crunching
through the dusty apex of the crater's rim, the tracks
to the rear forcing the vehicle forward so that the
heavy hard-vac mobile gunning unit wheelied into
the flat pit and charged toward him.

He got back to his knees.

Three minutes of oxygen left, and he got to his
feet, stood to attention, and saluted. Above, Earth
simmered in what had to be nuclear fallout. He heard
Hawker's broken and static-fractured voice penetrate
all the rampant radiation. "Sir—we've got—and
we—Gettysburg is—" The vehicle swung up beside
him. He walked toward it. The air-lock light flashed.
He focused on the light. Allowed himself a moment
of rage. Lifted a stone and smashed the light.

Got himself under control.

And made himself ready to be a colonel again.

20

The generator gave out three hours later, and the temperature in the cellar plummeted. Cam pushed the blanket away and got to his feet. Lesha looked at him, shivering from her spot on the floor. He lifted the flashlight and shone it toward the steps. The ice had melted. As he walked to the table, his feet squelched through two centimeters of water. The cellar smelled of earth, and he saw a pill bug, like a little armored tank, walking along the wall.

"We need to warm up in my truck."

Lesha's eyes narrowed. She struggled to her feet and looked around the cellar, but did so in a dazed fashion. Roosevelt lifted his head and stared.

Cam pulled out his cell, checked the little monitor, but the display was still telling him service wasn't available. He slid the phone into his pocket, lifted the water bottle, and drank. At least they had food. And water. But how were they going to get out of here? How could they get through all that snow blocking the roads? Surely as a government priority Blunt would find a way to rescue them soon.

He walked to the steps and peered at the cellar door. Light glimmered under its crack. He struggled upstairs, careful of the small slicks of water on the gray risers. Lesha followed. Out the corner of his eye he saw steam from her breath.

Eight more steps and he reached the top. He gripped the brass knob and pushed the door open.

He saw fog, not particularly thick, but oppressive, phlegmatic in its flow through the dim Texas morning. He felt each individual particle alight on his face, the backs of his hands, and down his neck.

He shivered. "It's all melting."

The heavy snow on the fields glowed—the impression was of more light coming from the ground than the sky. Out beyond the swimming pool, where the land dipped, water collected on top of the accumulation, in some places a meter deep. The Navasota River, flowing just beyond the stand of trees to the west, had risen above its banks.

He glanced over his shoulder to the east where the land climbed into a cornfield. The cornstalks, bludgeoned by snow, now tilted, some leaning against each other, cobs and leaves saturated with wet. He turned back to the Navasota. How high would the river rise? Would they have to go up the east hill? And if they went there, how would they stay warm? All his firewood had been blown away by the hurricane. Maybe they could drag some of his wrecked house over for a fire.

They picked their way through his demolished home. Roosevelt came up the stairs behind them, walked to the house's edge, leaped from the floor to the ground, and immediately got stuck in snow, sinking right to his chest. Once the dog had assessed his predicament, he bounded in a series of leaps to the nearest puddle and drank.

As Cam reached the edge of his house, he saw a framed photograph lodged under some broken plaster—his parents, in the days before the accident. He reached for the photograph. His fingers closed stiffly in the cold and he lifted the photograph. Would he always lose things, then? First his parents? Then his life's work? Now his house? He turned to Lesha. Would he lose her as well? She seemed to sense his thoughts. She clutched his arm. He heard music, but it wasn't the Builders' music this time. It was Lesha's music, quiet, serene, and steadfast.

She released him, jumped to the snow, and helped him down.

They walked past her vehicle until they came to his. High overhead he heard the screech of a kestrel, and looking up he saw the creature circling, its wing feathers splayed like fingertips. Why would the Builders want to destroy such innocence and beauty? How did they evaluate worth?

The integers of his plan tumbled through his mind in a disjointed fashion as Lesha helped him into the driver's seat of his truck. He inserted the key into the ignition. It hummed to life and he turned on the heater. The heat coming from the below-dash vents was like the breath of welcome summer. Yes. His plan. For a demonstration. But just how was he going to sell it to Blunt and the others? Sell it to them he must. For their own good.

Lesha climbed in the other side of the truck.

He turned on the radio and heard a country music

station in Kansas. Also a Spanish language station in Austin. But they didn't receive any signals from the immediate area.

After fifteen minutes, they got news, and through the various reports, he pieced together what he and Lesha had missed.

Widespread damage had occurred in eastern Texas and western Louisiana. Over five million people were without power. Cell phone networks were down. Looting was widespread in Houston, and the National Guard had been called in.

In related news, there was word about the sun. Dr. Nolan Pratt had been interviewed. The sun's temperature was now rising dramatically.

There was word about the Moon. Colonel Timothy Pittman, theater commander, said a second Builder communication attempt had failed, resulting in the disappearance of three scientific team members, and the death of at least one. Dr. Renate Tennant was reported as missing. Pittman wouldn't speculate on a possible military response.

The fate of the Princeton Team saddened Cam greatly. He was particularly sorry about Renate's disappearance. Why did it have to be this way? Why wouldn't the Builders at least try to talk to them? He took a deep breath and sighed. Why take Renate away from them when she had just been a scientist doing her job? And his house. He glanced over. A pile of wreckage. Where was he going to live? How was he going to find the courage to start over, particularly if the sun was going to bloat into a red giant and consume them all? He turned to Lesha. What kind of future could they possibly expect together when the future seemed to be quickly running out? He lifted his chin. A demonstration. If only he could convince the powers in Washington that it was necessary. He was upset, but tried to control it. He had to think. Had to somehow figure out a way to stop all this.

Roosevelt pawed at the door. Lesha let him in and he climbed into the backseat of the quad cab.

The heat made Cam sleepy, and he drifted off.

He must have dozed a long time because when he woke, he saw that all the clouds had cleared. The sun, setting to the northwest, now touched the horizon. What startled him was how the horizon had changed. It was all water. Five wood ducks—a mother and four ducklings—paddled across the new lake to the west of his house, serene and untroubled. The trees by the river were now half submerged, the water's smooth surface reflecting their branches. He couldn't see his swimming pool, nor his diving board—both were underwater. The water crept toward his house, and was rising so quickly that within the next minute it extended its reach by another fifty centimeters.

"Lesha?"

She moaned, turned. Looking at her, he saw that a strand of straw-tinted hair had become caught between her lips. He pulled it free. She opened her eyes. She looked at him, her cheek against the headrest. The wood ducks quacked. She glanced.

She sat up and gripped her knees. "What do we do?"

"We should climb the hill."

They got out of the truck. The snow had turned slushy.

They had blankets. And a bit of food. They had matches, but everything was too wet to make a fire. They reached the top of the hill and saw that the small valley on its eastern side had also filled with water.

Lesha said, "We're becoming an island."

He got down on his knees and moved slush aside. It squished through his fingers, and the cold, that which had penetrated his fingers for the last three days, came back quickly. Lesha got down on her knees beside him and they pushed the slush aside until they had made a small hollow for themselves.

Then they trudged back and forth to the house, using its wreckage to construct a shelter, even though the broken pieces of wood were sharp, splintery, and dangerous with exposed nails. Occasionally he looked up at the sky, wondering when a helicopter would come.

Once they were finished, Lesha attempted to drive the truck into the cornfield, but couldn't get past the first part of the incline. The truck's wheels sank into the slush, then into the mud, and finally spun and spun.

They stayed in the truck as long as they could, but eventually the water eased around its tires, and as the final light left the sky and the first stars appeared, they got out and climbed the hill to their makeshift shelter.

Much to Cam's surprise, the air was a lot warmer,

bizarrely so, having risen ten degrees in the last hour. He thought that at least they wouldn't freeze to death, even if it meant the sun was reigniting itself due to gravitational pressure.

The gold hydrogen band appeared a short while later, rippling, flexing, shining as hypercharged particles drifted away from the sun.

The night was long and uncomfortable. To pass the time, Lesha recounted her early life in California: herself and her four sisters growing up in Orange County, her father leaving them when they were young, her mother having to work two jobs, a lab tech during the day, a cleaner at night. "It just about killed her. We lived in a two-bedroom apartment. That was hard, the six of us in such a small space."

They dozed on their little platform. Roosevelt crawled in between them, and the dog was like an electric blanket.

Cam woke a little while later, went outside, and had a look. The Moon, like a dollop of orange sherbet, rose. Navasota floodwaters had climbed above his house. He saw some of its wreckage float away. Lesha's truck was now submerged, and the back half of his own vehicle was underwater. How high would it go? He heard trickling water everywhere, including underneath their makeshift floor.

He walked a little ways up the hill and gazed down the other side. An island, and a shrinking one at that.

An hour later, the water was so high it had submerged both trucks, and only the uppermost branches of the trees along the Navasota were visible in the moonlight. All the snow had melted. The temperature was around twenty-five degrees Celsius. The sky had clouded over again.

Lesha now stood beside him clutching his arm, staring out at the water. Menacing little whirlpools formed on its surface. Farther out a dead cow floated by, lit by the orange moon.

The flood rose until finally they were standing on a small disk of muddy land an inch above the surface. Water threatened from every direction. He tried his cell phone but still got no service.

At last the flood lapped at their ankles. As the water consisted of snowmelt, it was bitterly cold.

"I lived in San Francisco for a while," said Lesha. "When I was going to school. In a basement apartment. Do you remember all that weird rain the West Coast got eighteen years ago? My apartment flooded. I was walking around ankle deep. You wouldn't think it possible in a place like San Francisco, with all those hills."

She had barely finished telling him this when from the north he heard the *blup-blup-blup* of a rescue helicopter. That's when he felt another pain in his head. Blue light seemed to crowd around from the edges of his eyes. He lost all feeling in his body and collapsed. His head tilted to one side. His shoulder cramped. He had that crazy sense again that his body was expanding in every direction. He heard a phrase or two of the music. Then saw written in the ripples the helicopter made against the water the beautiful and poetic mathematical cuneiform he had seen on the television in the hospital. A grin came to his face. It turned out Navasota was going to be conducive to contact after all. He had a gut feeling that something dramatic had happened, that some fundamental shift had occurred, perhaps with Alpha Vehicle or with the Builders themselves; the spark of this new contact was searing and direct, and felt jumper-cabled into his mind. He turned to Lesha. The enormous and all-encompassing peace came to him. The last thing he remembered as unconsciousness slowly overtook him was Lesha—the beautiful California blonde—leaning over him, calling him, and Cam not being able to hear her over the curious two-to-one music that flooded his soul.

21

It was like an absence—like the way things were before Cam's birth, and the way they would be after he died. But out of this absence there emerged a sense of them again, the Builders, whoever or whatever they were, peering down at him, wondering about him, trying to figure out what they were going to do with him. He thought when he opened his eyes he would see a hospital room, that maybe he might be back in his special wing at Johns Hopkins. But when his leaden lids finally rose he didn't see a wardroom at all. He was floating free in space. A bright light illuminated a foreshortened view of the Earth, and it was as though he were staring at the planet through a fish-eye lens; and with this vista of Earth, it appeared as if the Builders, in the dark sleep of this new contact, were trying to communicate with him again; and in fact, it wasn't a fish-eye lens but a magnifying glass; and through this magnifying glass—though everything was blurry—he grasped his first real view of the Builders.

They appeared as bands of purple light angling

down through the universe, two dimensions, three dimensions, and hyperdimensional, all at the same time, glowing, happy, benevolent, not aggressive, like the plus in a plus/minus equation. The purple bands slanted through the starry heavens like an indigo aurora borealis.

At last he saw a more conventional view of Earth. And in this view he witnessed a series of detonations along the Pacific equator. And it was the oddest thing, because first there were two detonations, then three, then five, and it was like the Builders were trying to communicate to him with this basic sequence of prime numbers after all, only doing it with nuclear strikes. He couldn't understand it. What had happened? Weren't they going to show him the symbols anymore? Were they so disappointed that they had to use this primitive and ultimately puzzling expression of the prime number sequence?

Then he woke up in his same old room at Johns Hopkins, and forgot most of what he had seen.

Dr. Ochoa and Lesha, when they came to check him a short while later, acted weirdly. They tiptoed around him as though they thought he had an embarrassing disease.

When Lesha finally came to him alone an hour after that, she acted even more oddly than before. And stranger still, she wore a silk head scarf tied in babushka fashion over her hair. "They're recommending a hat. Not that we'll get much of it this far northeast of Washington, but they say a head scarf is a good idea. And when I'm outside, I use this." She pulled out a surgical mask. "The levels aren't too bad, all things considered." He was now under the impression that she had previously provided him with some context, but that this context was now lost somewhere in his confused memory. Later she said, "That's why they took so long to come get us. They had their hands full with other things." He couldn't make sense of this either. He must have been awake at some point, and simply didn't remember the missing pieces.

"I'm like a broken radio," he said. "I'm getting only part of the signal."

"You didn't get what I said about the PRNC attacks?"

"No."

She looked at him closely, and he had to admit, he liked her in a babushka, especially one that was so colorful, because it brought out her feminine features beautifully.

The tale she told petrified him with its freakish Kafkaesque turns: the breakdown of communications between the Earth and the Moon because of the runaway radiation coming from the slowly bloating sun; Pittman ready, willing, and able to take matters into his own hands; the nuclear launch against Alpha Vehicle; the Builder obliteration of Gettysburg with what Lesha called a spontaneous chain reaction five hundred meters above the installation; then a series of spontaneous fusion events in the Pacific, with no evidence of launch or trajectory. "Like the local hydrogen atoms all decided to get together on their own." And finally the PRNC's big mistake, believing American forces had launched against them, retaliating against the continental U.S. with their own nuclear assets, destroying six American cities, including

Washington; and America then taking out Shanghai, Beijing, and Tianjin before diplomats on both sides got the hawks to simmer down.

"Blunt and the others were lucky to get out of Arlington alive. And the president was lucky to get out of Washington. I guess Greenhow paid off after all. What's odd is the pattern of initial Builder attacks before the PRNC launched. They didn't target cities. They detonated in a sequence. All events occurred over the equator in the Pacific. Which makes you wonder why the PRNC launched in the first place, or if they were just looking for an excuse. Initially, there were two Builder detonations ninety-two kilometers apart. Then there were three more detonations. Then there were five final detonations. In other words, these sequences represent the first three prime numbers, two, three, and five."

And that's when he remembered the strange vision he had had, of detonations in the Pacific. "What time did Pittman launch?"

"Early yesterday morning. Just a little before you had your attack. I can't help wondering if there's a correlation between the two."

He thought of his gut feeling, his sense that something dramatic had happened, of this new contact's searing and direct feel, and understood she had to be right. More unsettling, though, was this whole new mode of expression.

"The prime number sequence is worrisome."

"How so?"

"Because they're using nuclear detonations to convey it."

She looked terrified by the implication. "So you

think they're actually trying to communicate with us via nuclear exchange?"

"That would be my guess. They're picking up on Pittman's lead. And that could be devastating if they decide to talk to us again."

Ochoa rechecked him an hour later. After the examination, the doctor said, "You seem much better than after your last episode. Maybe you're getting acclimatized to it. Are you up to meeting the president?"

Cam glanced out the window, where the effects of the slowly bloating sun had become evident. He was surprised by how bright everything was. The park across the street was like an overexposed photograph. Cars moved up and down Jefferson as if through the highest setting in a tanning booth. Take a small room, wall it with stadium lights, and that's how bright it was. The light stunned his eyes, and he squinted; he felt his headache come back, but none of his confusion.

"As a matter of fact, I was hoping you would ask me that."

"Why? Do you have an idea?"

"Yes. A big one. One that just might reverse the flow of hydrogen from our sun after all."

22

In Moonstone 47, Hawker and Callison stared at Pittman as he recounted Haydn's death, the edited version, how Haydn had willingly overdosed himself with morphine so he could give his air to Pittman. He couldn't understand why neither of them seemed to believe him. Hawker was an older man, ruggedly handsome, dark, but with a chin perhaps too small for the rest of his face. Callison was much younger, eighteen or nineteen, a fresh grunt with a round face—so young he had an oily complexion with a few pimples.

"I'll make sure he gets all the posthumous honors. I'm proud of him. And the whole Marine Corps can be proud of him too."

No, they didn't believe him at all, he could see it in their eyes.

They started back for Gettysburg. He explained to them how he had exercised the nuclear option, and Hawker grimly said, "We saw the flashes, sir."

The silence inside the Moonstone after that was like granite. He could tell that both Hawker and Callison were scared. He would have expected it from Callison, but not from Hawker, who revealed after some questioning that he had seen action in Mongolia during the PRNC War. "Mostly up in the mountains. With a cyber-enhanced unit. I was good at it. Those units are nothing like the armor we're wearing up here, sir. You have to be careful because you're vulnerable in certain circumstances. I miss it." All this was said softly, as if Hawker was remembering comrades fallen in the Khangai Range.

Talking about the PRNC War brought all his present political grievances to mind. "You know what I hate about the PRNC? I hate how they have to be consulted about every move we make up here. At least with all this radio interference, we didn't have to legitimately ask them permission to use the nuclear option. You know what I think? I think we should have finished them off when we had the chance. Unconditional surrender is what we should have asked for. Or at least we should have sufficiently armed the democratic south so they could move in and take over. Po Pin-Yen sticks in my craw."

As the Moonstone hummed over the lunar surface, disturbing sediment that had remained unmolested for millions of years, Pittman climbed into the bubble and spotted Earth. His throat tightened. Had one of those sparks indeed been Philadelphia, where his ex-wife and children lived? And was he to blame? He felt momentarily dizzy, and had the odd sense that there was somebody inside his head now, that there was somebody watching him, maybe the big silver eye.

"Have you had any communications from any other units?"

Callison said, "No, sir. All this haywire radiation from the sun has made communication difficult."

The radiation monitor hissed with greater intensity when they got within three kilometers of Gettysburg. As they entered the east arm of Shenandoah Valley, the Earth's light illuminated the lunar surface with a blue glow. The vibrations of the wheel-and-track system became crunchier, as if they were driving over peanut brittle—and ducking down to look out the big front windows, Pittman saw that the surface had been melted into black glass. Half of Bunker Hill was blown away. The radiation monitor hissed more persistently.

Callison murmured into the radio again and again, "Gettysburg, do you read . . . do you read?" His voice was soft, fretful, even as the tension thickened inside the hard-vac vehicle.

Pittman finally put his hand on Callison's shoulder and said, "It's all right, son. You can stop now."

They rounded the southern end of the blasted Bunker Hill and found a black crater. Gettysburg was no more. He was horrified. The nausea rose in his throat. Yet it was a tableau of destruction that inspired him as well. For this was war. Action, reaction. Offensive, counteroffensive. The deadly mathematics of the thing resonated in his soul.

At ground zero, the dirt had been swept away, and the sides of the crater looked like black asphalt, with no sediment anywhere. Recessed into the side of the crater to the north was a bas-relief of Gettysburg's deeper structures, like a cross-sectional diagram. The only thing left intact was part of the tower, some of its platform balancing on a single support, like a house burned to the ground and the second-floor bathtub still supported by the drainpipe.

Yes. Perfect. War was all about existence and non-existence. Deadly mathematics. He thought of the yin-yang symbol he had back in his desert home, carved from stone, a gift from the Democratic Republic of Canton at the end of the war with the north. Though he knew that yin and yang symbolized the passive and active forces in the universe, it now also seemed such a perfect summation of everything he was going through right now, and he didn't know why he hadn't seen it before. Existence. Nonexistence. Yin. Yang. He heard Haydn's voice in his head. "It's more than just three-card monte, sir." The voice sounded real, loud. He turned around to see if Haydn was actually there. And in turning a strange thing happened. He saw a brief impression of purple bands floating through the universe. Real but illusive. A hallucination? No. He didn't hallucinate. He wasn't that kind of man. He also had a sense of *them* now. The Builders. Trying to understand him. And in trying to understand him, recognizing something of themselves.

"You're not the only ones who can wage war," he murmured.

Hawker swung round. "Sir?"

"Pull up to the SMCP access lock. We'll assess the damage from there."

The Inter-Lunar Rescue-Vehicle *Pennsylvania*, the

spacecraft Bruxner had called from Earth before communications had completely disappeared, established Moon orbit ten hours later. Contact with the craft was so sketchy by this time, even despite its relative nearness, they had only a small radiation-free envelope in which to establish pickup coordinates. No news of Earth, because the radio clouded over too often. By this time, Pittman, Hawker, and Callison had determined that they were the only ones left alive.

Pittman generally wasn't a superstitious man, but he was made nervous by the ILRV's name, *Pennsylvania*. Sheila, Becky, and Tom were in Pennsylvania. So were Haydn's parents. As he recalled the position of that particular spark midway along the Delaware River, he grew more convinced than ever that it had to be Philadelphia.

They headed west toward Crater Cavalet as they waited for the *Pennsylvania*'s descent. Like a good soldier, Pittman wanted to assess not only the damage to Gettysburg, but damage to the enemy as well.

All the scarring his magnificent Moonstones had ripped into the area around Cavalet had been cleared away as if with a sandblaster. Moonstone 47 crunched over the dirt. The crater's rim was badly degraded, with small crenellations everywhere. It reminded Pittman of a Sumerian ruin he had once seen during the Euphrates phase of the PRNC War, one that was five thousand years old and so badly worn it was no more than a mound. The crater's rim couldn't have been more than thirty meters high now. The sediment along the slopes had fused into

black glass. The radiation monitor chattered into the
red, but as they were being protected by the Moonstone's magnetized armor, they continued on.

The hard-vac vehicle hit the slope with a minimum
of bounce in its shock absorbers. It climbed. In thirty
seconds it was at the top.

When he saw the *thing*, unscathed and peaceful at
the bottom of the crater, it was as if sharp fingernails
clawed his heart. The nuclear blast had blown away
all the dirt around Alpha Vehicle, and a lot from
underneath, but, from a tactical standpoint, the silver
sphere was in the exact same position, and remained
undamaged. Checking his biomonitor, he saw his respirations increasing. His right fist, seemingly with a
mind of its own, punched the nearest thing it could
find, the diagnostic console calibrating oxygen flow
to the fuel-burning unit, and the screen went pop,
flashed, then stabilized. The awful sterling-tinted
eye, bristling with its antigravity, wrapped in mystery, unwilling to talk to them, too *good* to talk to
them, was infuriating in its tranquility.

It was treating him like a nuisance. Like a child.
Like he wasn't important. Like it didn't respect him.

Like it didn't *honor* him.

But then he got the sense that it was staring at him
in a completely different way. It wasn't just its general, omniscient, wide-angle stare, but a focused scrutiny, something that was meant only for him. At first
he was daunted, but then fascinated.

"Drive closer."

"Sir, the radiation is really bad," said Callison.

"I don't give a damn. The thing's calling to me. It
wants to tell me something."

So Callison reluctantly drove the hard-vac vehicle down the inside slope of Crater Cavalet. The runnels were now gone, blasted into oblivion. The computer pinged softly, a danger signal, warning them the radiation was close to breaching their magnetized armor.

"Maybe we should turn around," said Hawker.

"Do you hear it?" said Pittman.

"Hear what, sir?"

"That music."

Callison and Hawker looked at each other. "We don't hear anything, sir," said Callison.

"Stop. I'm getting out."

"Getting out?" said Hawker. "Sir, your body armor doesn't have near the same magnetized field the Moonstone does. You're going to be putting yourself at risk."

"I'll be okay for a few minutes. It wants to talk to me. It's the old game, Hawker. Like three-card monte."

"It's communicating with you, sir?"

Pittman felt suddenly privileged. "I think it is, Hawker. I really think it is."

So Callison stopped the Moonstone, and after some extra air lock precautions, Pittman stepped out onto the surface and walked toward his silver nemesis, his suit pinging warnings all the way. His anger disappeared as he got closer to Alpha Vehicle. He thought it might reach out to him, the way it had to Dr. Conrad that first time, that it might draw him in and show him the wonders of the universe. But he remained on the outside. Inside, outside. The antonyms occurred to him spontaneously, like the fren-

zied thoughts of an obsessed man. He felt saddened
that it wouldn't let him in. And the music he was
hearing wasn't anything like the music in Gettysburg
after the blue wave of the Worldwide Crash. For it
sounded as if it was being played in reverse, still the
two-to-one motif, but backward, haunting, chilling,
music for the end of the world.

Then he stumbled on something.

And looking down he saw carved into the blast-
blackened grabboid basalt the yin-yang symbol, the
same thing he had been thinking of just moments
ago, and realized that he had at last become as privileged as Dr. Conrad, that they had finally entered his
mind, even if they were trying to tell him something
entirely different.

Corporals Allen and Sihem, unexpected personnel
aboard the *Pennsylvania*, arrested him the moment he
boarded. Sihem explained that his and Allen's presence had been ordered, when, just before they took
off, Greenhow had detected nuclear events on the
Moon. "You had no presidential authorization to em-
ploy the nuclear option."

They read him a list of charges, but by this time
he'd been awake nearly twenty-two hours, and was
too preoccupied with how he had failed to defeat
Alpha Vehicle to really listen to the litany of rubbish
they had brought with them. Also too preoccupied
with what Alpha Vehicle was trying to tell him. He
had never taken the yin-yang symbol seriously before. To him, it was just so much Eastern hocus-
pocus. But obviously they had plucked it from his
mind for a reason. They wouldn't have gone to all

the trouble of scratching it in the Moon's surface otherwise. He thought of the stone representation he had back in his desert home. Know your enemy. He was definitely going to have to do some research.

Sihem was a short man, didn't look like a Marine at all, had dark hair, an olive complexion, and Sephardic features. Allen was clearly an armed escort, built like a tank, with an expression as hard as a Minnesota lake in January.

Pittman tried to get information about possible nuclear events in America, but Sihem said he would be debriefed by the proper authorities once they were safely within the skin of Earth's atmosphere.

By this time, they orbited the Moon. Through the special polarized glass, the sun looked strange, with its great hydrogen band spinning away like a stream of golden confetti. He wanted to tell Sihem that things would have been different if his unilateral decision to launch had resulted in a victory. But who was Sihem? It would be like arguing with a Wal-Mart clerk about the price of detergent. So he sat there. And closed his eyes. And slept. Had never lost his Marine habit of sleeping anywhere at any time—one never knew when one was going to get the chance again.

But he slept with a troubled conscience.

At the end of ten hours the radio woke him.

"Control, copy for reentry."

The pilot, a man named Finbow, went through braking burns, telemetry, and angle of descent. They skidded across the atmosphere. The nose cone flared, reminding Pittman of the bonfires he had enjoyed with Sheila and the kids when they had vacationed on Cape Cod. The sky went from black to blue, and after so many weeks of the Moon's haunting darkness, it was like lifting the lid on a coffin. Everything was blue. Some puffy clouds floated by in the distance.

Control finally used some bandwidth for nonessential items, and he got his Orbops debriefing from, of all people, Brian Goldvogel, who seemed to love every minute of it.

"In response to your unauthorized attack, Tim, the Builders detonated a prime-number sequence of nuclear explosions along the Pacific equator, misinterpreting your launch as an attempt to communicate. The military junta in the PRNC mistook the Builder response for a preemptive strike by the U.S., and responded with strikes against New York, Boston, Washington, Atlanta, Chicago, and Philadelphia." A piece of his soul crumbled at the mention of Philadelphia. "The U.S. then took out Beijing, Shanghai, and Tianjin as well as a half dozen PRNC launch facilities. The only good thing that came of it was that internal factions loyal to the Democratic Republic of Canton overthrew Po Pin-Yen's ruling junta."

That Po Pin-Yen had at last been deposed was indeed the only bright spot in all this, and his heart rejoiced for a few moments.

They landed at Peterson Air Force Base, not far from where he lived. Corporal Allen helped him out of his seat, cuffed his hands behind his back, and accompanied him to the hatch. When the hatch opened, the heat struck him with nightmarish force. The light was so blinding he had to squint.

As he walked down the stairs, his legs unsure in

the strong Earth gravity after so many weeks on the Moon, he felt consumed by the need to get to Philadelphia as soon as possible. A compulsion, the impetus of which he felt coming from outside himself. As if the Builders were going to insist that he witness his own handiwork. He didn't want to believe that Sheila, Tom, and Becky might be dead as a direct result of his own unilateral decision to launch.

Allen was now joined by a second guard, this one in a military police uniform, the name Roadman stenciled above the breast pocket, a man half Pittman's age wearing government-issue sunglasses, a special kind meant to block out intense radiation—that's how bad the sun was getting. Roadman looked like a human fly because his glasses were so big.

If only Pittman could convince his superiors to let him go to Philadelphia immediately. He would make sure his kids and ex-wife were all right, then gladly spend whatever time in the stockade they required.

They led him across the tarmac and he looked out at the desert. He saw the low hills near his house, two gentle ones and then one that was more a mesa, shimmering in the ripple effect of the heat. Sweat drenched him in seconds.

Other military police led Hawker and Callison away to a different vehicle. Hawker glanced over his shoulder as he walked away. And it was as if Hawker was the only one old enough and wise enough to understand the true situation: that sometimes decisions had to be made down-chain when the links up-chain had been severed by unforeseeable circumstances. Down-chain, up-chain. Dark whispers rustled through Pittman's mind. As Hawker reached the big black vehicle that was going to take him away, he saluted Pittman.

Only it wasn't just Hawker standing there anymore. There was another man. Standing in hard-vac armor. His armor had been penetrated by what looked like weapons fire, and green StopGap had bubbled out to fix the leak. The man held his helmet in his arm. Haydn. Pale. Blond. Some blood down the front of his suit. Dead. Alive. Inadvertent. But intentional.

And Pittman knew the purple bands were somewhere up there judging him for it.

23

The Secret Service didn't take Cam and Lesha to Washington this time because Washington was gone.

They took them to Camp David in a military helicopter instead. The Builders were gone again—it seemed as if his Navasota episode had been brought on as a side effect of the nuclear exchange, the communicative efforts of the fusion events in the Pacific spilling into his own consciousness, then ebbing away as the Builders at last decided to dismiss this particular round of diplomatic dialogue as short-lived and bizarre. As such, it was important he convince the president of his plan, because he felt it was the only way they could reestablish communication with the hyperdimensional beings.

As they came down on the retreat's front lawn, the grass was brown, and the surrounding conifers as dry as talc. Inspecting the trees, Cam saw that the effects of the bloating sun had defoliated the uppermost branches so that each tree's peak was ragged, bare, and skeletal. The helicopter landed. Everything outside was light-blasted. Even through his dark polarized sunglasses, the entire Camp David grounds were awash in radiant whiteness. The effect was bizarre, like standing inside a giant lightbulb. He knew that despite the military helicopter's thick steel armor, radiation that customarily fell outside the boundaries of what was previously the norm must be getting through. So bright in fact were the grounds that he at first didn't see five tanks stationed at strategic points around the installation, not until he was standing outside on the lawn.

Having never been to Camp David before, he wasn't familiar with its setup, but knew the underground bunker was a section of the complex most visiting diplomats never saw. It was big, beneath the skeet range, and included not only domestic quarters but also several professional offices. It housed a medical clinic, a movie theater, a swimming pool, and a situation room. It was to this situation room that white-helmeted military police escorted Cam and Lesha.

Several people were already there, including General Blunt, Oren Fye, and Brian Goldvogel.

To his great surprise, a half dozen delegates from the People's Republic of North China were there as well, all wearing tailored gray suits with little PRNC pins in the lapels.

Cam took a seat and leaned toward Fye. "I thought we didn't have diplomatic relations with them anymore."

"There's been a coup. Po Pin-Yen's ruling junta has been overthrown by a more moderate faction of the army. The decision to launch against us, particularly when all the initial nuclear events occurred along the equator, was widely opposed. In fact, you could say it was a flashpoint for trouble that's been brewing a long time." He motioned at the gray-suited Chinese. "They're here to help. These are their top scientific and military advisers. They finally understand that we're all in this together."

President Langdon, Chief of Staff John Gielgud, and Secretary of Defense Leroy Congdon arrived a short while later.

General Blunt got up and summarized events: Alpha Vehicle's arrival on the Moon, the construction of the towers, the various attempts to communicate, the military actions, and the red giant progression in the sun. The Chinese had earpieces, and Cam heard the faint burbling of Mandarin. General Blunt, in the tone of voice of a grandfather describing a favorite old memory, introduced Cam.

"Dr. Conrad is the world's top expert on hyperdimensionality, and also the only man who has had any direct contact with the Builders." Blunt then went on to describe how this contact had been quantified using various scanning devices to track significant and unique changes in Cam's brain, particularly his sylvan fissure. "He's here today to explore with us possible new ways of either reopening communications with the Builders or in some way reversing the red-giant process in the sun. Without further ado, I give you Dr. Cameron Conrad."

Cam rose and went to the front.

He began by acknowledging the president, the chief of staff, the secretary of defense, the gathered Orbops personnel, as well as the PRNC observers. Then he launched right in—his speech was now back to normal.

"The solution, coincidentally enough, lies in my own frontier work, the Stradivari Project." He understood that he was immediately met with skepticism—they thought he was pushing his own agenda again. He hastened to correct this misconception. "On the Moon, before the Builders destroyed all my equipment, I was trying to generate something called anti-Ostrander space, a kind of curved space-time specific to hyperdimensionality first postulated by Dutch physicist William Ostrander back in 2055. In studying the effects of anti-Ostrander space on various particles, or at least looking at how these particles behaved in anti-Ostrander space, I hoped to come to a greater understanding of hyperdimensionality and how it might be used to explain some of the deeper and more perplexing mysteries of the universe. One of the difficulties in explaining cutting-edge physics is that it's primarily expressed in mathematical language, and so to comprehend it through the analogs of the five human senses is nearly impossible. Often, to describe things to laymen, I must rely on metaphor and simile, and to do this I want to tell you about something that happened to me when I was a teenager. When I was fifteen, my father suffered a stroke. Part of his mind was permanently damaged and he couldn't process his reality or his world in the same way anymore. He lost a great deal of his mental facility, and so you could say he was like a two-dimensional being trying to process a four-dimensional world, and that he simply didn't have the necessary conduits or filters to make sense of much of what he saw. Taking that to the next level, human beings, as a whole, don't have the filters to properly interpret, at least not without complicated and artificial mathematics, the presumed hyperdimensionality of the Builders. For one reason or another, I've been given brief sensory glimpses of it. Inside Alpha Vehicle I saw the entire universe as if mapped out in a small oval; but it was more than just this sight analog. It was a feeling. And it was this feeling that has led me to the conclusion that the Builders are hyperdimensional."

The president interrupted. "Yes, but what does hyperdimensionality mean?"

How to explain this to the president so he would understand. "It's the potentiality of all things, all the time, all at once. Within the confines of anti-Ostrander space we find these properties. And it is within this kind of setting that I believe the Builders operate. I believe, based on the subjective corollaries the Builders have allowed me to experience, that they are in fact manipulating the nature of hyperdimensionality to achieve the effects we're now seeing in our own sun. Which brings us to the primary reason we're all gathered here today. Why are the Builders bleeding the hydrogen out of the sun and accelerating it into its red giant phase, and is there anything we can do to stop it?"

The room grew still as they waited for him to continue.

He took a moment to collect his thoughts. "On the way here, I read Dr. Nolan Pratt's most recent report. He's now identified eleven other main sequence stars within the local Milky Way that have been kindled into red giants. Similarly, larger stars in more further-flung neighborhoods of the galaxy have been acceler-

ated into supernovae. I wish I could answer the first
part of the question, why the Builders are doing this,
but I have no idea. Whatever the reason, it means
the Builders have major engineering capability on a
pan-galactic scale." He turned to Leroy Congdon.
"Which means we must conclude that from a military standpoint, we're outmatched by a considerable
margin, and that to even consider military action
against them is, to say the least, counterproductive
and, as Colonel Pittman's unauthorized launch has
shown, even dangerous. As I've said before, they
could easily destroy Earth if they wanted to. If they
traveled twelve million light-years instantaneously,
bending time and space to do so, does anyone seriously doubt that they could crush us in seconds if
that was their ultimate goal?"

He tried to keep the tone of reprimand out of his
voice because he knew he was walking a political
tightrope. He was glad to see that the president and
the secretary responded with grim grace.

Congdon, in his gospel baritone, said, "Colonel
Pittman has been discharged from duty and is facing
a military court-martial."

The president said, "If not military action, then
where's that leave us? I don't have to remind you
that the political stakes are fairly high at this time."

Cam nodded. "Yes, I know. And I understand that
emphasis must be put on results of a concrete political and strategic nature. Which brings me back to my
original work on anti-Ostrander space. If we upscale
my Stradivari equipment, and place it at a calculated
spot somewhere along the outflowing hydrogen spi-

ral, we can reverse the hydrogen's flow and send it back to the sun. The Stradivari equipment will create a large anti-Ostrander space field. By creating an array of a dozen or so generators—and by the way, the cost would be fairly cheap because we already have the Brookhaven designs—we could create a field large enough to slow and possibly reverse the hydrogen bleed."

He glanced at the president. Would he buy it? And would the panel of backup scientists answering to him confirm it? The pugnacious little Langdon was staring at him now, and the president's eyes reminded Cam of burning coals. Langdon glanced at Blunt. "General, does Orbops possess the necessary launch capability for the mission that Dr. Conrad is suggesting? And if so, how long will it take?"

Blunt stroked his small white goatee. "While our operations on the Moon have significantly reduced our lift potential, we still have the resources for a launch of this nature. You're looking at . . . twelve boosters, then, Dr. Conrad?"

"For the units themselves, yes, a dozen. We would need another five boosters for scientific, construction, and supervisory staff. If we went to full-scale production at the Henderson-Lang Orbiting Assembly Bay, and called in extra crews to work around the clock, I believe we could get the Stradivari generators finished in a month. When you take travel and installation time into account, we should have the whole system up and running by the end of September. Red giant effects, according to the Omega Sol equation, will culminate in early October, so that should give us a two-week margin. By that time, the system will be operational and pumping hydrogen back into the sun.''

One of the Chinese delegates had a question, and it came through the translation speaker overhead. ''And how, exactly, is the Stradivari field supposed to send hydrogen back to the sun?''

Cam nodded. ''As I previously mentioned, we hope to create a wide swath of anti-Ostrander space. The environment inside anti-Ostrander space is something that's not well comprehended by lay people, but let me try my best to explain. If you were inside anti-Ostrander space, you would notice some extremely strange properties. For one thing, no matter where you were, you would feel like you were at the bottom of a gravity well. On Earth, you throw a ball up into the air, and it comes back to you. In anti-Ostrander space, you throw it to the right and the left, and even downward, and it would come back to you. In other words, all matter is boomeranged back to where it came from. If we made our own field continuous with the same field the Builders are using to drain the hydrogen, we'll initiate a backflow.''

Brian Goldvogel spoke up, his tone skeptical. ''If the Builders are as powerful as you say they are, what's to stop them from blasting this new apparatus right out of the sky?''

Cam's lower lip came forward and his eyebrows rose. Goldvogel was going to play the devil's advocate, was he? All right. So be it. Time for the other side of the coin.

''Nothing. If the Builders want to get rid of us, we

ultimately can't stop them. But there's much evidence to suggest that they're trying to understand exactly who we are. Some asked why did Alpha Vehicle come to Gettysburg when it finally wound up in Crater Cavalet, twenty-five kilometers away? It's been suggested that my own presence at Gettysburg could have been a factor. And in view of the evidence thus far, my own work in Shenandoah might have had something to do with it. Remember, Stradivari Team was trying to create an anti-Ostrander environment, and day by day I grow more convinced that this is the exact kind of environment the Builders inhabit. In other words, they may have intuited some part of their own innate way of existence, and so they investigated. Unfortunately for everybody concerned, their moonfall inadvertently destroyed the bulk of our equipment."

Goldvogel's patience looked tried. "So you're saying that all this could be a waste of time if the Builders don't buy it?"

"I'm saying they still might try to communicate with us if we foster the right conditions. With a new Stradivari, we might further that cause. I think they've been trying to communicate with us all this time and are just having a hard time understanding us. We have many examples of their attempts. The Worldwide Crash, for instance. My own time inside Alpha Vehicle. The recent nuclear exchange."

Goldvogel remained unconvinced. "What about Dr. Tennant's second communications attempt. Alpha Vehicle murdered one Princeton Team member, and the others are presumed dead. I wouldn't exactly call that communicating."

"Have you read yesterday's report on that?"

Goldvogel's face reddened. "I'm afraid I haven't."

"The Builders left an interesting clue at the site of the second attempt, another example of a possible communication attempt, the grooves running parallel to each other on the Moon's surface, the so-called runnels. We've now had all kinds of analysts study these grooves, including musicologists. The items sent in Dr. Tennant's more comprehensive second attempt included, among other things, a recording of Mozart's Fortieth Symphony in G Minor, Köchel 550. The musicologists have established precise relationships between the Moon grooves and many notational aspects of Mozart's Fortieth. They say it's as if the Builders tried to respond to Mozart's symphony with a notational idiom that reflected the composer's work. This further supports the notion that the Builders are trying to communicate with us, and leads me to believe that they're trying to discern our precise nature. If we promote the right conditions we might make a breakthrough."

The president spoke up. "But why are they trying to discern our precise nature? If they're just going to fry us in our own sun, why would they care?"

"Because as they are alive themselves, they recognize the value of life."

Oren Fye's voice was hard. "Considering that over three hundred thousand died in the Worldwide Crash—considering all the damage and death caused by Hurricane Delilah, not to mention the nuclear exchange, and the four murdered Princeton Team members—"

Cam raised his hands, preempting Fye's objections.

"I believe it's a matter of priorities for the Builders. We can assume that because several other local stars have been accelerated into their end-stage phases, the Builders' specific intentions don't necessarily focus on Earth. We don't know why they're doing what they're doing, but they must have a reason. And maybe the reason outweighs the preservation of a species like our own. I think the essentials for the Builders lie in a single question: 'Why should we bother saving you when we have much greater things at stake?' I believe we touched on this hypothesis in our last meeting."

The notion still had a sobering effect on everybody.

"Do you have any further guesses on that?" asked John Gielgud. "I mean, what would they have at stake?"

"I still don't know. But considering how vast their engineering project seems to be, I think it goes way beyond our petty concerns here on Earth. In my own contact with them, I've sensed this. At the same time, I realize that they've divined something in us. They've tried to establish the exact parameters for what they've seen in us. They've tried to reach us by various means of communication we haven't fully comprehended. Let's be thankful that with the recent nuclear exchange, despite the casualties, they seem to be trying again. With an upscaled Stradivari attempt, we just might encourage further overtures." He shrugged. "And we'll just have to hope that any new dialogue isn't as destructive as previous ones."

PART THREE

The Wreckers

24

As such things went, Pittman's cell was spacious, and included a small bedroom and office. He had computer access and tried to find out everything he could about the nuclear strike against Philadelphia, but there wasn't much. The Army was keeping tight wraps on the outflow of information about the disaster. He tried to get through to Sheila and the kids, but most of the Bell Atlantic grid was down, and the air was too thick with radiation, both from the nuclear strikes and the Builder-molested sun, for cell phones to work.

He did, however, get through to his lawyer, Gary Starling, who lived in Las Vegas—close-range cell phones seemed to be working—and explained his situation. He needed to get out of here. He had to go to Philadelphia. It wasn't only his worry and love that was driving him. Alpha Vehicle was in his mind now, and it was telling him to go.

Starling agreed to represent him. "I'll have my assistants dig around for precedents."

As he sat in his cell at Peterson Air Force Base

with the Bleed's eye-smarting light coming through his window, he found a new piece of information. For Philadelphia, the PRNC targeting mechanism had malfunctioned by seven percent, and detonation had occurred three kilometers east of the city across the Delaware River in south Jersey. This meant his ex-wife and family had three more kilometers of buffer, and this bolstered his hopes greatly.

He tried to gain access to Greenhow for satellite imagery, but his old passwords were now void. So he attempted to Google Philadelphia through Google Earth, but the Philadelphia shots were old file ones, taken three days before the strike, and all the familiar streets were still intact.

Starling, an older man, tall, fond of Italian suits, came for their first face-to-face three days later.

"There's an old incommunicado provision I found on the books. The Brazil Engagement." Pittman became appropriately solemn at Starling's mention of the bloodiest jungle conflict ever, particularly because it was the war his father had died in. "Colonel Robert F. Spencer was isolated in the Roosevelt River Basin in March of 2103. Brazilian forces had taken out his communications, destroyed all his supply dumps, and his men were running short of food and succumbing to disease. He had in his arsenal two tactical nuclear weapons, and the standing order stipulated he could fire them only with the consent of his superior officer, General Dennis Drayna. But as he was incommunicado, and in dire straits, he fired the larger of the two without that consent so he could break the Brazilian stranglehold. The military arrested him the moment he got back to battalion, but his defense attorney got him acquitted using the incommunicado defense. So we have an extremely strong precedent in *Spencer vs. the USMC*, and I think it will stand."

Up against *Spencer vs. the USMC*, the prosecutorial offensive didn't get much beyond the pretrial stage, and the insubordination charge was dropped. They let Pittman go after four weeks. Right around the same time, he learned that Dr. Conrad and a crew of scientists had gone on a mission dubbed Guarneri, and that they were now trying to communicate with the Builders using techniques of hyperdimensionality pioneered during Stradivari. They were somewhere between the orbital planes of Earth and Venus, attempting to negotiate a last-minute reprieve. And that was good, because reports kept coming in about how the Van Allen belts were shredding because of the bloating sun, and unrestricted radiation was reaching the Earth in ever greater amounts, and that time was generally running out for everybody.

It was in this atmosphere of looming disaster and potential salvation—another dichotomy, disaster, salvation—that military authorities gave Pittman some civilian clothes at Peterson, along with his dishonorable discharge, and then had an officer drive him back to his home five miles away.

The next morning, when he woke, he didn't know what was wrong with the sky. Was it gray? Was it blue? Was it brown? Was it green? It was filled from horizon to horizon with an awful haze, and the wind was strong and blowing dust and tumbleweeds across the desert. He felt ill in a way he had never felt ill before. Enervated. Weak. Tired. As if his body was simply too heavy for Earth's gravity.

He went outside in jeans and an olive USMC T-shirt, walked to his chin-up bar, and tried to do some chin-ups. He could only do three before he gave up. He wondered if the radiation from his un-protected excursion in Crater Cavalet was starting to catch up with him, or if, like Dr. Conrad, he was having a Builder-related attack of some kind.

When he dropped to the ground, his legs crumpled beneath him and he sat cross-legged in the dirt while the wind blew around him. He felt diminished. His hand, with a mind of its own, wrote two words in the dirt. Existence. Nonexistence. He had no idea he was doing it until he had finished. He was surprised that they were in his head, because he was convinced they had made him write those words. He was their sworn enemy, and he thought they would try to stay away from him. But maybe the old adage was true. Opposites attract.

He took his cell out and tried Philadelphia for the twentieth time, the old familiar 215 exchange coming automatically to his thumb. But he got the same message again. Service was currently unavailable. Bell Atlantic was working on the problem. Because Phila-delphia and its environs were now under military control, Ma Bell had no idea when the problem would be fixed. Then he looked at the words again. Existence. Nonexistence. The two necessary and counterbalancing principles of war. Maybe he was a lot more like the Builders than he wanted to admit.

He closed his cell and put it in his pocket. He dragged himself to his feet. Too many weeks on the

Moon. Or was it the radiation, the megadoses not only from Crater Cavalet but also the copious becquerels slipping through the slowly shredding twin magnetic girdles of the Van Allen belts? Maybe he was getting old. Next month he would be fifty-five.

He glanced at his garage. Time to go.

He went into his house and packed some clothes. His gun. Some extra rounds because who knew what kind of lawlessness he was going to encounter in postholocaust Philadelphia. Packed his raft, because he planned on paddling into town via the Schuylkill River to avoid as much of that lawlessness as he could.

Then he went to his den and looked at the yin-yang symbol carved in stone. It reminded him of two tadpoles swimming around each other, one white, one black, darkness and light, life and death, yes and no, existence, nonexistence. He felt certain he was the dark part, the yin part. As well-meaning as he had always tried to be, he had ended up bringing evil into the world. He was negation. A destroyer.

He reached up and touched the symbol.

After a few more moments of nearly religious contemplation, he got his bag, went out to his truck, and started the long drive to Pennsylvania.

25

Cam was weightless in the scientific command vehicle *Tecumseh*.

He couldn't sleep because he had a gut feeling that something wasn't right. Ever since the Builders had fiddled with his sylvan fissure, a sense of precognition pervaded his consciousness, perhaps the filter needed to discern the higher dimensions and rarefied space-time continuums in which the Builders operated. He opened his eyes, his anxiety mounting.

Across the tiny dorm, he saw Lesha, upright, strapped in her cot. Her face looked younger than it usually did, puffed up by constant free fall, edged in the scarlet murk of the night lamps. He heard the steady hush of the ventilation, and smelled the faint reek of vomit—a few crew still hadn't gotten their space legs.

He felt scared but didn't know why. He was in deep space, at a midpoint somewhere between the Terran and Venusian orbital planes—but had been here for the last week. Guarneri—his deep-space field array named after another famous Italian violin maker in honor of string theory—was about to go online, and all systems checked out, and he anticipated great success. He had all the people he wanted, all the original surviving crew of Stradivari. So the work was fine. Still, something was bothering him.

Then it came to him—the way Mark Fuller had looked at him today. The turn of his head as his long blond hair had danced in weightlessness, the usual light in his eyes gone, his pupils dilated, the overall insensibility of the young researcher's expression unnerving in its immobility.

His heart rate climbed. He leaned forward.

He looked down the dorm, a cramped space that was more like a corridor, the sleeping harnesses with blue padded nylon straps staggered from one side to the other. In the sanguine dimness of the red night lamps, he saw that Mark was gone, his harness straps floating free like the tentacles of an underwater creature, his small paper-wrapped pillow drifting above like a blue packing envelope.

He looked around and saw other sleeping crew members: Dr. Jeffrey Ochoa, Lieutenant Colonel Oren Fye, Blaine Berkheimer, Lewis Hirleman, and a few new technical support personnel, Stella Watson, Daniel Uttal, and Jacqueline Ceci. Many were under the influence of a mild sedative, the only way they could sleep in weightlessness.

He unclicked his harness straps. The presentiment of bad things to come wouldn't leave him alone.

He pushed himself free and maneuvered to the throughway below everybody's feet, a tube that was made crowded by personal hampers Velcroed here and there. He maneuvered around the hampers. His mouth was like a desert and his eyes ached from the dryness inside *Tecumseh*. He reached the end of the throughway and somersaulted into the much wider hub tube.

The hub was a cylindrical shaft that ran up and down the whole length of the spacecraft. He looked up, saw tiny violet lights quartering the shaft into four ninety-degree sections, the lights, like Christmas lights, providing a sense of space and orientation. Then looked down. Below he saw the access hatch to the *Tecumseh's* engineering section, and heard the hum of its fusion generator beneath the disk-shaped bolted door.

He looked up again and sensed Mark somewhere up there. Intuiting things in more than the usual four dimensions, a gift the Builders had *inadvertently* bestowed upon him.

He reached for a handhold and pulled himself along. He suffered momentary vertigo as the violet guide lights flicked by one by one. His uneasiness persisted. Drifting upward, he had the unsettling sense that all of *Tecumseh* had suddenly become a death trap, and that he would be lucky if he ever saw Earth again.

He passed the various bays—exercise, navigation, kitchen, sanitation—and slowed as he came to the PRNC observer bay. He peered inside. He saw John Quang, Loftus Hua, Carol Ng, Betty Hum, and Foster Chong. They were all asleep. Safely bundled in their blue straps.

He continued upward until he arrived at the science bay, dubbed Cremona, after Bartolomeo Guarneri's hometown, the largest bay in the whole craft.

He went inside, and the narrow aperture immediately opened into a large polycarbonate sphere with a comprehensive view of outer space. Fit into the interior was a gridwork of girders. Various workstations had been installed along these girders without due regard for the official up and down, so that some were at right angles to others, and a few stations were even upside down from their neighbors. Through the polarized dome, he saw the sun, an angry white ball that now looked as if it had an infection, throwing off the occasional gold, orange, and red spectra, the view filtered by the protective magnetized field around *Tecumseh*.

As with the hub, violet lights outlined the various girders in Cremona. These should have been the only lights burning. But in the sphere's designated northeast quadrant, he saw the glow of white halogen lights emanating from behind Station A, the largest and most important Guarneri interface.

Like a monkey in a monkey house, Cam pulled himself from girder to girder until he finally maneuvered to Station A. He peered around the partition and saw Mark strapped to one of the stools. The stool's base was snug in a locking rail, the brake pulled into position so Mark wouldn't drift up and down the rail.

Mark typed with unsettling speed at the main interface, his fingers so quick they were a blur, his rapidity unnatural. The young physicist's face looked gray in the blue light coming from the screen. His blond hair was tied in a ponytail with a red elastic band, and it floated straight out from the back of his head. His eyes were insensible. Though Cam was well within Mark's peripheral vision, Mark didn't turn.

"Mark?"

Mark still didn't turn. It was as if the young man was in a trance.

Cam maneuvered farther into view, and he thought that he might sense the Builders, that maybe this was the beginning of it, the Builders communicating through Mark now instead of him. He glanced at the screen to check what Mark was typing, and saw that it was dense machine language, the amber lines crawling onto the screen with lightning speed.

"Mark?"

Mark didn't turn. What was going on? Was this the Builders? This didn't *feel* like the Builders. This felt like something bad, and Cam's enhanced sylvan fissure seemed to quiver with apprehension. It looked like Mark was writing new code into the Guarneri nodes. Those nodes were so precariously balanced that any new background language was bound to destabilize them.

"Mark, what are you doing? Any new code has to be strictly authorized by me, you know that."

But Mark remained insensible. Only when Cam put his hand on Mark's shoulder did the man stop typing. His fingers lifted from the keyboard and remained poised there. Then Mark turned.

He was pale, and had dark patches of exhaustion under his eyes. Cam had to wonder if he had spent other evenings unattended in Cremona. Mark, whom he had known for the last eight years, and whom he had mentored at Brookhaven, looked as if he didn't recognize Cam at all.

"Mark, are you all right?"

"Fine."

"What are you doing?"

Mark didn't respond. He turned back to the screen, his head swiveling as if on poorly greased ball bearings, and began to type at the same phenomenal machinelike speed.

"Mark, you're going to have to stop."

He put both hands on the junior scientist, but this time Mark swung quickly and pushed him away with considerable force.

As Cam wasn't latched to anything, he flew end over end through the three-dimensional gridwork of workstations, knocking his elbow badly on one of the girders before he stopped himself. He again stared at Mark, his heart pounding, his fear like a sudden fever, and saw that the young man had resumed typing, raised slightly off his stool, as if, like a predator, he was getting ready to pounce at something.

Cam logged on to the nearest comlink and sounded a general alarm. A tone, something like the lowest note on a marimba, resonated throughout *Tecumseh*. As he waited for others to arrive, he realized the success of the mission was now in jeopardy.

Oren Fye and Dr. Jeffrey Ochoa were the first to come. Then Lesha, Blake, and Lewis, followed by the new recruits. At last the Chinese observers arrived.

After a considerable struggle, and a few contusions and scrapes, Dr. Ochoa, with a daring lunge, administered an injection.

Only then were they able to pull Mark away from the console.

Only then could they start assessing damage.

26

The science bay was cleared and all the stations secured.

While Mark was taken to the surgery to be examined by Dr. Ochoa, Cam stayed in Cremona and went over the various Guarneri nodes with Lesha.

Lesha had strapped herself into the stool next to him. "Node one is clear."

"Just because it appears clear doesn't mean it really is. It just means we can't find any evidence of tampering. But it's got to be there somewhere."

They went over node 1 a number of times but couldn't find anything even remotely suspicious, so finally went on to the next node. Line by line they went through it. He found no sign of modification, or corruption, or . . . sabotage? Node 2 appeared to be clear as well. So did node 3. Yet he sensed it was like going into an old house in a bad area of town—the cockroaches had to be right behind the walls. Where had all Mark's furious typing gone? And why would Mark want to sabotage?

Cam turned to Lesha. "You befriended him more

than I did. When you were doing the basic Stradivari research protocols together, did he ever exhibit any untoward behavior about anything?"

Lesha shook her head. "He was always fun. He always knew how to joke."

"Did he ever express any resentment toward me? Or the role I had him play in Stradivari?"

"No. Never. He has the highest regard for you. We all do."

"Then what's gotten into him?"

She shook her head once more. "I have no idea."

He motioned at the screen. "And where did all his extra background language go?"

She pondered the screen. "He must have hidden it. Or encrypted it."

"If it's encrypted, he's done it so well it's invisible, or locked away, and I don't have the key to open it."

They investigated the fifth and final Guarneri node and found no evidence of tampering, alteration, or sabotage. With the diagnostic complete, Cam locked the whole system down, unconvinced it was clear, even though their diagnostic routines had told them otherwise. Then he and Lesha maneuvered to the surgery to see Mark.

Mark was now strapped to a wall-mounted gurney, his eyes half-closed, his arms bent at the elbows so that his hands floated in front of his face. As with every other area in the *Tecumseh*, the surgery was small, with a total of six gurneys that hinged down from the walls, three on each side.

Dr. Ochoa sat at the lab bench going over test results. As Cam and Lesha entered, he turned from his screen, his sudden shifting making him strain against the safety belt he had around his waist. His green eyes had solidified into intense orbs of focused wonderment. Cam inferred that his discoveries had been remarkable. Of particular interest was the way the doctor had his patient shackled by the ankles to the gurney with titanium cords.

"Where's Oren?" asked Cam. "I thought he would be here."

"He's gone to . . . alert General Blunt. He sure is glad we have that new pierce-communications system to get through all this radiation. It's perfect for an emergency like this." Ochoa cast a nervous glance at Mark. "Were you successful in securing any of the nodes?"

"They look clear, but I don't think they're secure at all." He nodded toward Mark. "His codes are there. We just can't see them. They're like a time bomb waiting to go off."

Ochoa's lips pursed. He paused, and finally took a deep breath. "He's been implanted."

Cam looked more closely at Mark. "Implanted? What do you mean?"

Ochoa turned around and motioned at the laboratory readouts. "His brain is producing abnormally high quantities of adrenaline, cortisol, and glucagon. Before I worked for Orbops, I was employed by VIP-Med at the Directorate of National Intelligence, so I know about these things. Much of my work involved blue-sky implant research. It's nothing new, really. We've been doing it for nearly two hundred years, ever since Dr. Jose Salgado conducted his experiments with his so-called stimoceivers back in the nineteen fifties. Someone's implanted Mark. It was obvious to me the moment I first saw him typing like that. I didn't want to say anything until I ran some tests. I've got the labs, and I've also X-rayed his head." He asked his screen to maximize an image, and a second later a ghostly gray X-ray appeared on the screen. "They've made it out of translucent material, so it's fairly hard to see, but if you look down here, at Mark's cerebral cortex, it's the lozenge-shaped unit right here."

Cam maneuvered closer. "You guys implanted him?"

"Us?" Ochoa was surprised by the suggestion. "No. I recognize the design, though. Our operatives were constantly muling plants like this out of the PRNC before, during, and after the war. This one's autonomous. It's been modified from a more basic design. It's complex. It's loaded with commands. You can see fresh scar tissue up through here, in his sinus cavity. It probably crawled in."

"So, wait a minute. The Chinese put it there?"

Ochoa looked away. "Talk to Oren. I'm just a doctor."

"The Chinese on board?"

"The PRNC is a complicated place right now. The new government has a tenuous hold at best and there are many loyal supporters of the previous junta. We knew the risks, but the benefits at the time seemed to outweigh them."

"How recent is that scar tissue?"

Ochoa gazed at the image. "I'm not a radiologist, but I would have to guess no older than a week."

"So in other words, we have a Chinese operative aboard."

"We vetted them all scrupulously." Ochoa's lips tightened once more. At last he scratched the back of his head. "But apparently not scrupulously enough."

In free fall, with his skin puffed out, the considerably overweight and bald Fye looked like a man-sized infant. During his time in space, he had developed a soft hacking cough, and this new signature sound now replaced the previous one of a long, lilting sigh.

They were in the mess bay. The situation was difficult. The Chinese on board knew something was amiss. John Quang peered in through the access corridor, the third time he had done so, looking embarrassed, as if he had barged in on the wrong birthday party. Fye swiveled his fat, doughy face toward the chief Chinese observer, and Quang backed away, reminding Cam of a gopher going back into its hole.

If circumstances had been different, and the stakes not so great, Cam might have descried in the current turn of events an exquisite irony, or at least a dark humor that deserved acknowledgment. In its way, this was Moonstone all over again, another demonstration that perhaps the human race didn't deserve to survive after all. Cam was fighting to save things, while those he had to work with were hell-bent on wrecking them. He didn't understand it. He was flabbergasted by the unfathomable Machiavellian logic that was in play here. Between gentle hacks, Fye tried to explain it to Cam and Lesha.

"Restitution," he said, as if it were a kind of panacea. "You have Boston and New York. You have

Philadelphia, Washington, and Atlanta. You have Chicago. We're all appreciative of the great human cost. The president thinks of that every minute of the day, and so does the First Lady. But do you have any idea of what the loss of those cities means to the United States in terms of their economic value? And, yes, I realize the PRNC lost Beijing, Shanghai, and Tianjin, and we all grieve and mourn their countless dead, and the president has extended his special sympathy to the new rulers in Beijing. But there comes a time when any nation at war must consider reparations, and hold its aggressors accountable."

At this point, the impossibly dry air inside *Tecumseh* exacerbated Fye's lungs into a fit of space asthma, and he coughed for nearly a minute, stopping only when he had inhaled some of the puffers Dr. Ochoa had prescribed for him.

"The president and his closest advisers know they can never bring back all those lives, but as I say, at some point they have to consider the good of the country, and how they might at least repair the economic damage that the former rulers in Beijing have caused. I'm pleased to say that the new government has decided to be responsible. It's agreed to restitution. We're not the great power we once were, and we have to look after our own house. It's not just the loss of six primary cities. The whole reason for the PRNC War—New Sumeria selling off its U.S. dollars and buying PRNC Yuan, that whole realignment of the Middle East with the Far East, and the subsequent economic isolation of America—that's come at a great financial cost to us. I don't have to tell you how high the deficit is. And so we've used the PRNC's unprovoked attack to . . . what's the word the president used? Leverage? Influence?''

Fye went back to his customary sighing, now that he had his coughing under control. ''Bear in mind that we have many friends in the PRNC, and we always knew that it was just a matter of time before they went the same route as the Democratic Republic of Canton. So when the overthrow came, I can't say that we were really happy about the loss of six cities, but at least there was a groundswell of support for us, as well as for the DRC, and we capitalized on it, even to the extent of structuring certain economic outcomes in regard to . . . uh . . . the Guarneri mission.''

Cam was even more flabbergasted. ''Economic outcomes?'' The phrase was vintage Langdon-speak. ''The sun is going to go red giant in less than three weeks and you're talking about economic outcomes?''

Lesha glanced at Cam. ''This is unbelievable.''

Fye raised his chubby white hands. ''Dr. Conrad, Dr. Weeks, money is always a concern. And so we had the new government in the PRNC—the factions supported both by ourselves as well as the DRC— guarantee that the U.S. will have full exclusive rights to any technological offerings the Builders might produce for us when and if we are successful in reestablishing communications with them. Now it seems as if the new government in Beijing doesn't have as firm control over its people or agencies we would have hoped or expected. It appears that someone on board—someone loyal to Po Pin-Yen—has tried to undermine our objectives. And in fact, while you were investigating the node problem in the science bay, I spoke to the president using the new pierce-wave relay—what a dandy system—and the president assures me that he's doing everything he can to gather all the extra available intelligence we can on John Quang, Loftus Hua, and the other team members of the observer force to see if they ever had any previous party affiliation with the Po Pin-Yen regime in Beijing. As much as you might deride the president's legitimate concerns about economic outcomes and alien-based technological gains, I think it might be a better idea if, at least for the time being, you retire the more unfortunate aspects of your left-leaning ideology. For the time being it might be better if you focused on the science."

Questioning Oren Fye's role aboard the *Tecumseh*, and puzzled about the exact contribution he was making toward the Guarneri Project, Cam now understood the phlegmatic man's presence with chilling clarity. He was here as political officer. Cam lifted his chin, assessed his own role, and decided, for different reasons, that Fye was right. He should concentrate on the science.

"I was unable to find any corrupting code in the software. Whatever Mark fed into the system now seems to be completely invisible. But I have no doubt that it's there somewhere."

"Neither do I."

Cam shook his head in mystification. "Why would they want to sabotage something like this?"

Lesha said, "Don't they understand everyone might be fried in the red giant if all this doesn't work out?"

Fye's eyebrows rose. "The president had his strategists at the DNI study possible PRNC objectives, and they all tend to agree that Pin-Yen loyalists want to obtain the Guarneri plans, and then implement their own communications attempt in the hope of securing for themselves whatever technological booty the Builders might offer."

Cam grew still. He glanced at Lesha. She'd gone pale. She sucked her lower lip under her upper one, an unconscious gesture that, combined with her freckles and big blue eyes, made her look girlish. She spoke. "So, in other words, the leaders who Cam has entrusted with his efforts, not only in the U.S. but in the PRNC—the exact same ones who are supposed to save us from the red giant event in the sun—these leaders have willfully engaged in a proxy war that is going to reduce our chances of salvation to practically nil." She threw up her hands and turned to Cam, exasperation in her eyes. "We might as well close the whole project down, Cam. Langdon got greedy and now John Quang and company have filled the *Tecumseh* with macrogenic brain implants that are going to crawl their way into our cerebral cortexes. The Builders should abandon us. We're primitive. We don't deserve to live."

Fye sighed deeply. "The president has never subscribed to defeatist attitudes, Dr. Weeks. And he's always been a man for contingencies. In a situation like this, he expects unconditional loyalty. I admit, with scientific as well as economic concerns, Guarneri has always been a two-track program. But neither of you need concern yourself with the economic track. Let's just say the economic track is my problem. As far as the two of you are concerned, your objective hasn't changed. You're to create an anti-Ostrander environment that will boomerang at least some of the bleeding hydrogen back into the sun. The secondary and hoped-for result of this first objective will be to illustrate to the Builders that we can not only think in higher dimensions but also operate in them as well. The final expected yield is to reestablish communications with the Builders, get them to stand down, and work toward mutually beneficial trade relations." Oren Fye's voice hardened, and Cam was surprised because up until this time he had considered the Orbops lieutenant colonel passive and ineffective. Now he was showing a whole new side to his personality. "Your mission hasn't changed, Dr. Conrad. What's changed, I guess, are your obstacles. Let's see how flexible the two of you can be when it comes to adapting to new situations. Let's see if you can succeed in your mission despite what appears to be an organized sabotage attempt by agents of the former Po Pin-Yen regime."

Cam stared at Fye, feeling a new admiration for the man, but still perplexed by the problems they now faced. "How do you expect us to do that when we can't even see the code that Mark has apparently inputted into the Guarneri nodes? And how can we possibly begin to guess the intent of that code?"

Fye lifted his plump index finger, a digit that reminded Cam of an uncooked breakfast sausage, and waved it a few times in his face. "Good. This is exactly what I want to hear. We ask questions, and answer them one by one. You see, Dr. Conrad? You and I aren't so different from each other. We observe, we ask questions, we come up with hypotheses. We either prove or disprove those hypotheses through experimentation. Simple grade-ten science. It's amazing how well it works in all facets of life." Fye cleared his throat. "To answer your first question, we have to get Mark to help us find the code. Once we find the code, the second question will answer itself. I have, stowed behind a panel in the engineering section, a wide range of weapons, serums, and other tools. Also available to me are certain systems that will interrupt whatever behavior modification programs the Chinese implant has initiated in Mark. This is what I mean when I say the president plans for all contingencies. What we have to do is make Mark his old self again. This might take some doing, and unfortunately he might suffer some long-term health effects, but considering everybody's future is now measured in weeks, I think this is a small price to pay."

Fye motioned to Cam.

"You'll of course have to be present when we . . . talk to Mark. I'll need someone there who has complete knowledge of the Guarneri nodes. And I'm afraid we'll have to make it known to the crew that the entire PRNC observer staff might in fact pose a threat. To that end, you'll all be issued weapons. Not that I expect you'll have to use them. Any misguided weapons' fire might result in a hull breach, and I'm sure the Chinese understand the danger of armed confrontation aboard the *Tecumseh* as well as we do. Your weapons will be more for a show of force. Like when Pin-Yen sent his carrier task group into the Pacific, and in response we shifted the USS *Terpsichore* and USS *Rondon* from other theaters to observe. My own experience tells me that often, saber rattling is enough.''

27

Pittman drove along a rural road in Pennsylvania. The rain came down hard, and he couldn't see much past his hood. What was odd was how bright it was. In a rainstorm, it was generally dim, but what he saw before him was pure whiteness, as if he were driving through a big bale of cotton. This weather, they said on the radio, was a direct result of climate change from the bloating sun. Time was growing desperately short, and everybody was pinning their hopes on Guarneri.

He gripped the wheel—the wind wanted to blow the truck off the road. He was afraid he was going to run into something. The rain made his windshield opaque; his wipers couldn't cope. And the heat! He was stripped to his boxers, had the air conditioner on full, but was still dripping with sweat.

It took him another ten minutes before he reached Blossburg, Haydn's hometown. Buildings came into view as if through a white glaze. A drugstore. An auto garage. An animal medicine clinic. The local coal miners' office. A mall with box superstores. He proceeded into the older section of town. No one was about. With the convergence of three new hurricanes pummeling the East Coast, the first making landfall in Florida, the second in North Carolina, and the third—bizarrely, terrifyingly, and historically—in Connecticut, everyone was battening down.

He soon came to the Haydn residence. The blue spruce out front had blown over, and was angled across the walk. Cones lay scattered on the flooded grass, some floating in their own puddles. He parked the car at the end of the drive, reached for his jeans and T-shirt, pulled them on, then yanked on his cowboy boots. He could hardly get into them because they were so wet. He uttered a few dispirited obscenities, then got out of his truck.

He closed the door and headed off through the rain to the porch. He knocked on the door. The knocking sounded faint, overpowered by the roar of the wind and rain. So he rapped louder, and after a minute, a middle-aged woman came to the door.

She had on green denims, and a flower-print summer shirt with yellow daisies mixed with green garland. She was plump, and peered at him through thick glasses, her face flushed, the first three buttons of her blouse undone, her damp red skin just the other side of full perspiration.

"I'm Colonel Pittman," he called over the howl of the freakish weather. "I was Lieutenant Haydn's commanding officer on the Moon. I tried to call but the lines were down. I was with the lieutenant when he died."

It was as if at first she didn't register anything, for she just continued looking at him, her pale eyes blank, her face as still as a pond on a calm day. But then the corners of her lips turned downward slowly. Her eyes glistened with sudden moisture. She stared at him for several seconds, and he didn't know if it was because she knew about his unauthorized nuclear strike, its attendant consequences, and his subsequent discharge—all public knowledge, thanks to the media—or because she could sense, the way mothers could sense things about their children, that he had murdered her son.

"I'm Vivian Haydn, Gunther's mom." Her voice, though small, was deeper than expected, throaty but fragile. "It's just me and Joe now." She motioned toward the interior of the house, her hand limp, her wedding ring too tight around her finger, a mark from a missing watch indenting her fleshy wrist. "The kids are with their own families." Then she looked out at the weather and said, "We're all trying to make . . . peace with this."

He nodded. "Ma'am, I'll just take a moment of your time."

She made way for him and he stepped into the hall. He looked around. He saw framed photographs of children, three in all, the last showing a much younger Gunther, twelve or thirteen years old, blond brush cut, blue eyes, a smattering of freckles over the bridge of his nose, his shirt patterned with hick-town checks.

A young German shepherd came out of the kitchen, his claws clicking against the hardwood floor.

"This is Gun's dog," said Vivian. "Butch, say hello to the colonel."

The dog came up to him, friendly as could be, panting, and shoved his nose into Pittman's palms. "He didn't say he had a dog."

Pittman felt awkward as he patted Haydn's dog; it came back to him with poignant force, the monochromatic surface of the Moon, the sharp demarcation of gray ground and black sky, Haydn's suit foaming away with lime-green StopGap as the man went down face-forward. "Ma'am, he died bravely. I just want you to know that."

She shuddered nervously, her hands, seemingly of their own accord, rising, clasping, wringing, then freezing into a deformed and misshapen gesture of prayer. "Come into the kitchen, Colonel. Joe's in there."

He followed her down the hall into the kitchen. The windows had been boarded up. As there was no power, Joe sat at the kitchen table by the light of a few candles, working his way through a bowl of split pea soup and six crackers. He peered up from his lunch. He was many years older than Vivian, close to sixty, with grayish brown hair styled in a combover. His spoon was poised halfway to his lips.

Vivian said, "Joe, this is Colonel Pittman, from Orbops. He's done us the honor of paying a visit." She was speaking to her husband as if her husband had lost touch with reality.

And—oh God—it was terrifying, the change that came over Gunther's father, because he suddenly pushed out from his chair, stood to attention, and saluted Pittman with a hard but shaking hand. His jaw clenched, his lips tightened, and two seconds later, tears came to his eyes.

"Sir, it is indeed an honor to meet you. Gunther had nothing but the highest words of praise for you. You are a household name in Blossburg. And you did the right thing; don't let anybody tell you otherwise."

Pittman was momentarily confused. Did the right thing by shooting Gunther in the back? Then he realized Mr. Haydn meant the nuclear strike. "We were incommunicado and in dire straits, like my attorney told the media, and we had no choice."

Joe gestured to one of the kitchen chairs. "Please, Colonel, join us for lunch. Viv, if you want to get the colonel a bowl of soup."

"I can't stay long. I have to get to Philadelphia."

"Philadelphia?" The man said the city's name with a mixture of alarm and mystification, and he now inspected Pittman with bulging eyes that seemed to glow with quiet panic. "The military's not letting anybody in or out of Philadelphia."

The shrill quality in Joe's voice told Pittman he was a man who didn't handle calamity well. "I'm not anybody."

Joe stared at him a moment more, and his panic seemed to ebb as he absently brushed some cracker crumbs from his tie. Why a tie? Why now? It wasn't an attractive tie, brown and broad, with a stain on it. "No, I guess you're not." And then, more conversationally, added, "I think Gun mentioned you had family there."

"Yes."

In a more conspiratorial tone Joe asked, "You heard the casualty figures?"

As always, Pittman put on a brave front, even

though he was worried sick about his family. "I have."

The two men stared at each other solemnly. The silence lingered.

Vivian interrupted with an excess of nervous energy. "You sit yourself down, Colonel. Have some soup. It's not out of a can. I make it myself. We have a camp stove we're cooking on now. The power's been out awhile."

Pittman sat down. "Are you getting radio out here? I haven't heard any in my truck. I assume you have batteries."

Joe's nostrils flared, and his chin dipped, and he looked like a man who was considering the quality of goods at a flea market. "We're getting a little out of Pittsburgh from time to time." Then he looked up at the dim ceiling and out to the hall. "But not since these storms have blown in."

At the counter, Vivian ladled soup into a bowl. Pittman felt suddenly hungry, the overpowering need for food asserting itself for the first time since Iowa.

"And what have you heard? Anything more about the Guarneri mission?" Because that was everybody's obsession these days, the last great hope, a flotilla of flimsy spacecraft out by Venus trying to save the world at the last minute.

Joe peered at his wife. "Viv, what were they saying about that the other night?"

Vivian fiddled with crackers. "It's all in place and ready to go."

"And then that other thing . . . what was that other thing they were talking about?"

"I don't know, Joe. I don't know what you mean."

A trace of irritation appeared on Joe's face. "You know . . . that thing they were talking about."

Vivian let her hands drop to the counter in sudden frustration, her eyes closing briefly as if at the pinch of a migraine, accidentally knocking a cracker to the floor. "Joe, they were talking about many things. I don't know what particular thing you mean."

Butch walked over and ate the cracker off the floor.

"That thing about the atmosphere."

"The cold trap?"

"Yes, the cold trap." Then, with some sullenness, he asked, "Was that so hard to remember?"

"What's the cold trap?" asked Pittman.

Joe leaned forward. "Part of the atmosphere." He pointed to the ceiling. "Way up there. Any water vapor trying to escape the atmosphere turns to ice and drifts back down to Earth once it hits the cold trap. They say we need that cold trap. Without that cold trap, all our water will evaporate and drift off into space." He leaned back in his chair and put his hands flat on the table, looking as if he were the sole possessor of a mystical knowledge. "But now it's gotten so hot, it's not a cold trap anymore. It's not a trap at all. It's not stopping our water from drifting off. They say millions of gallons are being burnt off every day. It's the first step in the boiling of the oceans." He pointed to the ceiling again. "This Guarneri thing they have floating out by Venus . . . I don't know what good it is." His brow settled cantankerously. "And the last thing we should have done was gotten the Chinese involved."

Vivian put his soup in front of him. "Joe, let's not

talk politics. I have every confidence President Langdon is going to fix the problem."

Joe's face creased with mounting irritation. "Langdon's nothing but a big-money patsy."

After this cynical pronouncement, the kitchen fell silent. Vivian joined them. Pittman ate.

He listened to the rain outside. A big crash came from the backyard, and all three looked up. They then went back to eating soup. Butch settled on the carpet by the mudroom.

Pittman couldn't help thinking this had once been a big boisterous family home—just like his own place in Philadelphia—and now it was all gone. Here was Vivian, overweight and halfway through middle age; and Joe, a fussy old tyrant who was plagued by his own forgetfulness. And now the two of them had nothing left to believe in. He decided it was time to give the Haydns something to believe in again.

He started without preamble, his voice soft but firm.

"We'd just reached our objective." He gave them a brief description of the scene, the way the tower leaned like the Leaning Tower of Pisa. "Not right. Unnatural. With no regard for gravity. These aliens, they're stranger than anything you can imagine." He described for them the rise in temperature inside Moonstone 32, and how distress calls came in from the other operational units, and how they had been forced to bail. He sketched in for them Moonstone 32's astonishing end. "Just melted, then froze up, like someone stepping on a bug, then letting it dry in the sun." All that time he heard the low thrum in his ears; the same low thrum Haydn always heard.

Going completely off topic, he asked, "Gunther ever complain of any ear problems?"

Joe and Vivian looked at each other.

"He had the tinnitus something awful," said Vivian. "We took him to doctors but they never figured it out, not even the ones in Philadelphia."

Pittman considered the thrumming again. Was it guilt whispering in his ear? Or were the Builders trying to talk to him again?

He dismissed the phantom physical ailment and continued his story. "We were running away from the tower because we were afraid it might launch further attacks against us. Newlove didn't make it out fast enough. He burst into flames. Your son and I headed for this small crater, seeking cover. I made it there first. I was trying to figure out what we were going to do. I realized immediately that we had an air problem. We had to walk back to Gettysburg because our Moonstone was gone. I'd left some Moonstones at Gettysburg for rescue response, but I couldn't get in touch with Gettysburg because radiation from the Bleed was hampering our signal. As it turned out, all the Moonstones there had been destroyed anyway, so we were on our own. I decided that somebody had to get back to Gettysburg so we could launch our nuclear assault at Alpha Vehicle. It was the only chance we had."

He began to feel the insufferable heat and humidity again. Also extremely uncomfortable about the lie he was about to tell. He addressed Joe directly.

"And that was when your son volunteered to give me his air, sir. I said I didn't want it, that I couldn't take it, even though I realized that the only way we could realistically continue the mission was to have the commanding officer get back to Gettysburg. But before I could argue further with him, he used his med-pak and injected a lethal dose of morphine into his body. I stayed with him right to the end. He wanted me to give you the message that he loved you. He was a soldier's soldier. He knew and understood the importance of our mission. I disconnected his oxygen only when he stopped breathing. You have to understand that there was nothing I could have done to save him. The last thing I wanted was his death. He was a fine young man. And he died in the most honorable way any man can die, serving his country. I'll always remember him. And we should all honor him."

Both parents, having stopped eating several moments ago, now grew still. Vivian spoke first. "So . . . you took his air?"

Vivian's eyes had widened a fraction. Joe's jaw was moving ever so slightly from side to side. Candlelight brightened their faces from below.

"By the time I did, he was already dead. I wouldn't have taken it otherwise."

Both parents remained still for several more seconds, staring at him. And it dawned on him that they knew Gunther far better than he did, understood what he would do in a situation like that, and what he wouldn't do. The look in their eyes told him that something wasn't jibing for either of them. They knew he wasn't telling the truth. Truth. Deception. And the notion that maybe he had done some bad things in his life after all.

Vivian finally spoke again. "And did he suffer?"

He now felt relieved. At least he could offer a few comforting medical facts. "Opiate overdose is one of the most comfortable ways to go. The central nervous system shuts down quietly, and as you can imagine, there's absolutely no pain. Once his biomonitors told me he had gone into respiratory arrest, I disconnected his oxygen. The United States Marine Corps offers its sincere condolences. I made a monument for him. The thing about a monument on the Moon, it's going to last forever. There's no weather up there, so nothing's going to wear it down. I know we can't bring him back, and I'm deeply sorry for his death, but please understand, your son made a brave decision. The Corps will be contacting you about the various medals and citations he will receive."

Vivian shook her head. "It doesn't sound like Gun. He's not the kind to give up without a fight."

When he was back in his truck heading toward Philadelphia, he felt the burden of his guilt greatly. It was true. He was a destroyer. It was as if the Builders had held up a mirror, and were now asking him for atonement.

28

Dr. Ochoa held a large syringelike instrument close to Mark's head, one of the tools Fye had in his bag of tricks. Cam floated next to the wall-mounted cot as Ochoa inserted the instrument into Mark's left nostril. Mark lay strapped in place, eyes partially open but insensible. Looking into Mark's eyes, Cam couldn't help thinking of his father's eyes after the stroke, like burnt-out lightbulbs.

Fye floated above them, head angled, legs drifting, elfin in his chubbiness. Cam glanced toward the hub. Blake and Lewis stood guard at the surgery hatch. Lesha was next to Cam, her hand resting on his shoulder.

Ochoa depressed the instrument's trigger. The instrument made a slight hiss, like pneumatic brakes letting out air, and Mark's face scrunched, not in pain, but as if an insect had flown up his nose.

Ochoa turned to Cam. "The nanogens need a little time to adjust to the new medium."

"And what's the new medium?" asked Cam.

Ochoa's eyes narrowed. "Brain tissue."

They waited.

After five minutes, Ochoa took a large needle and administered epinephrine directly to Mark's heart. Mark's back arched, his eyes went wide, his teeth clenched, and the corners of his lips curved downward in a spasm. He inhaled with a jerk, his breath scratching against his dry throat like fingernails against the skin of a tambourine. A semblance of sensibility came to his eyes, and he turned to Cam.

"What happened?"

It took them a while to explain things to Mark, and at first, as the nanogens went to work, rearranging his brain, he had a hard time putting it together. The blankness in his eyes, combined with a hint of perplexed alarm, told everybody the young scientist didn't remember much, had no knowledge of his midnight forays to Cremona, and couldn't recall one speck of code he had typed into the Guarneri nodes.

John Quang floated past the hatch, his flat Asian face illuminated to a pale shade of indigo by the violet guide lights. Blake told him to go away. Quang, not looking surprised, just nervous, mumbled an apology in the perfect English so many PRNCers spoke. This apology seemed to irritate Blake, for he feinted at the observer, as if he meant to hit him, and Quang maneuvered away, instinctively trying to swim, frog kicks with his legs, dog paddles with his hands—but stayed in one place until he latched on to a handhold and pulled himself up.

Fye reached into his kit and withdrew something else: an epipen-style injection device such as one might use on oneself during a severe allergic reaction.

"What I have here, Mark," he said, holding the instrument up, "is a form of scopolamine. It's going to help you remember what the implant told you. I'm sure you understand we have some hard choices to make. We don't know what you've put into the nodes, they're so well hidden, but they might compromise the whole mission. If we were to activate the anti-Ostrander field—and we have to activate it sooner or later or we're going to lose our chance—we might damage it in some unforeseen way, perhaps sabotage it completely, thanks to the new language you've backgrounded into it. So that means we've got to find and deactivate the code you've entered before we can proceed safely."

Fye gazed at the unit affectionately. "As I say, we have scopolamine in here. We also have some good old-fashioned LSD. There's nothing like LSD to unlock the mind. And of course at VIP-Med, nanogens are all the rage, so we've got some of those, too. These nanogens are going to search out deep memory. Stuff that's right in your subconscious. We just want you to talk, Mark, that's all. And type. We've hooked up this keyboard, and anything you remember you can type in here. It'll download immediately into a segregated file of Guarneri, ready for upload when Dr. Conrad has cleared it. Do you think you can do this, Mark? Everybody back home is really counting on you. The sun goes red giant if you don't help us."

Mark gazed at Fye with his lower lip drawn so that his bottom row of teeth showed, looking like a man who had just been asked to jump out of an airplane. He nodded but the nod was fretful, and tiny in its range of movement, a spasm of the neck that made Mark's cranium duck a few times.

Then Fye handed the unit to Ochoa and the doctor injected the VIP-Med cocktail of relaxants, hallucinogens, and nanogens into Mark's arm.

Now another veil came over Mark's eyes, a deeper, more meditative one, softening the jangle of razor-edged adrenaline that had been crawling around the periphery of his pupils after the epinephrine. He grew less agitated, and as this artificial calmness spread through his body, he turned to Cam, as if hoping Cam would get him out of the surgery.

Fye made a general announcement. "If we could clear the surgery." Because they had spoken about this, too, how the "need-to-know" rule had come to roost, and how it was important that the Chinese find out as little as possible about what was going on.

All nonessential personnel drifted away.

Once they were gone, Fye said to Cam and Ochoa, "That John Quang. Not his real name at all. Wouldn't you know it."

As Mark slipped more deeply into a dream zone, the submerged part of his brain started to remember the implant's previously transmitted instructions.

Over the course of the next couple of hours, Cam and Mark went systematically through Guarneri node 1. It reminded Cam of strip-mining for iron, having to take huge truckloads of ore to a processing plant, then sending it through the separator, only to come up with a proportionately smaller nugget of useful information. Often, the code that Mark typed seemed to be mixed, or have nothing at all to do with Guarneri, and they had to straighten it out, re-

write, polish, and test until the system-read gave
them a green light and a correlate.

During this time, Fye disappeared for an hour and
a half, then came back to check on progress.
"Anything?"

Cam sighed as his lips came together. "Take a
thousand shredded documents. Then laboriously
tape all the documents back together. If you get it
wrong, you have to start over. That's a lot of taping.
And, Oren, I don't think we have the time if it's just
me and Mark. Vet a few more of my people."

Fye's lips pursed. "Have you gotten *anything*
useful?"

"So far, it's just a lot of encrypted transmit code
with special boost capability to get it through the
radiation." He motioned toward the hull. "They've
got something out there, a stealth-capable orbiting
communications relay using the same new pierce design, and it's fairly close by."

"So they're sending all our plans back home." Fye
shook his head. "I knew that pierce design shouldn't
have been a joint venture. Is it still sending?"

"Not now that I have a lock on it."

"So in other words, they can't compromise us
more than they already have."

"Yes, but that's not the point."

"And the point is?"

"We're running out of time."

Fye considered this with raised eyebrows. "So just
go ahead and start Guarneri up?"

Cam's brow creased. "We can't do that."

"Why not?"

"Because I've found a number of suffixes in seven

backgrounded lines that indicate a sabotage program, as we suspected. It's extremely easy to blow something like the Guarneri array sky-high. We're dealing with subatomic reactions here. If it's not controlled precisely, any of the arrays could turn back on themselves and self-destruct. I'm seeing suffixes that tell me the Chinese, once they've finished with their transmits, intend to destroy Guarneri. It's as if those elements in the PRNC that are still loyal to Po Pin-Yen don't understand the danger we all face."

Fye studied the screen. "They don't want us to get the upper hand once and for all. And with Builder technology we would." The large man turned to Cam, and in a philosophical tone said, "The PRNC War is still going on, Dr. Conrad, even in spite of the overthrow. It's just going on in a different way. And they're good. They're a formidable and worthy adversary. Do you know how many times we checked John Quang? And since you broke this whole thing open, you can't imagine how much manpower we've put into getting new information on him. We've lost several good agents. But it's been worth it. We even got a nugget or two on Loftus Hua. They don't know it yet, but they're both scheduled for VIP-Med treatment as well."

Cam nodded, now accepting that he was a soldier in all this. "In the meantime, we've got to find a way to further penetrate this program and disarm it. I'm focusing specifically on the destruct program, but it's like eking information out of thin air. Given enough time, I think Mark will ante up. You've got enough medication?"

"Yes."

"And I'm going to need more people."

"Who do you want?"

"We'll start with Lesha Weeks. If I can't do it with her, I'm going to have to include Blaine Berkheimer. Meanwhile, I think you should make it known to the president that he's got to get in diplomatic contact with elements of the old Po Pin-Yen regime and tell them that what they're doing is suicidal."

Fye shook his head, as if Cam were woefully unschooled in the ways of the world. "It's not going to happen, Dr. Conrad. If Po Pin-Yen doesn't get his way, he doesn't give a damn if the sun goes red giant."

After eight hours, they moved Mark to the dormitory for a rest. Cam's thoughts dwelled on the Builders.

Did they sleep? Did they eat? Did they breathe? Bleed? Or reproduce? Were they pure energy, or pure information, so many zeros and ones constructed in a massive array that spanned NGC4945?

"I sometimes wonder if they might be white holes," he told Lesha as they maneuvered an exhausted and only partially conscious Mark down the hub.

"White holes? Cam, white holes are theoretical. They're mathematical doodling."

"Just because we've never detected one doesn't mean they don't exist. Look at it this way. Black holes suck in all matter and energy. White holes do exactly the opposite, according to the theoretical models. They *produce* matter and energy. They are the gods of the galaxy. Look at Alpha Vehicle. It reflected all light. It had a gravitational *push*. It produced all those Moon towers, and the Moon towers then went on to produce energy cells. Matter. Energy. Positive outflow."

"So you think Alpha Vehicle is a white hole?"

"It's not beyond the realm of possibility."

It was while they were maneuvering Mark into the access chute of the dormitory that Cam noticed a small spot of blood a centimeter across near the young scientist's carotid artery. It reminded him of the red dot artists put beside their paintings when they make a sale. The spot of blood quickly widened, and a second later, Cam realized a weapon had been used.

He swung around and looked up the hub, but didn't see anyone. He swung back around in time to watch globules of blood float from Mark's neck. He watched helplessly as the spot widened into a hole, then a gash, and finally into a gaping wound.

An explosion of blood splashed into the weightlessness of the hub, and automated spill-mites emerged from the recessed spots along the wall, a swarm of two or three hundred turquoise units that swirled through the spray, gobbling every last bit of it. Lesha cried out. Mark had an odd lurching seizure. Cam put his hand over the wound, like the Dutch boy and the dike, trying to get it to stop. But the wound kept widening, and finally his hand fit right in.

By the time the grisly episode was over, and there were only a few spill-mites circling around, and Fye was rushing toward the scene from Cremona, his corpulent frame reminding Cam of a beluga whale, it was too late. Mark's head dangled by only its spinal cord and a few threads of flesh.

29

Outside New Hanover, Pittman saw something flopping on the road. He pulled over to investigate.

He got out and, making sure he had his gun ready, walked around the hood to have a look.

It turned out to be a seagull. He knelt next to the creature. It couldn't fly away, nor even walk away. It was missing a lot of feathers, had a festering sore on top of its head, and was bleeding from its mouth. After a short hobble, it squatted and looked up at him, scared, breathing fast. The webbing between its toes was coming apart. It started to choke, and during this spasm, it coughed up bloody tissue. Pittman sighed. He knew the seagull suffered from radiation sickness, and had most probably flown up from Philadelphia, where the levels from the bomb blast had to still be fairly intense.

Rather than waste a bullet, he wrung the creature's neck. In doing so, he couldn't help thinking of Haydn.

On the outskirts of Philadelphia, the rain-filled gutters ran with white residue—nuclear fallout. A lot of roofs were missing. He opened his window. The smell of dead bodies—a smell he remembered well from operations during the PRNC War—was enough to gag.

River Road wasn't more than a couple hundred meters from the Schuylkill River. He found a small business—a neon sign place. The big gate was chained and padlocked. He didn't let the gate stop him. He bashed through it with his truck. He drove across the gravel parking lot to the shipping yard and soon came to the water's edge.

He stepped onto the lot, walked around to the back of the truck, got his raft out, and took it down to the riverbank.

He saw a few dead bodies float by. He pulled the dinghy out of its sack and laid it on a small muddy part, where a couple of dead birds had washed up. The stench of the river was horrendous. He went back to his truck, got the paddles, his knapsack full of supplies, and a box of extra ammo, then returned to the water's edge. He pulled the dinghy's rip cord and the raft inflated.

He pushed the dinghy into the river, walking in up to his knees, certain the water was full of disease by now. He jumped into the raft and paddled farther out to the middle.

After a while, he drifted under the archways of the old Manayunk commuter rail bridge, and once he got past it, the destruction to the city became more apparent.

Houses and buildings had been flattened, and numerous cars and other vehicles lay toppled or gutted up on the road, the charred scent of melted automobile upholstery reaching him all the way down here on the river.

As he reached Market Street a while later, he finally got a glimpse of the downtown skyline, or at least what was left of it. Many of the tall buildings were gone. Yet oddly, some had been spared, as if by the chance of their design and position they had miraculously withstood the blast. Many of the remaining buildings looked badly gutted by fire. One was severed halfway up. Another had been shorn of its outer layer of glass so that all he saw were the girders underneath. Warehouses and factories along the river's edge had been flattened.

He didn't want to look at it. It told him Sheila, Becky, and Tom must have had little chance.

He maneuvered around the great lumps of concrete, steel, and asphalt that made little islands in the Schuylkill. He understood the chain of events clearly, and knew that this rubble, now piled in the river, had once been Philadelphia, and was here as a direct result of his decision to launch a nuclear strike against Alpha Vehicle. The farther along he got, the more clogged the river became.

It took him close to an hour to get to Philadelphia's south end, his old neighborhood, built on the former site of the Philadelphia Gas Works, not far from the General Frank Ibert Building, where he had worked for many years developing orbital warfare strategies. He felt weak as he paddled the dinghy toward shore. Was this radiation sickness from his ground-zero excursion in Crater Cavalet getting the better of him again, or was this simply the novel regret he felt—unusual in a warrior like himself—for having caused all this destruction?

He placed his boot in a muddy flat next to the river's edge, and it sank up to his heel, not in mud, but in wet ashes. Three dead bodies floated next to what looked like a melted piece of pink insulation.

He walked up the riverbank into the neighborhoods. He took heart. While many buildings had been destroyed, others remained standing, sticking out of the rubble like gappy teeth. All the street signs had disappeared. This particular subdivision, until ten years ago bulldozed rubble from the Philadelphia Gas Works, was rubble once more. All the debris was soaking, and gray ashy water flooded large portions of the neighborhood.

It took him most of the afternoon to find Tiago Avenue, where Sheila and the kids lived. He finally found it by recognizing a part of the Tiago Park Clubhouse, where all the local moms took their kids to day care. The clubhouse had only its foundation left, and part of its west wall. He walked south on Tiago for three blocks until he came to Delmar Street, or at least what he thought was Delmar. He stopped and surveyed the last two blocks of Tiago. His heart beat with hope because a number of the houses at this end were still standing.

As he traversed the final two blocks, his pace quickened, and his eyes focused through the gloom on what he thought for sure was number 19.

While the second floor had caved in, the first floor stood intact. He walked up the drive. A car he didn't recognize was half-backed out of the garage. The garage had toppled on top of it. Debris cluttered the driveway, in some cases a half meter deep.

He walked to the side door. He pulled it open and ash shook loose. He tried the inside door but it was locked. He found a brick and smashed the window. He reached inside and turned the latch. He had to shove because debris blocked the door on the inside. At last he got it open.

"Sheila?"

The house was quiet and smelled of furniture rotting in the damp. Steps led to the basement on the right, and he saw that the basement was full of water. The steps immediately before him led to the first floor. He climbed. He tried the light at the top of the stairs but it didn't go on. He picked his way through debris to the kitchen. The cupboards were open and all the food had been looted. Water trickled through the ceiling, and the plaster up there sagged.

"Kids?"

He went through the kitchen into the vestibule, then the living room where he picked through yet more debris. The entertainment unit had been pushed over. He saw Tom's junior league baseball trophy, lifted it, and brushed all the dirt off. He finally got an inkling of how Joe Haydn must feel about Gunther.

He put the trophy down and walked into the dining room.

The silver had been left untouched, as if in this age of the looming red giant, silver no longer mattered.

He went back into the hall and ventured to the den.

Sheila's sewing machine lay toppled on its side.

Becky, an archery enthusiast, had taken her longbow—or at least someone had—but her target equipment and a quiver of arrows had been left in the corner.

He sniffed the air. It had a faint electrical smell but otherwise didn't reek of dead bodies. He took that as a good sign.

He learned from survivors that military officials had turned the Museum of Art into a morgue and triage center, so that's where he went to look for his family.

As he reached the top step, he gazed out at the grounds. Soldiers dug various mass graves, not only in the space out front, but farther away, in Eakins Oval. He was sad to see that in Eakins Oval the statue of George Washington had been blown on its side. Bodies were sheathed in black plastic body bags, the polymer laced with chemicals to stop the spread of disease, and to contain the smell. The rain slanted down, and it was bathwater warm. He felt faint, nauseated, and knew that the radiation was starting to take its toll.

Inside the museum's grand front foyer, a military triage unit had established phalanxes of waferscreens on trestle tables. He waited in line to use one. Those in front keyed in particulars, and some were offered a chit while others were turned away. The emergency lighting did little to dispel the gloom. People looked hungry and dispirited.

Pittman finally got to a terminal and filled in the fields, starting first with his children. His body sagged as he saw on the waferscreen that they were both marked deceased, Becky a DOA, and Tom succumbing to massive internal hemorrhaging shortly after arrival. He could have cried but he didn't. It was as if the Builders had dried the capacity for tears right out of him.

Sheila was a different story. She was marked in critical condition. Her location was gallery 161. He wasn't much of an art lover, and didn't know the museum that well. He accessed the floor plan and saw that gallery 161 was to his right. He took his chit and headed that way.

He had to go through a number of other galleries, and they were full of sick people lying on the floor, with too few nurses and doctors going from one to the other. He wasn't sure what they were doing about sanitation because the whole place stunk of human waste.

At last he came to gallery 161, and it was large and spacious, and hexagonal in shape. He presented his chit to one of the military clerks, and the clerk, struggling in his radiation suit, and doing ten things at once, waved to the west side of the gallery. "She's over there. Bed sixteen. Under the van Gogh."

He walked over and found his ex-wife lying under a blanket on a bedroll. Hanging above her was a painting he actually recognized, Vincent van Gogh's *Sunflowers*. It hung inside a protective case. No one was looking at it.

Her head was bandaged and he saw only her right eye and mouth. The skin around both was blistery, scorched, and red. She looked at him with her one uncovered eye, but didn't seem to recognize him.

"Doctor?"

He sighed. "No, Sheila. It's me. Tim."

She grew agitated. "Tim?"

"The thing tells me the kids are dead." And he didn't mean to make it sound as if he were blaming her, but maybe he did, just a little, even though in his heart of hearts he knew he was the one to blame.

Tears brimmed in her one good eye. "Oh, Tim, I'm so sorry."

"Were you in the house when it happened?"

"No." She reached up. "I can't see anything. You're all blurry. Could you find a doctor? This pain is bad."

"Where were you?"

"You mean when the bomb hit?"

"Yes."

Her lips quivered and her hand sank to her chest. "We were on our way to Lincoln Field to see the Eagles. We were just exiting the expressway, and it hit, and the car went dead. It was so bright. I couldn't see a damn thing. Like a flashbulb. My eyes stung, and I thought at first it might be this sun thing that's going on." In a more quavering voice, she asked, "We're going to be all right with that, aren't we? This Guarneri thing's going to fix the problem, isn't it?"

He didn't think his ex-wife was going to live long and so told her a lie. "I've learned through some of my contacts that Guarneri's been a success." He paused. "So . . . the kids."

She nodded woefully and her tears came more quickly. "After all the brightness disappeared, I saw it. I wouldn't exactly call it a mushroom cloud, more like a huge white wave of fire and debris, and after that, the car was pushed right off the expressway into Roosevelt Park, along with a lot of other cars. We were trapped there. I got burned all over my face. It took about two days for someone to come, and by that time . . ." She got choked up. For several seconds, she couldn't go on. "By that time, Becky was dead. They put me and Tommy on this big military truck with a lot of other injured people, and it took us about eight hours to get to the museum because all the debris blocked the roads. Tommy lasted another day." Her face creased in anguish. "Then my poor baby died."

Pittman sat with Sheila through the night, scarcely able to believe that he had personally been responsible for the deaths of his children. His eyes clouded with tears for a while, as if the Builders had decided to give him back the ability to cry after all. But then a blue light seemed to envelop everything around him, and he knew the Builders were with him; he felt not a peace, such as Dr. Conrad had described, but a resignation. It felt like the dark side of the yin-yang symbol. Then the visitation passed. And he once again found himself waiting for her to die.

She died early in the morning.

He went back to the river to get his dinghy.

He paddled upstream much of the night until, at dawn, he came to the abandoned neon sign factory.

His truck was still there.

He got in his truck and started heading west.

Back to the desert.

Back to face the coming red giant by himself.

30

A day later, with Mark's body now commended to deep space, Cam sat at Station A in Cremona going over the scraps of code the late junior scientist had dredged from the subconscious reservoirs of his mind. Cam wasn't a forensic software specialist, but he certainly felt like one, gluing together bits of language the way an archaeologist might reconstruct a shattered Grecian urn.

Parts of the language in three less infected nodes might be reversed, he decided, and when he mentioned this to Lesha, who was sitting next to him going over her own bits of recovered language, her delicate brow rose, and for the first time since Mark's murder, he saw hope in her aquamarine eyes.

He pointed. "I've isolated this strand, and by breaking it down, I've managed to sever the command sequence so the bit can't pass on instructions to node four. But there's got to be a faster way. Some of what I'm seeing tells me there's a master key, a mechanism that will throw the tumblers all at once and get the code to retreat from Guarneri in a piece.

If we can isolate that mechanism, we can go ahead with the sequenced acceleration and define our anti-Ostrander region. If that happens, the hydrogen flow reverses—at least enough so that the Builders might take notice."

Some of the hope faded from her eyes. It was a long shot. At the same time, it was better than no shot at all.

He glanced over her shoulder where tethered beyond the science bay's large polycarbonate dome he saw the survival modules, now turned into holding cells. They were secured by life support umbilicals, and acted as improvised brigs for the Chinese observer staff. The white lozenge-shaped objects drifted twenty-five meters behind them; one was upright, and Cam saw Foster Chong staring at them from across the void. He knew Foster was an excellent scientist, and loyal to the new regime, a man who was trying to do good in his life; but they couldn't take any chances.

Lesha asked, "So how much time do we realistically have?"

Cam turned from Foster and stared at the code. "Forty-eight hours would be pushing it."

"So if we had this hypothetical master key . . ." She glanced toward the hub access bay. "I wonder what's taking Oren?"

"He's extremely thorough when it comes to his work."

"I hate to say this, but I'm glad he's here."

"Yet will the Builders judge us harshly?"

"You talk of the Builders as if they're gods."

"Define God."

A short while later, Fye appeared at the hub access hatch. "He's been sufficiently softened, Dr. Conrad."

Cam glanced at Lesha. How he hated this. It wasn't supposed to be like this at all. It was supposed to be a reaching out between two galaxies, not one long sad comment on the barbarity, stupidity, and short-sightedness of humankind. And yet he would *not* give up.

He unstrapped himself and drifted free of his stool. Lesha did the same. He remembered the music. Sweet. Sighing. Tender. Compassionate. Positive. And if the Builders could make music like that, tried to communicate with harmony and melody of such mystical caliber, then they must be capable of for-giveness.

He pulled himself over. Fye's face was set, had a fleck of blood on it. Violence? Sure, why not? After Mark's near decapitation by a vicious little PRNC macrogen, what was to stop the emotions from boil-ing over? This had nothing to do with the beauty and sublimity of First Contact. This was all about war.

The three went to the surgery.

John Quang lay strapped to one of the hinged-down gurneys. His face had been badly beaten and his left eye was swollen shut. In his other eye—a haze. He was in the half sleep of Fye's insidious truth cocktail. As Cam floated up to him, Quang lifted his chin. Lesha hovered in the background. Ochoa looked on from his workstation.

Quang was a middle-aged Chinese man with broad flat cheeks, a strong chin, and small rosebud lips. His scalp, shaved bald at the beginning of the voyage, had now developed a blue-black stubble. Cam had to wonder what drove a man like Quang. Why jockey for position in a politburo that had seen its day? Did Quang truly believe that despite his reckless course of action he could save the day for Po Pin-Yen? Or was he ultimately afraid of what Po Pin-Yen might do to his family?

And, speaking of family . . .

"Lieutenant Colonel Fye tells me we've located your wife and children in Beijing, Dr. Quang. We're holding them in a safe house. Pearl, May, and Kingsley—we have them all."

Quang's good eye widened as Cam listed family names.

"We have our own implants," continued Cam. "And these particular implants are set to eat brain tissue. Slowly. Over the course of a few days. So that as the sun bloats like an infected pustule thanks to the misguided attempts of Po Pin-Yen, as well as the monopolizing efforts of my own government . . ." Fye put a restraining hand on his shoulder. Cam glanced over. Fye gave his head a covert shake. But Cam was beyond caring. "Thanks to your own deposed regime, and the grasping and nearsighted strategies of the Langdon Administration, as the sun bloats, these implants will make a leisurely dinner of your family's cerebral tissue. They'll suffer horribly."

He sat back and contemplated Quang.

"I've just made an interesting discovery, John, only I don't know how to go about utilizing it. I hope you have the good sense to help me with that. If you don't, your family dies. I'm sorry about this. I apologize for using this kind of barbaric coercion on you, and I don't condone it at all. I'm a scientist. I've never understood political violence. But what I *do* understand is that this corrupting code Mark's entered into the Guarneri nodes can be reversed using a tumbler mechanism. This tumbler mechanism can break strategic information links with a single turn. I'm not sure if it works on a node-by-node basis, or if you can turn all the nodes at once. Let's find out. Here's the keyboard, John. Help us. You can still be a hero in all this."

Cam and Quang stared at each other for several seconds. He saw fear in Quang's one good eye. It seemed as if Quang was questioning everything he had ever done in his life, had reached that moral crossroads where it wasn't enough simply to follow orders, and to bolster the old dogma no matter what the cost; he had reached that threshold where he had to think for himself.

"And my family?" The Pin-Yen agent's voice was raspy with emotion.

"You can save them," said Cam. "Isn't that right, Lieutenant Colonel?"

Fye nodded. "Dr. Conrad's right, John. It's all up to you."

Quang turned away. "Dr. Fuller's implant malfunctioned."

Cam nodded. "We suspected as much."

"Its stealth element failed. Dr. Fuller was never meant to get caught."

Cam thought of his own unusual prescience. "What about the background language?"

Quang shook his head. "You Americans, you're all alike."

"John, you've been taught to think that way all your life."

"America suffers in the chains of its own political ideology."

"None of that's going to matter if you don't disable the sabotage codes and make Guarneri operational. Don't you realize that this is your last chance? Politics has nothing to do with it. We've measured the rate of change in the sun. It's documented. You've seen it. Time is running out."

But Quang insisted. "We have our own modules in place. It won't take our technicians long to modify them. We'll make First Contact."

"I don't think so. I've checked the log. Mark wasn't able to send half of what your people need before I stopped him. And has it ever occurred to you that the Builders wanted me to stop him? The old PRNC regime hasn't got a chance. None of us do. Not unless you enter this tumbler language."

"I'm sorry. I can't do that."

Cam turned toward Fye. Fye took another needle from his bag and jabbed it into Quang's arm. Quang went all rubbery. Then Fye took out a combat knife and unexpectedly stabbed Quang through the fleshy part of his thigh. Quang jerked upward, his face scrunching in agony as the spill-mites came out of the walls again and fed on his blood. Cam felt nauseated. Lesha groaned behind him. Ochoa watched impassively, as if he had seen a lot of this kind of thing as a doctor for VIP-Med.

Fye reached for a floating waferscreen, pulled it in front of the Chinese, and tapped it to life.

A small living room in Beijing. A woman, boy, and

girl—tied to chairs. Fye spoke at the waferscreen. It took a while because of the transmission distance, and because the new pierce array had to reassemble the radiation-fractured signal, but soon, American operatives cut the boy's ear off, then the girl's, then two of the woman's fingers. Lesha left. Cam wanted to leave but knew he couldn't.

John Quang looked at the screen in alarm. His shoulders sagged and he nodded. "Give me the keyboard. They have to be unlocked one node at a time. It might take a while."

Fye pulled the keyboard from the wall and shifted the gurney into a sitting position. He moved the waferscreen out of the way and unhinged the input monitor so that Quang could see it clearly. Cam maneuvered around to follow the PRNC operative's work.

Because Quang was so drugged, and weak from blood loss, he made a number of mistakes, but he always corrected things. He worked first on node 5, shifting back and forth from normal script, to superscript, to mathematical script.

Over the next half hour, Quang unlocked node 5. He also helped untangle a lot of node 1. Cam believed that he might yet succeed. But then Quang hesitated. He glanced up at the floating waferscreen, then at Fye, and finally at Cam, and seemed to have an epiphany of sorts.

Cam felt his uncanny prescience again. "He's going to try something."

Before any of them could reach Quang, Cam saw the operative's tongue shift in his mouth and dislodge something from behind his molar. A second later, Fye grabbed Cam and pulled him to the access chute along the surgery floor. Ochoa dove too.

A second after that, he heard a small detonation.

He looked up. Blood floated everywhere. Also brain tissue.

The spill-mites swarmed with renewed vigor.

31

Loftus Hua pledged cooperation the instant Fye showed him the linkups to his own family. As the Chinese second-in-command lay there strapped to the gurney, tears collected in his eyes, then floated free. His family moaned on the waferscreen. Cam glanced at Fye, then at Ochoa.

Ochoa leaned forward and administered a shot of something. "To steady his nerves and focus his concentration."

A few minutes later, Hua—short, chubby, with cherubic features—settled and asked Cam where he wanted to begin.

"We're going to work on the tumbler software hampering node four. Here are the schematics from the node one and five tumblers. I know you're not as well versed in the system as John was, but John's already helped us with these, so you might get some ideas from what he's done."

In spirit and inspiration, the node 4 tumbler mechanism was similar to the mechanisms in nodes 1 and

5. In other words, it was a key. But all keys were cut differently, and the difficulty lay in the details.

Fye got tired—Ochoa had been keeping him up on special drugs for the last seventy-two hours—and, as the situation now seemed stable, the Orbops man went to the dorm for some much-needed sleep.

Ochoa, too, went to rest.

Blaine and Lewis stayed with Cam, acting as guards.

Lesha came in for a while. "We just got another communication from Blunt. Earth's meteorological systems are experiencing further heat-related hyperactivity. The oceans are awash in hurricanes. Five in the Atlantic, and eleven in the Pacific. Shipping has been halted. All air traffic has been grounded. There have been catastrophic temperature rises in Brazil. It's reached sixty-two degrees Celsius in Rio de Janeiro, and that's in the shade. People down there are doing anything they can to get away, and we're now faced with a massive refugee problem. The ice caps are melting at an alarming rate, and there's been significant flooding along all coasts. Langdon and his advisers have left Camp David and are now in their underground bunker in New Mexico."

Cam now felt the burden he carried more than ever, but tried to stay focused on the task at hand. There was no use in panicking. He needed a clear head.

He and Hua worked all day and finally managed to get node 4 untangled. Ochoa gave them both a stimulant, and they worked through the night.

By morning, node 4 tumbled over, and they were starting to get the hang of it.

At that point they had a short rest, waking up two hours later to begin work on node 3. But node 3 seemed to be derived from a different plan altogether, and they got no further than two sequences when Cam said, "I'm lost."

Hua kept going. "I recognize some of it."

So the PRNC agent continued, and Cam was sure he was going to succeed.

The short, chubby Asian was just deciphering the last strand when he began to shake. His chin went back, his eyes rolled into his head, and his eyelids quivered. Hua's hands jerked away from the keyboard. Cam saw the code on the screen tangle itself up again. He lurched forward and tried to stop the code from reinstalling itself, but there was nothing he could do; he simply wasn't familiar enough with this particular design to arrest what was happening to the Guarneri software.

Hua, meanwhile, went into further convulsions. He finally started choking.

Out in the hub, the alarm pinged. Cam maneuvered to the hatchway and looked at the security console. The screen had defaulted to three views of the survival pod interiors, where the rest of the Chinese team members were imprisoned.

Foster Chong was having his own seizure; it was as if Foster couldn't get enough air. Carol Ng convulsed. Betty Hum quivered from head to foot, even as she bit her tongue. It became quickly apparent that the Chinese were under attack, that they had nanogens lodged in their bodies they perhaps didn't know about, and that Po Pin-Yen, understanding the operation was blown, had turned these nanogens on to stop further compromise.

It was over in a matter of minutes. Hua's arms floated lifelessly away from the keyboard. The Chinese in the survival pods were like dead hatchlings inside large white eggs, skin blue, eyes wide with burst blood vessels, the latest casualties of the PRNC War.

Any chance of figuring out the rest of the tumblers was all but gone.

They ejected Hua's corpse quickly. "Those macrogens could have multiple-target capability," explained Fye. They unhooked the survival pods and let them drift away. "We should seal the observer bay as well. I'm afraid we'll have to make it a dead zone."

Cam felt a pang when they tumbled Loftus Hua out the hatch. It didn't seem fair. Loftus was an unlikely hero, and he had met an uncalled-for end.

Twenty minutes later, everyone congregated in Cremona.

"We go ahead," said Cam. "We know that three of five nodes have been purged of corrupting software. This might be enough to operate at least some of the generators safely. I think at this point we salvage what we can. We haven't got the time to do anything else."

They alerted the rest of the fleet.

Half the engineering crews, now that all the work was done, set a course for Earth. The operational crews stayed behind, a total of ninety-eight people spread out over many millions of kilometers in five different spacecraft.

In a coordinated chain of start-ups, one field after another was sequenced. Cam watched the readouts on the Station A terminal. Accelerators 1 through 6, indicated by square icons, flickered into the green one by one. But generator 7 surged into the red. The operations craft *Geronimo* reported an explosion, followed by a chain reaction, which resulted in the entire obliteration of the accelerator. Eight and 9 fired the way they were supposed to, but 12 and 11 fed back, with the same resulting obliteration, some of the PRNC code still working its ugly sabotage. As for 12, it blinked into the yellow, and Cam worked furiously with some additional background language. He finally got it into the green. By the time he turned to Fye, his forehead was moist with perspiration.

"It's not optimal. But the readings tell me we're seeing gravitational anomalies consistent with the theoretical properties of anti-Ostrander space inside the target zone. This window here indicates the target zone is expanding to reach those alien-created zones closer to the sun that show similar gravitational anomalies."

Fye studied the readings. "With three of the generators down, we must be experiencing a reduction in strength. What about the hydrogen band?"

"It's too early to tell. I'm going to send our first probe."

He sent their first probe, really no more than a superfast projectile with an odometer linked to *Tecumseh* by laser relay; and as the probe entered the anti-Ostrander space field, it began to send back atypical readings, so that it didn't travel as it would through normal space, covering only millions of kilometers, but reported traveling distances that measured 1.4 light-years, the readings sent back instantaneously, not in 1.4 years, in keeping with the whole hyperdimensional setup. In other words, as theorized, anti-Ostrander space was smaller on the outside than it was on the inside, an indication that a curved space-time phenomenon was in effect. And within this wide region of curved space-time, some of the hydrogen bleed from the sun at last showed the reversal Cam had promised. The data came in, and the boomerang effect was proven. He realized, with a sense of awe, that he was viewing the universe in a fundamentally different way.

Fye wasn't convinced. "All I see is space." His tone wasn't calm anymore. His face had gone red, and he peered out Cremona's polycarbonate dome with a mix of perplexity and annoyance, as if he thought he had been outsmarted.

"It's not out there," said Cam. "It's here, on the screen, on the instrument readings. In the interplay of quarks and gluons at the boundary of the field. And we have something else here. Something I've only wildly speculated about but which we're seeing at the boundary's edge. Do you know anything about virtual particles, Oren?"

"No."

"Virtual particles are particles that don't exist yet, but have the potential to exist. This is what I find so exciting about this. Some of the sun's hydrogen is twinning itself. We're seeing something here that's never been seen before. The creation of matter. There's an old scientific maxim: matter can be neither created nor destroyed. But all the matter in the universe had to come from somewhere. We now see that virtual particles are leaping into existence out of the hyperdimensionality of anti-Ostrander space."

"Uh . . . okay."

Cam's lips tightened and he grew momentarily impatient. "As a species, you and I are equipped to live only in a particular space and time. Here, matter can be neither destroyed nor created. But the Builders live simultaneously in all times in all spaces, including the one you and I now inhabit. In the higher planes that the Builders also inhabit, matter seems to be created all the time. Just as it is destroyed. Existence and nonexistence. The only two propositions that make sense in an overall theory of the universe. It's a crazy theory," he said, thinking of Niels Bohr again, "but maybe it's just crazy enough to be the only theory that can explain it all."

Fye remained unconvinced. "How does this stop the sun from going red giant?"

Cam wanted to tell the Orbops agent that the slowing of the hydrogen drain was beside the point. He was tempted to finally admit to Fye that Guarneri was the equivalent of the Wright Brothers' *Kitty Hawk*, and that what they really needed was something like an airbus because they were dealing with the sun, and the sun was huge, and this whole question of concrete political and strategic gain was nothing but Langdon-speak anyway.

"Guarneri is a lens, Oren. It's going to bring the Builders into focus. But more important, it's going to bring *us* into focus for them. The Builders are actually going to see us for the first time through a medium they can understand. They've tried numerous ways to contact us, but they've finally dismissed us because we were too indistinct for them. If we can prove that we're capable of showing ourselves, we just might stop this whole situation."

A pathological coldness came to Fye's eyes. "You've lied about this, haven't you? The hydrogen reversal is going to turn out to be incidental and insignificant, isn't it?"

Cam peered at his equations. "I haven't lied. I've told you, Blunt, and the president what you needed to hear so I could get this job done."

"You're not reversing the hydrogen. And that's how you sold this mission."

"I'm reversing some of it. And I had to sell it any way I could because it's the only chance we have."

"The only chance *you* think we have, at least."

"Once we have meaningful communication with them, I'm convinced it will work itself out."

A line came to Fye's pink brow. "Yes, but what if it doesn't?"

"If anybody else has a better idea . . ."

"Excuse me. I have to contact New Mexico."

"About what?"

"About how you've lied to us."

"Don't do that. There's no point in upsetting the apple cart this late in the game."

"We'll let the president decide that."

While Fye was gone, Cam fretted about the outcome. He considered the possibility of mutiny, going ahead and doing what he had to do despite whatever the president decided on. He stared out the polycarbonate dome at deep space. He tried to feel the Builders. If only they would come to him again. Give him some sign. Reach through the multiple dimensions in which they lived and finally proclaim the human race worth saving. But they felt distant, inaccessible, and by the time Fye came back a couple hours later, his stomach was tight with anxiety.

Fye's brow was knuckled toward the middle. "They're not happy with you. They feel they've been misled. I'm to relieve you of responsibility."

A stab of panic shot through Cam's body. "What?"

"Nolan Pratt has submitted a report."

"And?"

"We've reduced the hydrogen drain by only six percent. It's statistically insignificant and won't make any difference to the red giant process going on in our sun. God, I wish I knew why they were doing this. Why us? Why our sun?"

"And you told the president that we're missing three of our accelerators?"

"Even if we had the other three online . . . the president was under the impression you'd given him ironclad guarantees. He's worried about the political fallout."

"Oren, listen carefully to what you're saying. Political fallout's not going to matter if we don't bring the Builders into focus."

"All I see is a big lie. Your own theoretical work was driving you all along. And we fell for it."

"I'm telling you, the Builders are going to notice this. It's the anomaly they've been looking for. This is like a black marble in a pile of white ones. They're going to notice. They can't *not* notice."

"I'm going to need all your access codes."

"So you're going to put me in cuffs?"

Fye looked away. "I don't want to die."

"Then just let me do my work."

"You want me to collude in mutiny."

"Yes, I do."

"They want you yanked. They say you've failed."

"In my gut, I know I haven't."

Fye frowned. "Don't talk to me about your gut. You're a scientist."

"Yes, but the Builders left planted in me a seed . . . an idea . . . that beyond the fringe of Euclidian, Newtonian, and quantum physics, way out there at the frontier, things are better explained by the gut than by mathematical equations so complicated that only a few people in the world can understand them. It's where physics meets the spirit. And they've sensed this in us. This is what hyperdimensionality is."

Fye, showing an originality that surprised Cam, didn't relieve him after all. "Carry on, Doctor."

"What about the president?"

The corpulent agent sighed. "I'll draft my resignation this afternoon."

Over the next fourteen hours, ninety-two Builder energy cells arrived. While Cam felt within himself the same indescribable sense of expansion again, he also felt immense relief because Guarneri seemed to be doing what it was meant to do after all. Just as Alpha Vehicle had come to inspect Stradivari, so these energy cells flocked around in shades that

flickered between ultramarine and turquoise to inspect Guarneri. Stranger still, they seemed to quiver
in and out of sight as they came close to Cremona's
polycarbonate dome. Cam understood that they were
really quivering in and out of time, reminding him
of the way electrons crossed transits instantaneously
in atoms, without traversing the space in between.
Each one was about the size of a car, and within
the ultramarine plasma, blue lightning branched in a
thousand rootlike patterns. Where he moved within the
Tecumseh, so they followed around the outside hull.
Were these the sensory organs of the Builders, then?

Fye grew anxious. "It's like we're in a small raft
surrounded by dozens of whales."

When Fye communicated with Blunt, he discovered that his messages came and went instantaneously. It was as if the mere presence of the energy
cells created a local medium of hyperdimensionality
that bent time and curved space.

"Langdon says he finds current developments
promising and asks that you resume your duties."

"So he hasn't accepted your resignation?"

"Gielgud turned it down. The president didn't
even see it."

While Fye might have felt anxious about being surrounded by this strange pod of space-faring blue
whales, Cam, for the first time since his Navasota
Builder-induced episode, experienced a release of
all tension.

Lesha told him he was being remote. "It's like
you've gone away some place."

He reached up and stroked her face, and experienced love not as an emotional reaction but as a

physiological change, a further sense that he was undergoing a great expansion, that though he was small on the outside, he was infinitely big on the inside. His love for her was like a thing alive, a phenomenon that had taken root so deeply and was so fundamentally a part of the universe's flux around him that he began to think that maybe it had a physical basis, that if they had instruments sensitive enough to see beyond the gluons and quarks, they might at last break through a barrier and observe a completely different realm of particles that had to do with love and other emotions. Crazy, but maybe just crazy enough.

His anxiety returned when the rest of the crew began to flicker. This happened a few hours after the approach of the last energy cell.

He pulled himself down the hub to the mess bay to get some juice, and found Stella Watson and Daniel Uttal investigating one of the vents, holding up a maintenance scanner.

"What's the problem?" he asked.

Stella said, "For reasons we can't readily explain, the oxygen-nitrogen mix of our air supply has changed significantly, and we're now registering more oxygen in the constituents. In other words, things are happening on an atomic level."

That's when Stella, dark, intense, with the body of an Olympic gymnast, flickered. She became like a Christmas tree light with a faulty connection. In addition, she and Daniel seemed to red-shift. Then blue-shift. Then become normal again.

"Did you see that?" Cam asked.

They were staring at him. Daniel said, "You disappeared."

"What?"

Then both of them flickered again, and they were again surrounded by red and blue. He realized it was himself who was actually doing the flickering. He couldn't help thinking of the 3-D comics he had owned as boy, what they looked like before you put on the red and green 3-D glasses, with all the images blurred by scarlet and beryl. It made him anxious, but he also thought that it was starting to happen, that for whatever reason, the Builders had chosen him yet again as a conduit.

Ochoa and Lesha took him to the surgery. Ochoa ran the battery on him. When the doctor was finished, he glanced at Lesha. Ochoa's face was set.

He said something to Lesha, but just as he spoke, the music started up again, and Cam was so startled by its return, he didn't immediately understand what the doctor said. It was like he was looking at Ochoa from the wrong end of a telescope. The music commenced with a single tone, and in timbre it reminded him of a piano, the pure crystal sound of a felt hammer striking a metal wire, perfect in its fullness and sustainability. This single tone was followed by two other tones, both the same pitch but each half the length of the first tone. This pattern was repeated for quite some time, one long, two short, as if this were the only possible combination. He couldn't help thinking of binary code, the on, and the off.

He went somewhere. He wasn't in the room anymore. For several seconds, the *Tecumseh* disappeared, and he floated in space by himself.

He looked around. He lifted his hand. He was

unprotected, adrift in the merciless void, but no tissue damage occurred. He took a deep breath and felt as if he were breathing something far more rarefied than air. To his right, he saw the sun festering like a boil about to burst, angry, red, awash with solar hurricanes. He saw slanting bands of purple immediately above him, the same purple bands he had seen during the last episode. These bands seemed both impossibly distant yet excruciatingly near. The Builders. He was overwhelmed by a sudden sense of anticipation. He knew that this was it, that a truly meaningful First Contact was about to occur.

Then he heard someone calling him.

"Dr. Conrad." The purple bands in outer space dimmed. "Dr. Conrad . . . can you hear me?"

He felt suddenly squeezed into a tight space, as if, having existed in all times and all spaces for eternity, he was now in a definite moment, a definite space, and that the overall dimensionality of his existence had been drastically reduced. The *Tecumseh* coalesced around him, red-shifting and blue-shifting, finally coming back into focus.

Lesha, Ochoa, and Fye leaned over him. Lesha's eyes were wide, terrified, and she said, "You vanished, then came back."

She gripped his hand; he loved the feel of her hand, the fleshy part at the ball of her thumb, the pressure of each individual finger.

The doctor made him understand that he was suffering from a dangerous arrhythmia, and was injecting him full of drugs.

"Arrhythmia?"

"It's like your body can't take the stress of what they're doing to you."

In other words, he wasn't necessarily designed to survive in hyperdimensionality.

Fye was standing over him like a buddy-soldier. "You've got to hang in there, Dr. Conrad. In the last two days, since you've been gone . . ." And Cam had to wonder, had it really been two days? Floating out there in space with the purple bands? Those spectral analogies by which the Builders seemed most comfortable in representing themselves? "And the energy cells are all over the place. Another ninety-two, and then another ninety-two after that." So, really two days? He decided that time, and the experience of time, were two different things, and that if he was ever going to understand the Builders, he would have to embrace the concept. "You spoke in the different languages again, Dr. Conrad. And Dr. Ochoa has detected increased activity in your sylvan fissure. The outflow of hydrogen from the sun has shown periods of stabilization, and we think the Builders are doing that. It's like they're trying to make up their mind. So you've got to hang on, Dr. Conrad. You've got to talk to them. Let them know we're here."

Yet as the chosen nexus for interdimensional contact, Cam couldn't hang on, even though the stakes were so desperately high. The arrhythmia got the better of him, and he realized that floating out in the void with the Builders had indeed been a great strain, and that some of his family history of cardiac disease might at last be catching up with him, just as Johnsie Dunlap had suggested after the first episode. An excruciating pain enveloped the left side of his chest, and he came screaming back to his own dimension with all the vulnerability of a biological creature in the grip of a heart attack he simply didn't have the wherewithal to fight.

32

Back on Earth, Lesha sat in a critical care room at Johns Hopkins staring at Cam, wondering if he would ever reemerge. Special equipment from Brookhaven National Laboratory had been moved in, instruments she used to measure what she was now calling the Fade. She couldn't explain it, only that it seemed to have something to do with what Cam had been saying about virtual particles fluxing in and out of existence.

The Fade was happening right now.

She analyzed the data on her screen. While certain particles around Cam seemed to materialize out of their own quantum potential, others were sucked into a subgravitational skin that was just below the event horizon of the whole bizarre phenomenon, and disappeared forever. Her equipment gave her an imperfect approximation.

In terms of naked visual assessment, he seemed to vanish, but only because he reflected with minute precision and exact resolution all the things around him, like Alpha Vehicle did. She tossed a pencil toward him as he faded, and the pencil was pushed away as if by a strong breeze, a hypergravitational effect similar to what Alpha Vehicle produced. Her heart contracted, and her throat thickened with anguish, and she was so afraid of losing him she could hardly breathe.

Dr. Jeffrey Ochoa came a few hours later.

As he entered the room, his lips were set, and his green eyes focused, drilling through the air with uncharacteristic intensity. Ochoa, usually so impeccably groomed, had let his beard grow, as if, with the end so near, he felt he could let himself go.

Coming to within a meter of his patient, Dr. Ochoa looked at Lesha with mounting anticipation. "Any sign of what we would call normal consciousness?"

This was the other thing—the way Ochoa spoke now, everything always qualified, each sentence, phrase, and word accompanied by implicit caveats, quid pro quos, and loopholes.

"No. But he's been flickering again."

"You understand this is beyond my expertise."

The heartfelt concern in his voice was genuine—it wasn't a question of medical responsibility anymore, but the compassion of one human being for another in a situation nobody could control.

"Did you get the scans back?" asked Lesha.

Ochoa's head shifted. "Yes. Would you like to see them?"

Lesha hesitated.

"Don't worry," said Ochoa. "I'll call the nurse to watch him."

Lesha said, "I'm worried he's going to flicker out of existence, or to a higher plane, or to wherever they are."

Ochoa gave Lesha's worry a moment, then said, "I don't know what to make of the scans. But you're a scientist. And you and him . . . maybe you can . . ."

Lesha took a deep breath and stroked Cam's head. "Sure."

A few minutes later, they were looking at slice-by-slice views of Cam's brain.

"None of the normal structures are visible," said Ochoa. "In fact, you can hardly make out the left and right hemispheres at all. As you can see, our scanning equipment has recovered nothing but a brilliant wash of light. Laser measurement has come back off the scale. We don't know whether it's a machine malfunction, a technical error, or in fact an accurate reading. If so, certain structures of his brain—those same internal structures that are now obscured by this . . . zone of light—can no longer be measured in centimeters, but must be calculated in parsecs. What's particularly striking is how his brain, like the universe, seems to be expanding."

Lesha stared at the scans. She saw the shape of Cam's skull. But within the cranial casing, his brain was like a star. She reached out and pressed her fingertips against one of the images. She wanted to go with him, wherever he was going, but she knew he had to make the journey alone.

She turned to Dr. Ochoa. "He's with them, isn't he?"

Dr. Ochoa lifted his chin as he contemplated the scan. "I certainly hope so."

The president came the following day. A small entourage accompanied him. There was no media, but

the presidential photographer was there, and he took
a number of stills of the leader standing beside Cam,
some with Langdon looking thoughtful, others serious, one with a cell phone pressed to his ear. Cam
stabilized dimensionally while this activity took
place.

It wasn't until the photographer went away that
the president actually came over and had a few
words with Lesha.

"I've spoken to Dr. Ochoa. You've seen the Fade?"

"Several times."

"Has Dr. Conrad shown even a trace of consciousness while you've been with him?"

"No. He's comatose."

"Dr. Ochoa says he can't get this arrhythmia under
control, that every time Dr. Conrad comes back from
one of these flickering episodes, it starts up." With a
bluntness the president was known for, he added,
"He says he might have another heart attack. And if
he does . . ."

She looked at Cam. He was now hooked to a venti-
lator. And a catheter. And a feeding tube. Despite
the feeding tube, he had lost weight. He looked like
an old man. Each day, she shaved his face. She
turned back to the president. Standing next to him
like this, she was again unsettled by how short the
man was, no more than five-one or -two. The scrutiny in Langdon's eyes made her quiver. World leaders were only human, but Langdon seemed to be a
breed apart. She felt the insistence of his will as his
eyes bored into hers.

"What's your gut feeling?" he asked.

Her eyes widened as she remembered the way

Cam always talked about gut feelings. Perhaps the president understood the universe after all. "I don't know if they're going to take him away for good, Mr. President, like they did Dr. Tennant."

"If they were going to take him away for good, he would have been gone by now. Like Dr. Tennant."

She shook her head. "If only he weren't weakening."

"Lieutenant Colonel Fye says you and he are . . ."

She nodded.

"Then do what you can to keep him alive. Sometimes it takes more than medicine. I know my wife prays for me every day. And it seems to help." He motioned out the window where the world was white with warm steam. He looked like he was about to say something but then gave up. His lips came together, and he glanced at his staff; she had the sense he just wanted to get away from them, that some time alone was all he really needed. "Guarneri has been destroyed, by the way. The Builders knocked it out at oh four hundred hours this morning." His face reddened suddenly. "If he's in touch with them . . . if there's anything he can do . . ."

Her body released low-level doses of adrenaline into her bloodstream at the news of Guarneri's destruction. "So the hydrogen drain?"

A tired grin came to Langdon's face. "Guarneri was only ever marginally effective with that."

"Oren was saying the drain was showing periods of stabilization. That the Builders—"

"Not anymore. It's back to previous levels."

"So . . . how long?"

The president rubbed his chin. "Looked at one

way, Dr. Weeks, we've already run out of time. People can't go outside without special protective glasses now. If they do, the radiation will damage their eyes permanently. Then there's the polar ice caps, heat stress in equatorial areas causing massive damage to large tracts of rain forest, an exponential increase in the number of hurricanes, and also in the number of cholera and diphtheria outbreaks. We have the disappearance of the cold trap and the shredding of the Van Allen belts . . . which brings me back to radiation. My scientific advisers tell me that a year of exposure at current levels will be fatal to most of us."

"So how long . . . before the actual red giant event?" she asked, and her voice to her own ears sounded soft, and weak with fear.

Langdon's eyes widened in speculation. "Unfortunately, Dr. Pratt now detects factors that were previously absent. The initial stabilization we saw just after Dr. Conrad experienced his first Fade bought us some time, but now the rate of reaction is doubling every eight hours."

"In other words?"

Langdon glanced at his waiting staff again. In a lower voice he said, "It could be any day now. And that's why . . ." He leaned closer, and for a few seconds his president's armor vanished. "That's why it's so important that you . . . as the woman who . . ."

She nodded. "I love him."

"Exactly."

33

Cam was back at Gettysburg—he wasn't sure how—and as he stared out the broad tower windows at the bleak lunar terrain, he saw that it was raining. Raining on the Moon, an impossibility, but perhaps now possible because of hyperdimensionality. It splashed on Bunker Hill and ran in rivulets. It cut channels and pooled at the bottom. He knew this couldn't be. There was nothing but the usual black sky above. It reminded him of all Delilah's rain in Navasota.

He lifted his arm and looked at the back of his hand. It glowed. Not with electric radiance, but with the luminescent flesh tones of a Rembrandt portrait, highlighted because everything was so dark in the tower.

The rain beat against the polycarbonate pressure glass. Lightning flashed and he saw for an instant dead bodies, blackened, and left partially skeletal by, he supposed, the nuclear blast that had happened here.

In the next flash, he saw the bodies resurrected in

their pressure suits, forming a column and walking around the far end of Bunker Hill.

He turned from the windows and looked around the tower.

He was in one of those dreams where he knew he was dreaming; yet at the same time the situation was a hundred times more vivid than any dream.

He walked to the companionway that led to the hub below. At the top of the companionway, he looked down and saw Lamar Bruxner—a ghost— illuminated from within by the same Rembrandt light, pale silver verging on white gold, glimmering as if underwater. Bruxner looked like he existed outside of time. Outside of space. The chief of support flickered, then disappeared, and Cam was left with nothing but an empty corridor.

"Hello?" he called.

He got no answer.

He descended the companionway and walked along corridor 9.

He heard snippets of Mozart's Fortieth Symphony in G Minor, two short and one long, a sigh a semitone apart—only the symphony didn't progress the way it usually did, the way he remembered it when his father and mother had taken him to hear it performed by the Houston Symphony Orchestra many years ago. Rather, it concentrated on those sections that used the opening motif, developed one way or another through various harmonic modulations, leaving the subsidiary material untouched, as if the balancing phraseology was so much extraneous information. Two short and one long. A musical exhalation, filtered through an overlay of echoes, so that the fragmented symphony washed up onto his ears in a series of ones and twos.

And interspersed with this fractured version of Mozart's Fortieth was that other music, the hypnotizing compositional work of the Builders, the music he had become so familiar with. In breaking it down, he heard the two-to-one proportions in the Builders' melody as well. And the bits and pieces of the Builders' music seemed to work in counterpoint with the uncoupled phrases of Mozart's symphony, so that he began to think that maybe Renate Tennant hadn't been so far off base after all, and had actually succeeded in effecting a communicative bridge using Mozart's music.

Two. One. Two. One.

Not binary—not the zero, one—but a reflected representation, because who could hear the zero? So they used two and one instead.

He came to the intersection of corridor 6. He peered down this hall to the common room. The music's character changed, became more visceral, scraping, seemed to emanate from the common room, the timbre now shaped through the vowel sounds A, E, I, O, U, over and over.

He reached the common room and he saw, speak of the devil, Renate Tennant, sitting at one of the tables.

Instead of wearing her usual Defense Department greens, she was in white, and she glowed with the same vigorous but elusive Rembrandt light, and he couldn't help remembering that in her second "send" to the Builders she had sent many examples of Rembrandt's work. Though her hair was done up in the same conservative way, she appeared decades younger, and he knew he was looking at Dr. Tennant as she might have been at twenty-three or -four.

She spoke to him in Cantonese. "Yes, I'm real. It's me." His ear immediately translated.

He approached. "You're younger."

"They've represented me at my mean age."

"Are you . . . alive?"

"I am. But not in the usual sense."

He reached the table and sat down. When he spoke next, it was in French. *"Pourquoi est-ce je suis ici?"* Why am I here?

She responded in French. *"Ceci est un premier contact, Cam."* This is first contact. "Before, I coveted it. But now I'm part of it. And part of them."

"Then I implore you, as their representative, stop the transformation of our sun."

In Greek she said, "The transformation of your sun will be a transient episode for all of you. You will continue. Your atoms are indestructible and will last forever, as long as they remain in their hypodimensional state."

"We wish to continue in our *current* state."

"We realize this now."

"We?"

Her next words were in English. "Your language is insufficient, and can't possibly describe, even through the use of a place-marker pronoun, our precise nature."

Cam tried to get his awe and wonder under control. "Why do you play this music all the time?"

Renate looked away. Out the big observation window, Cam saw the Sumter Module and Command Port, and it fluctuated between a destroyed version of itself and an intact one. "You hear the motif? The two and the one? We begin to see that you might understand. It represents the binary nature of the universe. We are existence. The others are nonexistence. These are the two fundamental choices in our universe. We are the will of the one choice, and they are the will of the other. We create, they destroy. Creation and destruction. It's the anvil upon which everything is forged."

Cam was immediately reminded of the creation-of-matter, destruction-of-matter virtual particle phenomenon in the Guarneri field, and his subsequent hypothesis of an existence-versus-nonexistence schematic for the universe. His eyes narrowed. But who were these *others*, then? For the moment, he pushed them from his mind and concentrated on the dangerous situation at hand.

"Then if you're existence, you know we want to exist."

Renate turned to him. "You never die."

"We wish to continue to exist in our present mode."

"It's hard for us to make sense of hypo-dimensional existence, just as it's difficult, I imagine, for you to imagine a . . . a habitat that occupies several different planes at the same time. We came to your solar system for the express purpose of utilizing your sun. But then emanating from this Moon, right down there in Shenandoah, we picked up a sudden flash, and this was Stradivari. So we came here, and we investigated, and while we inadvertently destroyed the field, we sensed in your mind—yes, your mind, Dr. Conrad—something that made us hesitate. Say you are a prospector. You are walking over the ground, and the ground is made up of base particulate of no striking interest. You dismiss the whole tract. But then you see something flash. You walk over and find a diamond. The diamond is big, and the diamond speaks in a language you can understand. Suddenly you look around at the drab patch with new interest."

"So Guarneri . . ."

Here the language became a mix of Greek and Latin, like Omega Sol, but he found he could untangle the hybrid syntax with surprising quickness. "Your own effort was enough to make us realize, or perhaps to shock us into believing, that alpha species on planet omicron in the system you call Sol was perhaps satisfactorily developed enough to save. Particularly when we discovered evidence of curved space-time and gravitational manipulation out by planet beta. I could describe what you have done in your own mathematical language, but we understand, as you do, that mathematical language reaches a point where it must adapt other, more poetic strategies. And so, when we saw your small example of anti-Ostrander space by planet beta, we knew that you were taking your first tiny steps toward . . . *commutatio*." She seemed to consider the metaphorical worth of the word in its original Latin, and let it stand.

Cam asked, "Is there any way you can help us?"

"You will be preserved. Is that not help enough?"

"Preserved how?"

"In your natural habitat."

"So planet omicron. Earth."

"Yes."

"And what about Omega Sol?"

She looked away. "Omega Sol will be stopped."

"And what about all the millions of people who have already been killed in the Worldwide Crash and the August nuclear exchange?"

"They aren't dead. They exist. Just in a different form. And a different time."

"You can't bring them back?"

Renate's eyes narrowed as she continued to gaze out at the fluctuating SMCP. "No. They now serve the universe in their altered form. They are part of the overall balance. For we and the other are light and shadow, and we balance each other out. We and the other are yes and no. We and the other are black and white. Nothing balances something. Something balances nothing. We are positive and they are negative. We are existence and they nonexistence. Together we are force versus lack of force. We are a chaotic shifting of *back* and *forth*. This is the fundamental scheme of the universe. We are on, they are off. Together we are binary. We, who have done this to your sun, are of the first part. Together with the other part we are life and death. All those millions of dead you speak of must play their role in the balance of the universe. Just as those of you who remain, the living, must also play your role."

"And what role is that?"

"Existence. Existence and nonexistence, you see. That's all there is."

"So you can't bring back the dead?"

"Not in hypodimensionality."

"But you will stop Omega Sol?"

"Omega Sol and its quick reversal are just a matter of manipulating matter and energy."

"Why are you turning main-sequence stars into red giants in the first place? Why are you changing larger stars further afield into supernovae?"

"You're a scientist. You can't guess?"

"It doesn't make much sense to me."

"From where you stand, no, I imagine it wouldn't. But when you get to what you would most probably term the thirteenth and fourteenth dimensions—and bear in mind that dimensions can't be numbered this way because dimensionality is a continuum, a string, like on a Stradivarius violin, capable of microtonal glissandi—but when you get well beyond the dimensions where space and time have been left far behind, you begin to see that there is a fundamental dissonance as well as a harmony to the universe. Harmony and dissonance. You have no math to describe what I'm talking about. Here at the bottom of dimensionality, where you and your kind dwell, we heat stars to their end-stage sequences for the sake of producing elemental building blocks that help us address the dissonance, and to encourage harmony. When stars are heated to their end-stage sequences, they produce all kinds of heavier elements, everything from carbon and oxygen to lead and gold. These distilled particles help us fight our war."

"War?" said Cam, and was so surprised by the notion it came out in a half dozen languages at once. "You're fighting a war? With whom?"

34

Pittman took his time getting home, meandering through the country over the next week and a half because he wanted to see it one last time—America, the greatest country on Earth.

A kilometer outside Grand Island, Nebraska, he got out of his truck and threw up. He vomited blood. Radiation exposure, most probably from his surface excursion in Crater Cavalet, was at last catching up to him. It seemed a fitting end that he should be shredding into nonexistence like the Van Allen belts. On his hands and knees in the coarse gravel, he looked up at the sky, and it was white with a blanket of ruffled silver clouds. Over by a stream, he saw a dead coyote with flies buzzing around it. He finished throwing up and, pressing his hand against his truck's front fender, struggled into a standing position.

He looked around at the surrounding fields and discovered a farmhouse in the distance. He didn't see any vehicles around the house. The house looked deserted. Abandoned. Empty. The red giant was upon them, and everybody was hiding.

He tried not to brood on his children, but his mind relentlessly circled back. Becky, dead immediately, and Tom, succumbing a day later. He walked to the driver's side and got in. And Sheila dead as well. He was the penultimate destroyer, a man who had murdered his own family.

He took out his gun and stared at it—a black, precise, well-oiled weapon. He released the safety, made sure he had a round in the chamber, then stuck the barrel in his mouth. The metal tasted tangy. A sudden jerk of his finger and that would be it. He finally understood that war wasn't the only answer. So simple. The single greatest principle any true warrior would have employed, but which he had failed to grasp, was to prevent war before having to fight one. In that respect, Dr. Conrad was a greater warrior than he.

And now . . .

Now it was too late.

Now the world had gone beyond the tipping point.

He took the gun out of his mouth and put the safety back on. Tears came to his eyes. He grieved for Becky and Tom. He grieved for Sheila. He even grieved for Haydn. He turned the ignition and the motor started. He put the car in gear and drove.

He came to a windmill installation just outside Laramie, Wyoming. The big turbines, field after field, were turning; but when he came to the utility station, he saw no cars, no one in the grounds or the windows, and the big security gate left unlatched and banging against the fence in the wind. The sound of the gate against the chain-link fence was a lonely one. This was what it would be like when everybody finally died. They said neutron bombardment would mercifully kill all living things before the flames of the red giant came. For two or three days before the inferno, the world would be empty. A giant ghost town. And there would be a lot of unlatched gates banging in the wind.

He continued west along Interstate 80 through Rock Springs and so toward the Nebraska-Utah border. He turned on his radio and got a station out of Salt Lake City.

There was a story on Dr. Cameron Conrad, how he was still comatose at Johns Hopkins in Baltimore. Doctors were baffled by his condition, and late last night he had survived a second heart attack. The announcer spoke of the flickering, reported that Dr. Lesha Weeks had been investigating the phenomenon, and had theorized about an "event horizon" surrounding Dr. Conrad, and how at the boundary of this event horizon, virtual and nonvirtual particles seemed to be at war with each other. They had a sound bite of Dr. Weeks speaking. "It seems that within the perimeters of this event horizon—and I use the term loosely—we see a conflict between particles that want to exist and don't want to exist. I believe through this event horizon we're getting a rare glimpse into how the universe operates on its speculated higher planes."

Pittman wasn't sure if he knew what the doctor was talking about. It was like she was asking him to see something that no one could ever describe in concrete terms. But he thought about existence and nonexistence, and how it seemed to reflect his yin-yang symbol at home, and it kept him preoccupied for a long time.

As he reached the outskirts of Salt Lake City, he saw several large smoke plumes in the downtown core. He bypassed the city to the south, occasionally catching glimpses of these plumes. What had happened to the fire department? He counted seventeen conflagrations in all. With things getting bad, had the fire department simply gone AWOL?

He saw three people walking along the freeway. They wore heavy long cloaks and big hats with broad rims—like so many others, they erroneously believed this kind of garb would protect them from the heavy radiation coming from the unfiltered sun, even though it had originally been advised simply for the fallout of the August nuclear exchange. They waved their arms. They wanted him to slow down. But he had nothing to give them, and when the tallest of the three lifted a piece of broken asphalt from the side of the road and hurled it at him, he sped up.

He entered Nevada a short while later. It was like returning to a place he hated, but also a place he loved. He took 93 South at Wendover. As he drove through the desert, he again couldn't help think about what Dr. Weeks had said, how there seemed to be a battle of particles around Dr. Conrad, ones that wanted to exist, and ones that didn't.

He drove through the night, and Nevada revealed its many sides to him. But mainly it was just the road he stared at, the heat-blasted asphalt showing up nearly white in his headlights, with the flick of the yellow dividing stripes, one after the other, overpowering and hypnotic. It made him think how narrow his own universe was compared to the one the Builders must inhabit.

He must have dozed, because the next thing he knew, his truck rumbled over the gravel shoulder and in a heart-jolting awakening he swerved to avoid the ditch. He swung the car back to the road, his eyes wide, then braked, only to realize that the sky was getting brighter, and that all the strange white clouds had finally cleared.

He wasn't sure what this meant. According to theoretical models, the sky was supposed to be awash in steaming clouds until the end. It wasn't supposed to get clear. He glanced to the left. Did they have it wrong, then? Because the sky was now clear, and he could see a long way. He saw telephone poles rising one after the other along the superstraight desert highway. He saw sagebrush. Low brown mountains collared the desert on either side. The sky was blue, a clear amethyst of gemlike intensity.

He tried his radio, but static blocked his signal.

Then the sun came up.

When he saw the sun, he knew the world was doomed, that he wasn't looking into the face of the sun but into the face of death. The star took up half the sky and was an angry red disk of fiery vortexes, shooting flares, and mushroom clouds. He saw sunspots, like sinkholes into oblivion. Storied old Sol seemed to writhe with a feverish infection. Yet for being so big, it wasn't as bright as usual, and cast a dim scarlet glow over the land. He swallowed. He perspired. It was rare for him to feel a fear so big. It left him shaken.

During the final stretch, he thought the sun was looking at him, judging him, condemning him for the murder of his children. Its awful sanguine eye penetrated to the root of his being.

He heard Haydn sometimes whispering in his ear from the other side of the Moon, and wished he could be with his adjunct in all that immense lunar silence and peaceful isolation because he needed a quiet, dark place to think.

The heat got so bad the asphalt grew gummy. He looked at the thermometer on his truck's ceiling and saw that the temperature had topped fifty-five Celsius. Even though his air-conditioning was working full blast, it hardly alleviated the miserable heat inside the cab. The desert around him looked like a photographic negative, and he knew that the strange light coming through this new amethyst atmosphere must be distorting the spectral qualities of the landscape.

When he came to his spread in the desert, with the large silver flagpole and Old Glory drooping in the windless day out front, he didn't turn up the long, dusty drive, with its sporadic one-inch gravel glowing like lava chunks in the light of the ungodly sun. He stopped on the shoulder and prepared himself to do what he had to do. He thought he might see jets come from Peterson, or at least see traced against the aquamarine depth the usual loose fabric of contrails. And he was certain he would hear the soul-lifting

song of afterburners. But it was as if Peterson had
ceased to exist. The only flying thing anywhere was
a vulture picking at roadkill. The feasting bird staggered away when it finally saw him and, as if overwhelmed by the heat, fell in the dirt, then struggled
into a sorry and somnambulant flight that took it
over the ridge.

Once he got his nerve ready, he drove up to the
flagpole and got out of his truck. The heat took his
breath away—like stepping into a sauna after rolling
in snow. He coughed a few times, the heat was so
bad. He walked to the flagpole and touched it. He
couldn't leave his fingers there more than a few seconds before the metal became too scorching.

He grabbed the guide ropes and lowered the flag.
It was a sad moment. He never thought he would
lower the American flag in his own front yard. Once
the flag was down, he untied it from its guide ropes
and folded it in appropriate military fashion until it
was nothing but a triangle of white stars on a blue
ground. He shoved the neat packet under his arm
and walked back to his truck.

And still, he couldn't get it out of his mind, those
particles   around   Dr.   Conrad,   existing   and
nonexisting.

He drove the rest of the way to his house.

When he tried the water from the kitchen sink,
nothing came out. So he got some bottled water from
under the sink and drank.

He went outside, stood in the middle of his yard,
and faced Peterson. By this time, the sun was a lot
higher, didn't seem to ooze with the same gelatinous
gush of ugly red light, and in fact he could look right

into it, squinting, and see that it wasn't really the sun at all, but a big hole into emptiness, just like Alpha Vehicle. Existence. Nonexistence. And the choice between the two. How could he have been so blind all his life to miss something so simple?

He put the flag on the ground, still folded, and gave Old Glory a salute. But as he gave the flag the crispest salute he had ever mustered, the thrumming in his ears got really bad, and he had to gather all his strength to clamp down on it. Then he realized it wasn't thrumming at all. It was a jet coming out of Peterson. He watched it approach. The jet was like a chapter from a life he had once lived but which he could hardly remember anymore. Yet it filled him with a nostalgic joy, an old soldier remembering old battlefields, and he realized that this was the moment.

He lay down on the ground, using the folded flag as a pillow. The jet flew over him, low to the ground, spooking a jackrabbit from behind some sagebrush. He put his gun in his mouth. He watched the jet pass by, then pulled the trigger.

35

Lesha moved aside the Venetian blinds in Cam's hospital room and looked across Jefferson Street to Patterson Park. The sun was in the south. The strange turquoise sky made the entire city look emerald, and the sun glowed with a redness that scared her. What puzzled her was the unexpected absence of clouds. In a world that was 70 percent water, the atmosphere should have been as violent and unstable as the inside of a teakettle approaching a boil. But it was remarkably calm, with only a few cirrus wisps on the horizon.

An hour later, as Cam continued to flicker in and out of existence, President Langdon called her on her cell.

"Has there been any change?"

She hesitated. "They've had a palliative physician come in to assess him. After the MI three days ago, they don't think he's going to recover."

"That bad?"

"Dr. Ochoa did further scans. The light inside his head is fading and he got a better fix on some of the key structures. It seems he's suffered a small stroke as well. Dr. Ochoa doesn't think he's going to live. The strain of the presumed contact is killing him."

At the other end of the line he heard the president sigh. "Keep him alive, Lesha. Keep him going. Because I have good news."

"You do?"

"You've seen the change in the sky?"

"Yes. Why is it so aquamarine?"

"Put simply, it's a field."

"A field?"

"The sun's radiation isn't penetrating anymore. Bombardment levels are back to normal. Blunt has launched a probe. It's sending back surprising data. A sphere has encircled the Earth. There's a magnetic component. This is helping keep out the radiation."

She divided the slats of the Venetian blinds again with her fingers, and a bar of orange light fell across her face. "What about the sun?"

"The hydrogen drain has slowed significantly."

"But we're still heading toward a red giant?"

"It would appear so. Dr. Pratt now predicts Christmas, so at least we have some time. Dr. Conrad is doing something right, so keep him alive as long as you can."

But as she got off the phone, she thought that this was easier said than done.

The sun traced its path through the sky, and occasionally, during the course of the day, Lesha walked to the window to have a look. By noon, it had become a more homogenous color and didn't appear so angry. By three, it had regained some of its customary golden hue. But by sunset, it had grown large again, and perhaps through an optical effect of the new atmospheric shield, looked more malevolent than ever, seething, foaming like a star gone rabid. She was glad when it finally set.

At that point, she left Cam for a while. She ate some military rations in a special area set up for staff. Then she went outside.

The temperature had dropped. It was still hot—as hot as the hottest day in equatorial Africa—but at least it was in a normal range, not verging on the unlivable. Mid-forties perhaps? An odd smell hung in the air, like chlorine and electricity mixed, as if the Builders' field juggled the subatomic particles of the atmosphere.

She saw stars for the first time since August. And then the Moon came up half-full, and it looked more gold than silver. The alien field magnified the Moon as if through a telephoto lens—craters, ejecta patterns, and mountains were visible to the naked eye. She thought of the nuclear blast at Gettysburg. Thought of Lamar Bruxner, and of his assistant, Laborde. She thought of Johnsie Dunlap, and tried not to feel sad—ultimately the nurse practitioner had been a hapless victim in an intergalactic miscommunication.

As she went back into the hospital, her cell phone rang once more.

This time it was Oren Fye. "Did you do something?"

"Like what?"

"Are you with him?"

"No, I'm downstairs."

"You'd better go up."

As she hurried to the elevator, Fye explained. "There's been a massive read. A bit like the World-wide Crash. But not as disruptive."

"And you're sure it came from the Builders?"

"We've traced its origin to the Moon, and they're the only ones up there right now."

"What are they after this time?"

"Every reference, every mention, every possible hit or permutation of a hit on Dr. Conrad."

"Just Dr. Conrad?"

"And everything that tangentially relates to Dr. Conrad. Particularly his work on hyperdimensionality."

She grew hopeful. This massive read was like the stirring of fresh weather, and boded well.

When she finally reached his room on the fifth floor, Cam's eyes were open, and as she came in, he was staring at her; but there was something not right about his eyes, an opaqueness, like the eyes of some deep-sea creature. This made her nervous. Was it actually Cam looking at her? Or was this . . . this *thing* . . . a Builder?

She checked the heart monitor and saw that the subtle and dangerous symptoms of arrhythmia, present since that fateful day aboard the *Tecumseh*, had disappeared, and that what was on the scope was a normal heartbeat. His respirations, for so long erratic, had stabilized, and his pulse was down to a normal resting rate of seventy-two per minute. His temperature, spiking, then dropping in the most whimsical fashion for the last several days, graded in at a sturdy thirty-seven Celsius.

Lesha's heart swelled. Cam continued to stare as

if he'd been transformed in some way. Serene. In possession of himself. He lifted his hand, inviting her touch, and she laid her fingers in his palm.

Dr. Ochoa arrived a few hours later. He had porters move Cam into a special room. He did more scans. And introduced chemical tags into his brain to better monitor electrical activity. He launched a microscopic nanogenic probe that followed his mind's many corridors, simply to calculate distance.

At the end of it all, he broke it down for Lesha. The president's face hung on a waferscreen, patched through for conference purposes.

"We were able to better visualize the structures of his brain this time, Mr. President," said Ochoa. "The nanogenic probe continues to indicate an inverse spatial relationship, and has reported traveling distances of up to ninety-five astronomical units. As for the chemical tags, they show his synapses firing at the deepest levels of his communicative centers, which would seem to indicate he's talking to somebody."

"What about this stroke he seems to have had, Dr. Ochoa?" asked the president. "I just the read the report on that now."

Dr. Ochoa hesitated. He looked first at Lesha, then at the president, then at the scans. "The site of the cerebral vascular accident has been isolated and disconnected from the rest of his brain. Not by me. By them. Other parts of his brain are picking up the slack for this damaged part. It's nearly as if the Builders have quarantined this area of his brain. They've introduced millions of nanogens into the damaged area but so far they're in a state of stasis. I'm seeing the same thing in the damaged areas around his

heart, nanogens ready to go. I don't know what
they're going to do. I think we should be prepared
either way. Because either way, it's out of our
hands now."

36

That the Builders should be fighting a war with someone astonished Cam. Were they fighting with these *others*, then? he wondered.

Renate got up from the table and walked to the observation window. She stood next to it, and usually, when a live, warm human being was next to that window, steam appeared on its surface. But Renate left no steam. Nor did she cast a reflection.

She turned around. "The nature of our enemy is as vast and complex as we are ourselves, and can only be accurately described using a numerical language not even Earth's most gifted mathematicians can understand. Since such is the case, I'll sum it up metaphorically. As you call us the Builders, so we call our other half the Wreckers. But to call them Wreckers doesn't tell the whole story. As I said, they are negation, the minus sign to our plus sign, the *off* to our *on*, the zero to our one. At these sophisticated levels your math breaks down and becomes so complicated as to be impenetrable. These two basic forces were formed in the negatively curved space-time that existed in the nonexistence that prevailed before the big bang. Together the Builders and the Wreckers comprise the engine of the universe. And we fight each other. Or don't necessarily fight each other but are in constant conflict with each other. The Milky Way is a new battleground for us, which is why you haven't discovered our interactions until now. Entire star systems form the hinterland to feed our positive-negative interactions, and such would have been the fate of your own star system if you hadn't poked your eyes like twin periscopes above the biological milieu of your planet. We saw you looking. The black marble among white ones, as you put it."

Cam considered for a long while, then asked, "So we're worth saving?"

Renate shifted, looked out the observation window. "Sometimes we choose stars, and there are planets around these stars, and there is life on these planets. Planets, stars, what you see with your telescopes are all part of the plane we ourselves call hypodimensional space, the first through fourth dimensions. Those creatures born at the omega end of the dimensional continuum can never occupy its higher reaches. It would be like asking a fish to live on dry land. Sometimes in order to create, we must destroy. This was the prevailing policy with the star you call Sol. But your demonstration near planet beta changed that policy. It has now been determined that the preservation of you and your people will add to the balance against the negative outflow of the Wreckers."

This sounded sinister to Cam. "Must we be your allies, then?"

Renate seemed surprised by the question. She turned to him. "Human, you delight me. You play chess on several boards at once."

"You're powerful."

"But we are good. If the Wreckers had come . . ."

"Will they ever come?"

"It's hard to predict the binary flux of the universe."

"You can't predict the future?"

Renate sighed. "You've got a long way to go before you understand the true nature of past, present, and future. Suffice it to say that in this backwater here, I think you'll be safe for a long period to come. We've put a screen around planet omicron. We've reversed the hydrogen bleed in your sun. At the end of ninety-two planetary rotations your sun will again be a main-sequence G-class star. You'll be safe. You personally will be restored. And your life will go on—in its present mode." She looked back out the observation window one more time. "As for the Wreckers, only the future will tell."

37

When Renate finally released him, he felt as though he were falling through a wide tract of outer space, with stars everywhere. But then he had the notion of a ceiling above. At the same time, he felt more comfortable. He could breathe easier. His heart beat in its regular fashion. The ceiling turned out to be a hospital room ceiling.

He slept a long time. And dreamed. Of his father. His mother. And of Lesha. These dreams were of a healing nature, and his mind, so long tightly wound because of the impending red giant, felt a peace similar to what he had felt inside Alpha Vehicle.

When his hospital room finally came into view a second time, Lesha was sitting in a chair next to him, her head bowed, her eyes closed, wearing a lab coat she had borrowed from somewhere. After so many days of scorching heat, she seemed cold.

The Venetian blinds were open. He looked out the window. He saw blue sky, and sunlight slanting down in its old yellow fashion.

Lesha lifted her head, opened her eyes, and looked

at him. It took her a moment to come out of her doze, but when she did, she leaned forward, her body seemingly released by a tight spring, and peered at him, surprised by something.

"Cam?"

"Are we back?"

She didn't seem to know what to make of his question, but in the context of everything he had just experienced, these three words made the most sense to Cam.

"Your eyes . . ."

He looked down at his body and saw that he had an IV drip in his arm and ECG sensors taped to his chest. He turned to the window. "The sun . . ."

She at last understood. "Yes, we're back."

"Will you marry me?"

Her face was momentarily shocked into immobility. It was a simple question, yet full of quantum potential. It was a yes-or-no question, a proposition like the Builders and the Wreckers, but within each fecund egg of a response lay a whole future, a path to follow, a territory to chart, a continuum in which to exist. He had a better understanding of what the Builders meant by the binary nature of the universe. Yes or no. And all the maybes that made up the gray areas of the universe were just way stations to either answer.

The answer had to wait. Ochoa peered around the door. When he saw Cam, he rushed forward.

"Dr. Conrad?"

"Hello."

"You're awake."

"I am."

Ochoa did the basic neurological battery. Months of the year. Backward from a hundred. Touch my finger. Touch your nose. Then he got on a special pager, even as Lesha wandered away and thumbed digits into her cell. Yes or no. The answer to his question remained unanswered for the time being. Dr. Cormier, the cardiologist, came in. Heart. Lungs. Breathe in. Breathe out. Can you sit up? He was a little shaky, his muscles a little atrophied, but wonder of wonders, he could.

Pages went out to lab personnel, diagnostic imaging techs, Rhona Lindsay, and a number of other allied health professionals.

For the next several hours he was surrounded by these professionals. They rolled in like a peculiar white-coated weather front, and behind them, Lesha, with her beautiful blond surfer-girl aura, peered at him, poised between trepidation and bliss. Between negative and positive. Between one step forward and one step backward.

The arrival and departure of these people was like so many thespians entering and exiting a stage; and when he and Lesha were at last alone together, it was like she had forgotten the question.

She gave him a history of the world, and of himself, for the last several days.

"You've had two heart attacks and a stroke, but we believe Builder nanogens are repairing the damage, and that you should have a complete recovery. As for the red giant, hydrogen levels in the sun have increased dramatically." He was still foggy, half his mind skittering along the edges of higher dimensions, and sometimes what she said seemed out of

context. "Also, the Earth's polarity reversed itself for
a few days, then righted itself, and after that, the Van
Allen belts regenerated."

One of the strangest things she told him about,
and what took him a long time to understand, concerned the Earth's orbit.

"It seems that as the Builders were tinkering with
the sun, stoking it, its gravitational pull weakened,
and Earth lost a bit of its grip. This resulted in the
widening of Earth's orbit. Mean distance from the
sun went from one hundred and fifty million kilometers to two hundred and twenty-five million. The
Builders then purposely kept the Earth at this greater
distance as they reestablished a main-sequence phase
in the sun. The extra distance cooled the Earth considerably, and reestablished the cold trap. In fact, it
got so tremendously cold at the poles that significant
portions of both ice caps have reformed. We haven't
seen ice caps like these since 1950. Some long-defunct
glaciers are advancing again. The reformed ice caps
are reflecting sunlight back into space, and this has
significantly reduced the effects of global warming.
Now they've pushed Earth back into position."

The president called him via video-conference line.
"You'll be pleased to know that units of the PRNC
Army still loyal to Po Pin-Yen have been defeated
in most outlying provinces, and that the new DRC-
supported government has established firm control.
Much of the credit goes to you, Dr. Conrad. The new
government backed you, and now that you've won
the day, it's paying them dividends in popular support. That's great news for America. It seems you've

given us some concrete political gains after all. Your country thanks you."

As Cam stared at the pugnacious little leader, he realized that the president might belong to the Wrecker side. Millions of people had died, not only in the Worldwide Crash, but also in the August nuclear exchange. Everyone on the planet was now at risk for radiation-related illness at some point in their lives. Personally, he had lost two great friends, Jesus and Mark, as well as his house. And the president was still playing politics? He understood better than ever why the Builders might have been so hesitant.

Dr. Ochoa collected all the test results the next day. "Your scans are normal. The stroke-affected part of your brain has been completely repaired by the Builder-introduced nanogens, and any damage from your two myocardial infarcts is gone as well. Your cardio workup is unremarkable. I want you to wear a Holter monitor for the next forty-eight hours, just to be on the safe side, but I think you have to be grateful to the Builders, Dr. Conrad. They've completely restored you."

He was left to sleep after that.

When he woke, he found Lesha by his side. "Yes."

He nodded. There it was. The answer he had been waiting for.

In the fecund egg of her response lay a whole future, a path to follow, a territory to chart, a continuum in which to exist. The choice had finally been made.

And he knew it would add to the positive outflow of the universe.